A Calculated Conspiracy

*To Sarah
My classmate and friend
Best Wishes always*

A Calculated Conspiracy

A Will & Betsy Black Adventure

David & Nancy Beckwith

SeaStory Press
Key West, Florida

A Calculated Conspiracy, A Will and Betsy Black Adventure
© 2011 by David and Nancy Beckwith
All rights reserved

Reproduction of this book or any part thereof is prohibited, except for quotation for review purposes, without express permission of the author and publisher.

This is a work of fiction. Names, characters, places and incidents either are products of the authors' imaginations or are used fictitiously. Any resemblance to actual events or persons, living or dead, is entirely coincidental.

Quotations from the following musical compositions appear in the text:
    John Bartus, *Keys Disease*
    Terry Cassidy, *Bat Tower*
    Howard Livingston & Mile Marker 24, *Mile Marker 24*
    Howard Livingston & Mile Marker 24, *Leave This Island*
    Howard Livingston & Mile Marker 24, *Red 69 Oldsmobile*
    The Barefoot Man, *Back To The Island*
    Terry Cassidy, *Henry and His Railroad*
    Michael McCloud, *Tourist Town Bar*
    Rolando Rojas, *Toda la Noche*
    Jose Feliciano, *Hi Heel Sneakers*
    C.W. Colt, *Key Western Cowboy*
    Arrow, *Hot Hot Hot*
    Yankee Jack, *Key West Serenade*
    The Young Rascals, *Groovin'*
    C.W. Colt, *Mi Amigo Mosquito*
    Bossa Rio, *Old Devil Moon*

Cover photo by Rob O'Neal

Printed in the United States of America

LCCN 2011943491

ISBN 978-1-936818-22-8 case binding
ISBN 978-1-936818-23-5 e-pub
ISBN 978-1-936818-24-2 e-pdf

SeaStory Press
305 Whitehead St. #1
Key West, Florida 33040
www.seastorypress.com

This book is dedicated to our precious Coco, a miniature long-haired dachshund. For fourteen years he brought smiles to our faces, gladness to our hearts and unconditional love as he zealously guarded our Vero Beach home from all threats, both real and imagined, of the outside world and steadfastly defended our Keys home from roving iguanas. Coco passed out of our lives but not out of our memories on October 31, 2011.

David & Nancy Beckwith

CHAPTER 1

The evening calm was deceiving. A veneer of contentment lay over the perfect tropical night at the Dolphin Marina. Will and Betsy Black had driven from Vero Beach that afternoon with their friends Jimmy and Henri Sue Bynum to spend a relaxing Fourth of July in the Keys. Guy and Penny Walsh had taken their car down, trailing their boat along with the two teenagers, Lexie and Laura, and the group had reconvened at the Dolphin Marina in Little Torch Key. The trip had been planned since last Christmas, which the Walshes and the Blacks had spent together. All anticipated a marvelous holiday weekend.

After dinner, Guy, Will, and Jimmy pulled some of the marina's resin chairs near the waterfront to enjoy the cool early-evening air. Guy and Jimmy each lit up a cigar to go with the remainder of a bottle of Chardonnay they had brought downstairs after dinner. Lexie and Laura disappeared, deciding to explore the dock to see if they could spot some fish. Conversation continued in a low-key, easy-going manner as they watched the shimmer of the water reflecting the light of the moon. Each was completely relaxed as the Keys disease took hold. In the background they could hear the bass notes of music coming from the Gulf side.

"I see there's a rock band playing at Boondocks," Guy said, referring to the tiki bar. "They'll be going until the wee hours. I understand Mile Marker 24's playing."

"If that's who it is, the place will be packed," Will said. "Howard's developed one hell of a following down here. He'll also be on Lower Sugarloaf tomorrow night for the fireworks celebration. I was playing one of his discs on the boom box a little while ago upstairs."

"It always seems strange how far sound will carry over water - that music is coming all the way from Ramrod," Guy said.

"Sounds like everyone's having a good time, but I'd rather be right here tonight, kicking back and making my own drinks with my own whiskey. It will be fun listening to them in person tomorrow night, though. As soon as I get the energy, I'm going upstairs to get a refill. Anybody need anything while I'm there?" Will asked.

Guy looked up at the sky and took a lazy drag on his cigar. There wasn't a cloud anywhere. He exhaled a big puff from his cigar. "I'm good right now. Damn, this is relaxing. The stars are always so clear down here. They just seem to pop out of the sky. I could get used to this."

"I already have," Jimmy agreed. "It would take a stick of dynamite to jar me out of this chair."

Suddenly, their tranquility was broken by the sound of an outboard motor pulling up to the far end of the marina dock. Almost before they could turn their heads to look, the boat quickly emptied. There appeared to be fifteen to twenty Cuban refugees who instantly took off across the pearock that covered the parking lot. Will panicked until he saw Lexie and Laura safe at the other end of the dock. The high-powered boat slammed into reverse, turned and immediately took off from the protected harbor back to open water. They could hear the motor jump into full throttle and quickly disappear into the night. The pilot never looked back as the cargo of passengers scattered in all directions.

A woman with a young boy holding her hand tripped over a rock in the grassy area of the parking lot. Will, Guy and Jimmy ran to assist her since most of the other Cuban immigrants had vanished into the dark.

Betsy, Penny and Henri Sue witnessed the landing from the porch of Hibiscus #1. The woman was shaken, but not hurt. "Gracias," was all she said.

Betsy dialed 911 on her cell phone.

Penny said she had read the illegal aliens coming in via the sea were instructed to find locals who could help them call immigration officials for processing. The current law initiated by the Clinton administration is known as the "wet foot-dry foot" policy. Simply put, Cubans who reached land before being caught by the Coast Guard, Navy, DEA or Border Patrol fell under the "dry foot" portion of the law, which meant they could remain in the United States. Those less fortunate who were interdicted at sea were rounded up and returned to Cuba.

Betsy added, "There have been many explanations as to why people take such huge risks to come to America. Many describe the Castro regime's failed political, economic and social policies. Others have said life in Cuba has simply become too unbearable to deal with. Some blame it on U.S. imposed travel restrictions. The discussions on the topic are almost as endless as the smuggling traffic from Cuba."

Then all was quiet again except for the thumping bass of the band coming from Ramrod Key.

CHAPTER 2

The day that had lazily ended at Dolphin Marina had begun on a different note as Will and Betsy raced at eighty miles an hour on the turnpike, eager to leave the mainland behind. Even going that speed, many cars zoomed by them.

Unnatural manufactured swells billowed and gradually melted into the horizon. These were not nature's beautiful free-form seas of blue water gracefully crested with white foam but boxy geometric houses that had been tinted terracotta red and sandstone. Occasionally, this uniformity was interrupted by an infrequent rectangle of a lone, out-of-place, desert sand house, highlighted by a lone, out-of-place, green roof. The darker green and desert sand seemed strangely inconsistent in this ordered environment and would momentarily catch the eye. Then the predictable terracotta and sandstone would continue monotonously once again.

"Here we are in Homestead. As long as I live I'll never become accustomed to this sight. Homogenated living without any cream - is this what all of Florida is destined to look like in the future?" Betsy asked.

Jimmy and Henri Sue had been friends of the Blacks since Mobile days when Henri Sue and Betsy had worked together as faculty members at the University of South Alabama. Like Will, the Bynums were originally Mississippians. The Bynums had relocated to Florida a year after the Blacks arrived, and when Lexie was born, they were Will and Betsy's natural choice to become Lexie's godparents.

As their SUV reached an overpass where the turnpike was elevated, this lofty position on the Florida peninsula gave them a panoramic view for miles. No matter where one looked the view was of rows and rows of houses on schematically laid-out streets where the developer's bean counters had evaluated the use of every square foot. These houses were designed from a list of painstakingly planned proven salable models. Landscaping was limited, controlled and uniform. Privacy fences to break the continuity were non existent. Swimming pools were not in the budget for houses in this price range. Three bedrooms, two baths, a bonus room, a two car garage. The American dream in paradise - with an unobstructed view of the turnpike. Who could ask for anything more?

"Would you rather live in a Four Winds model or the Siesta Key model? Maybe something sophisticated and English like a Wycliffe or Ashleigh? How about something sexy and Spanish like Palencia or Granada or Casa Lobo?" Will asked his fellow passengers sarcastically.

Betsy smiled. She and Will had talked about this topic often.

"A rose is a rose is a rose," Henri Sue said with a laugh. "These houses all look the same to me – like – kachunk, kachunk - they were stamped out of a mold. Speaking of roses, what do you want to bet that there's a Roseland model in that metropolitan wasteland somewhere, and there's nary a rose bush in sight."

"I bet with a little practice we could become mercenary Florida developers – the originators of the concept of transfer of wealth. And now for the snowbird who wants everything…for our next magic trick we have designed… drum roll please… the ever popular…Southern Comfort model…Hold your applause until the end of the trick."

"That would look right at home beside the Canadian Club model," Jimmy added.

"Or the Chardonnay."

"I'll drink to that but, seriously, look at this urban sprawl. A few years ago we had an uninterrupted view of farmland and groves. Now there's very little vegetation remaining. This is a recent transformation that has happened since Hurricane Andrew," Betsy said.

"I read an article recently in the *Miami Herald* that said within a very few years Miami-Dade County will be completely built out," Betsy continued.

"They're probably right," Jimmy agreed.

"I've always considered our home to be our refuge against the world, but I doubt I'd feel that way if I lived in the middle of this," Henri Sue said. "If you live there, you'd best be a teetotaler. Since they all look alike, if you ever got drunk you'd never be able to find your way home."

Will suddenly braked to avoid another motorist who had whipped into his lane without looking. He eyed a pickup tailgating him impatiently. He glanced to his right where they were in lockstep with a truck. A motorcycle zoomed by at breakneck speed to his left.

"I wish that son of a bitch in that pickup would get off my ass…"

"Will, watch your temper…," said Betsy.

"I'm going eighty, for God's sake. He acts like I'm doing forty. The bastard must have a death wish. The signs say to be careful because of the construction. Have you noticed, Betsy, this whole place is under construction year round? It never ends any more. You would think that at some point you would get a respite, but as soon as the lanes being worked on are completed, they start adding more lanes, along with new interchanges. Where's it all going to end? At the rate we're going there will be one big wide east-west highway that extends from the Gulf to the Atlantic. Will this growth ever end?"

"Doesn't seem like it! Retiring baby boomers want to live in Florida and in the process they have turned south Florida into one nonstop, never ending construction project – kind of like what you read about in China. I read that in the last five years China has initiated 53 billion square feet of housing projects," Betsy said.

"A mutual fund wholesaler who did a luncheon meeting a few weeks ago at my office to promote his international fund said Chinese activity is escalating at an average of ten percent a year – even from these heightened levels," Will said. "No wonder there's a worldwide shortage of concrete. Reading about China almost makes you appreciate Dade County, doesn't it?"

"I wouldn't go that far. I do wonder how long it will be before this out of control growth reaches the Treasure Coast," Jimmy said.

"It may be coming sooner than expected now that the Treasure Coast is becoming a mecca for biotech research. Thank you, Lord, for the Keys. It may soon be the last place south of Orlando where sanity reigns."

"Since when did funky and sane become synonyms?" asked Betsy.

"'Variety is the very spice of life, that gives it all its flavour – William Cowper,'" Henri Sue said.

Everyone laughed.

"Just a few more miles to Florida City and this will all be behind us until we pass this way again. Bye bye, rat-race mainland; hello, laid-back Keys. I can almost taste my first mojito. I'll gladly give my little patch of super highway back to some other desperate soul…they can all drive each other nuts with my blessings…though in most cases, it's a short drive. By the way, are you going to take Card Sound Road?" asked Betsy.

"Hell, yes! I've seen enough construction for one day," Will said. "I'm ready to see wetlands, woods and water. Until they get that new bridge complete over Jewfish Creek, as far as I'm concerned Card Sound is the only way to go. It's well worth the buck toll. Besides that I love the drive. Eighteen plus miles of absolutely nothing is a godsend after going through the megalopolis of Broward and Dade counties. So cheer up folks; we're over halfway to our destination."

"I'll never forget the first time Jimmy and I came down to Key West. We got to Homestead and thought we were almost there. Were we ever wrong! As stiff as I feel right now, I can see this trip hasn't gotten any shorter," Henri Sue said with a laugh.

"You ever wonder how a modern road and bridge like the one on Card Sound Road came to be in the middle of such a remote area?" Betsy asked.

"Yes, I have. It does seem strange," Jimmy said.

"It's also an interesting story," Betsy said as she described the origins of Card Sound Road.

The concept of Card Sound Road goes back to 1921 and the Florida land boom when a group called the Miami Motor Club was looking for a way to attract tourists and fishermen to the most easily reached part of the Keys. With the help of wealthy real estate speculators who saw an opportunity to take thousands of acres of worthless Keys land and turn a handsome profit, the Motor Club was able to persuade the county commissioners from Monroe and Dade counties to jointly float a $300,000 bond issue to build a road and bridge that would connect Florida City to Key Largo. The road project almost got abandoned when they ran out of money. The Dade side was completed so Dade taxpayers left Monroe high and dry to finish it. Monroe County had to float an additional bond issue on their own to complete their part of the project. The bridge on Card Sound Road was a wooden drawbridge until 1969. That's when the bridge that they were about to go over was opened. It was funded by the Department of the Interior as part of their Biscayne National Park project. There were plans at one point to build a toll road that would connect Key Biscayne to Key Largo, but that never happened.

After Betsy finished, Will said, "My wife, the historian!" as Betsy gave her husband a slightly irritated glance.

"Don't get your feelings hurt. I'm not heckling you –you are a wealth of information, my dear."

"Gee, and I thought you just married me for my pretty face."

"It is a good thing Key Biscayne and Key Largo were not connected," Jimmy said. "That certainly would have opened the floodgates from the mainland."

"By the way, I see the sign for the end of the turnpike," Henri Sue said.

"Great! I know we're not in the Keys yet, but when I get on US 1 and see the Last Chance Saloon, I feel like we are," said Will."

"Good old Last Chance Saloon. Now that's a landmark! We really ought to stop and go in there sometime, if for no other reason than just to say we've been there. After all, that is where the Conch Republic was born," Will continued.

"I've seen Conch Republic souvenirs all over the Keys. I guess I never really thought about their significance," Henri Sue observed.

"It's significant all right...besides being a multimillion dollar industry. Now that's a story – could only have happened in Monroe County. It was in 1982 – two years after the Biscayne National Park project finally became a reality," Betsy said.

"I thought you said that Card Sound Road opened in 1969 as part of the Key Biscayne project," said Jimmy.

"You heard me right, but it still took until 1980 for Key Biscayne Park to actually open."

"Monroe County has the distinction of not only seceding from the Union once but twice. The first was in 1982 when the U.S. Border Patrol set up an inspection point across from the Last Chance Saloon; the second time in 1995 when the 478th Army Battalion made the mistake of conducting training exercises in Key West to teach the troops what it would be like to invade a foreign island."

"We'd love to hear them both."

"I truly don't know which incident was funnier," Betsy said.

"Both were Keys original, that's for sure. But I really don't blame the 1982 *Moron County* officials for doing something outrageous to get the Federal government's attention. Do you know the story?" Will asked.

"Will, it's Monroe County not *Moron County*."

"Tell Henri Sue and Jimmy the story, Betsy, and let them decide."

"I'm not sure if I've ever heard either tale, so you've got my attention," Jimmy said.

As they drove, Betsy relayed the historical events surrounding the Last Chance Saloon. In 1982, the federal government determined that at least seventy percent of the illegal smuggling activity in the nation took place in the

Keys. They set up an inspection point across from the Last Chance Saloon and started to search every vehicle coming out of the Keys to see if it was carrying either illegal drugs or aliens. Cars waited in line for as long as five hours to get through the checkpoint. The traffic gridlock was miles long. As a result, the hassle soon started killing tourism. The officials of Monroe County tried reasoning with the Feds to no avail. The Border Patrol had an agenda they were committed to - come hell or high water. Monroe County officials even brought suit against the federal government in which they maintained the county line between Monroe and Dade counties was being treated illegally as if it were a foreign border instead of a county line. The court refused to give them an injunction to stop the searches. The only easy way in and out of Key West was Eastern Airlines from Miami. This route of Eastern Airlines was extremely profitable because every plane was full. People didn't care what the tickets cost. They simply did not want to sit out on a hot highway for hours waiting to have their cars searched.

"What a fiasco!" Jimmy said, shaking his head.

The whole scene turned into a circus when locals and employees of the Last Chance Saloon taunted the Border Patrol officers and DEA agents by shooting smoke out of a cannon and throwing bricks of firecrackers under their trailer and other similar shenanigans. The carnival went on, day after day.

Henri Sue laughed.

Finally in April, the Key West City Council had had enough. The affair then ratcheted up to a three ring circus. Monroe County seceded from the United States and declared it was now the Conch Republic. The mayor of Key West, Dennis Wardlow, was named prime minister. He immediately declared war on the U.S. Armed aggression ensued when Wardlow symbolically broke a loaf of stale Cuban bread over the head of a man dressed in a naval uniform. Exactly one minute later Wardlow surrendered and immediately applied for one billion dollars in foreign aid.

The news media from all over the world covered this story – and the partying escalated as everyone awaited the federal government's response.

"If you liked the 1982 story, you'll love the 1995 Conch Republic saga," Betsy said. "If ya'll aren't sick of stories, I'll tell you about it. It won't take long."

"I don't have any place to go…for another two hours," Jimmy chuckled.

In September, 1995, the Army Reserve's 478th Public Affairs Battalion decided to conduct a training exercise in which they would simulate the invasion of a foreign island. They chose Key West for the exercise. There was one tiny problem, however. They forgot to notify Key West that they were coming.

When the local officials saw the training exercises taking place, Dennis Wardlow, the ex prime minister of the Conch Republic, and his compadres decided that this was too good of an opportunity to pass up to get a little cheap publicity at the Army's expense. Therefore the Conch Republic was resurrected. Once again they seceded from the Union and declared all-out war. The insurgents of the Conch Republic then attacked by firing water cannons from fireboats and hitting people with stale Cuban bread. The following day they issued a formal apology and quickly surrendered in an elaborate public ceremony.

The Conch Republic refused to die. During the federal government budget shutdown in '95 there was one last attempt to milk the Conch Republic when the rebels under its banner attempted to invade Fort Jefferson out on the Dry Tortugas. Since the government was briefly shut down due to a lack of funding, Fort Jefferson was temporarily closed. Before the attack the Conch rebels raised money all over the lower Keys which was to be donated to the park to climax the invasion. There was only one problem - when they got to Fort Jefferson, there were no park rangers working that day for them to give the money to. The wannabe revolutionaries tried to enter the fort anyway and were cited for trespassing. Not exactly a passive group, the rebels retaliated with a lawsuit. When they did, the government saw the whole Conch Republic affair getting out of hand one more time and quickly dropped the entire matter – a fitting end to one of the most ridiculous invasions of all time.

"I think I'm starting to understand the nickname *Moron* County," Jimmy laughed.

"This is going to be a fun Independence Day."

CHAPTER 3

After a short stretch of US 1 through Florida City, Will saw the sign he was looking for.

CARS $1.00
CARD SOUND ROAD
UPPER KEY LARGO
VIA TOLL BRIDGE
NEXT LEFT

Card Sound Road was a very lightly traveled two-lane road with narrow shoulders. Within minutes they were in the middle of nowhere, surrounded by classic Florida brush. There was very little to see, and there didn't appear to be any particular place to set up a speed trap, so drivers seemed to pay very little attention to the posted speed limit.

"This toll bridge is going to cost us a whole dollar," Betsy commented. "That may not seem like a lot, but last year Lexie was meeting us down in the Keys for a long weekend. She came directly from school. We told her that

US 1 was a disaster with all the construction going on at Jewfish Creek. We suggested that she take Card Sound Road instead. We even reminded her of the toll. You're not going to believe this, but when she got to Card Sound Road and realized there was a toll, she remembered she did not have any cash to pay the toll. She had to turn around and go back to US 1 to find an ATM. Can you believe that child took off on a trip without even a dollar in her pocket?"

"Yes, I can," Henri Sue said. "My boys used to do the same kind of thing."

"I guess I must come to the realization that our children's generation lives on plastic," said Betsy.

"Anybody getting hungry?" Will asked. "We're coming up on Alabama Jack's – in the middle of scenic downtown Card Sound. Ya'll want to stop for lunch?"

"I'd rather get to Dolphin Marina so we can get unpacked before the rest of our crew shows up," Betsy said.

"Well, let's do this then," Will said. "We'll get some conch fritters and sweet potato fries to go. Their conch fritters are to die for."

When the sign indicated the Monroe County line, they could see Alabama Jack's. It was a ramshackle building that extended out on stilts over the water. Downtown Card Sound consisted of some commercial boat slips adjacent to a few equally time-worn buildings. Blink and you'd miss it. Crab traps and old trailers littered the side of the road. A crooked homemade sign next to a wooden phone pole announced:

LIVE BLUE CRAB

Next to it was a more formal sign telling them their location.

THE HISTORIC FISHING VILLAGE OF CARD SOUND, FLORIDA

Will parked on the gravel shoulder next to the wooden Alabama Jack's sign. A ragged stockade fence surrounded the building which was weathered and old; one end was two stories and the other was only one story. The flat roof gave it the boxy look that was so common for buildings in the Keys. The exterior of the structure had been painted as a blue sky and decorated with white clouds. There was no air conditioning.

"I'll be dog," Jimmy commented. "You can see the water between the slats in the floor."

The dining area had a bar and aluminum patio tables with glass tops that were scattered around the deck; striped deck chairs alternated haphazardly with resin furniture. Crab buoys hung from the inside of the stockade fence.

The order was soon filled and they were back on the road again, crossing the Card Sound Road Bridge.

"These are good conch fritters. I wonder who Alabama Jack is." Jimmy asked.

"Typical Keys confusing," Will told him. "First of all, Alabama Jack is dead – has been for years. Second, he wasn't from Alabama but from Georgia. Some of the Yankees called him Alabama Jack because to them, southern was southern."

"I guess we all do look alike," Henri Sue mocked.

"And sound alike too. I saved the best for last. Before he came to the Keys, Alabama Jack was one of the riveters who built the Empire State Building. He bought the lease on this property from a Miami plumber. He originally never had any intention of running a restaurant; he was just looking for a place to keep his boat."

Will soon hung a right and after travelling about eight more miles, they were back to US 1.

"Key Largo!" Will announced.

"That was really a good movie. It was just on TV a few months ago," Betsy said.

"Key Largo is the largest Key but is still unincorporated. All the local decisions emanate from Key West," said Will.

Betsy added, "Key West is almost 130 miles away. Town or no town, Humphrey Bogart made this place...And Lauren Bacall and Edward G. Robinson...And don't forget Lionel Barrymore and Clair Trevor...Even though not one scene in the movie was shot in Key Largo...It was all shot on a sound stage in Hollywood."

"I didn't know that," Henri Sue said.

"I didn't either until Robert Osborne told us when we saw it on TCM. By the way, as long as we're talking about Bogie – the African Queen is here in Key Largo. It's a tourist attraction."

"That's another place we ought to go sometime – if for no other reason, just to say we've seen it," said Betsy.

"We could do that and go out to John Pennecamp State Park one day. After all the Keys are the only living coral barrier reef in North America," Will added.

"We've talked about doing that, but never got around to it since Looe Key National Marine Sanctuary is so close to the Dolphin Marina," continued Betsy.

"There is also Looe Key Tiki Bar – now that's a local's hangout if there ever was one. I swear – their bar stools are scarce as hen's teeth from about eleven in the morning on – seven days a week," Will said.

Everyone laughed and said in unison "Keys disease!" and then laughed again.

As they were leaving Key Largo they crossed the bridge into Tavernier. Everyone was now starting to transition into the Keys. The feel of the mainland had definitely been left far behind. Will turned on the John Bartus CD he had brought for the trip.

> *Some folks say I'm wasting my life*
> *But I say I'm doing just fine*
> *You see, I've got the Keys disease*
> *In case you haven't heard*
> *I've got the Keys disease*
> *Mañana is the operative word…*

"Good choice," Betsy commented and began to sing along.

"We can start counting down the mile markers now. We're at mile marker 92."

"What's our destination?" Henri Sue asked.

"Mile Marker twenty eight and a half as the crow flies on the Overseas Highway. Thank you, Henry Flagler."

"Did ya'll see the History Channel show on the Overseas Highway?" Betsy asked. "This has been dubbed as one of the five most scenic drives in the world."

"I also read that it's the longest archipelago in the world connected by bridges – 43 to be exact," said Betsy.

"And we'll be going over all three of the longest bridges in the Keys today – Long Key, Seven Mile, and Bahia Honda," Will added.

"Another piece of trivia – after the 1935 Labor Day hurricane heavily damaged the Overseas Railroad, the State of Florida was able to buy the whole shooting match from what was left of the Florida East Coast Railway for only $640,000," said Betsy.

"Sure shows how things have changed. Any kind of house at all – I don't care how crappy and rundown – on water down here now brings almost that much," said Will who added, "And if it's on open water it'll bring a hell of a lot more than that."

"The 1935 hurricane was one of the worst in U.S. history…came right over Islamorada…over 400 people died. Would have been worse too if half the people in the work camps hadn't gone to Miami that weekend for a baseball game," said Will.

"We know all about Labor Day hurricanes, don't we? People in Indian River County are still doing repairs from Clarice," said Betsy.

"Yeah, that was tough, but thank goodness it wasn't a cat 5," Will said. "There's only been three category 5 hurricanes that have struck the United States and the '35 storm was one of these. Can you imagine if we had had a twenty foot storm surge like they did in that storm? Vero Beach would only be a memory. A lot of the loss of life in '35 could have been prevented if the bureaucrats hadn't dilly-dallied around on sending down the rescue train until it was too late. The train didn't even get under way out of Miami until after the storm had started. By that time it was too late. The train derailed in Upper Matecumbe Key. Upper Matecumbe was one of the keys flattened by that storm."

Before they knew it, they were at mile marker 82 cruising through Islamorada. Will stopped to fill the car with gas and find the local newspapers and then they headed for the Matecumbe Keys.

Before sharing the news from the *Key West Citizen* and the *Keynoter*, Betsy said, "It is refreshing to hear what is going on in the Keys – in most cases it is absolutely entertaining."

Once they started reading the papers, they were all laughing at most of the news items.

> Key West – Police pepper-sprayed a 45-year-old amputee who allegedly punched and bit her lover and then kicked and punched officers with her only arm.
>
> Key West – Police are looking for a woman who allegedly stole clothes from Sears and then drove through the parking lot with a store manager hanging on her hood.
>
> Key West – Two Key West men were trying to buy pizza Wednesday night when the employees started throwing napkin dispensers for no reason, they told officers.
> The two employees said the customers were angry when their change fell on the floor and started throwing things.
> The workers told police they had to throw objects back in self-defense.

Because officers heard conflicting stories and couldn't find a sober witness, no arrests were made, though all parties were issued case numbers.

Stock Island - A 25-year-old inmate was moved to the county jail's infirmary after losing 20 pounds over the last week on a hunger strike, sheriff's spokeswoman Becky Herrin said.

Key West – A 20-year-old man said he awoke Wednesday night on Smathers Beach to find another man, with his genitals exposed, squatting over him and trying to unbutton his pants.

Officers said the alleged victim and the alleged exposer were both intoxicated and had conflicting stories, so no arrests were made, though both were issued a case number.

Ramrod Key – A Boondocks employee was arrested on charges of stealing a case of beer from where he works.

By the time they drove into Layton the group was almost crying they were laughing so hard.

"Even the news down here is bizarre," Jimmy laughed. "Better slow down, Will, I see a cop car parked on the side of the road."

"You talking about the Layton police cruiser?" Will said. "That car has been sitting in exactly the same place pointed at the highway with no driver as long as we've been coming here. Notice as we go by, they even mow the grass around it. I seriously doubt there is even any law enforcement in Layton. That is why that Monroe County sheriff's vehicle is constantly parked there probably as a deterrent to speeders.

Layton has less than 200 people. You'll never guess who made Layton famous... Remember Zane Grey?"

"The guy who wrote westerns?" asked Jimmy.

"*Dick Powell's Zane Grey Theater*...I remember that. His books were the basis of the Lone Ranger and Sergeant Preston of the Yukon," said Henri Sue.

"The same. Zane Grey was a major fisherman...He fished all over the world. Layton was his favorite fishing spot in the Keys," added Will.

About as quick as it took them to blink, they were through Layton headed for Long Key. They were passing mile marker 67.

Everyone in the car was quiet, entranced by the beauty of the drive. The view was even more breathtaking as they drove onto the Long Key Bridge. Approaching the middle of the long bridge gave one the impression you were in a boat seeing shimmering blue-green tropical waters stretching to the horizon in all directions. Seagulls rode the wind currents as pelicans searched the waters below for fish. A Suburban in front of them was towing a twenty-six-foot boat with twin engines. Another boat sped in their direction along side the bridge. A few diehard fishermen were out on the old bridge that ran parallel to it on the other side. A sign stenciled on the concrete fishing bridge informed visitors:

NO TENTS OR TARPS ON BRIDGE

"You wouldn't believe how many people camp out on some of these old bridges and fish all night," Will said.

"There aren't enough adjectives to describe this view," Henri Sue said. "No wonder people come from all over the world to see it."

Eventually the bridge had propelled them back onto land, once again passing a spot on the road's shoulder where mountain ranges of lobster traps were being stored. The weathered slatted boxes were piled two to four high on land, waiting for the opening of lobster season.

"Won't be long until lobster mini-season will be here. It always starts the last Wednesday and Thursday in July," said Will.

"Some of the locals dread it. They call mini-season amateur days and claim every idiot who owns a mask and fins shows up to dive for lobster. And there does seem to be an inordinate number of people getting hurt, even killed, during mini-season," said Betsy.

Approaching mile marker 61, they were on Duck Key, which has a long, modern looking causeway that leads from the Overseas Highway out onto Duck Key itself. The Keys started coming faster after that – Grassy Key, Crawl Key, Deer Key.

CHAPTER 4

As they were crossing over the bridge into Key Colony Beach on Key Vaca to Marathon, Will suddenly slammed on the brakes, as did the vehicles in front of him. Three men were running across U.S. 1 chased by another waving a gun. The gunman opened fire and shot one of the three. Other shots were heard hitting cars and glass windows. Everyone ducked. The shooting seemed to go on forever. Finally, it was quiet – Will, Betsy and the Bynums slowly raised their heads above the dashboard to see what was going on.

A crowd had gathered around the shooting victim. Another crowd had caught and subdued the gunman. Sirens could be heard coming in both directions. Since traffic was at a standstill, people were getting out of their cars – some to see if they could help and others curious to find out what this unexpected scene was all about.

By the time Will, Betsy, Jimmy, and Henri Sue reached the shooting victim, an ambulance and the police had arrived. The victim was dead – someone had covered the body with a beach towel. The crowd holding the assailant was angrily shoving him toward the Monroe County Sheriff's deputy's car. The middle-aged man was shouting obscenities and appeared to be eager to shoot more people if he hadn't been stripped of his gun.

The entire scene was reminiscent of a movie set – Will and Betsy looked at each other in disbelief. Finally, Jimmy said, "Golly, I've never seen anything like this."

Some passengers on a bus several vehicles ahead of Will and Betsy's SUV had been cut with broken glass. Another more fortunate member of the trio being chased was shot in the leg. The third man was unhurt, but shaken.

"You see crime on television and the movies and read about it in the newspaper, but you never expect to actually be involved," said Betsy as she looked around the blood soaked area. "To think we were laughing about those petty criminal cases in the newspaper."

"I wonder why someone would chase people at gunpoint across a major highway in broad daylight thinking they would not be caught," said Henri Sue. "This is freakish – that guy could have hurt or killed a lot more people," she continued.

The deputies were questioning people as they worked the stopped line of vehicles. A deputy by the name of Davis approached Will, Betsy and the Bynums as they stood by their SUV.

"Did you see anything that might help our investigation?" he asked.

"Out of the corner of my eye, I saw the men running from my right," Will answered pointing at the Gulf side of U.S. 1.

"From that real estate office over there?"

Will pointed to a building with a sign that read:

CLUB TROPIC REAL ESTATE SALES.

"That's a great starting point! No one else has been able to pin-point the origin of this dispute," said the deputy. "What is your name? We may need to call you as a witness."

After Will gave the deputy his name and their Vero Beach address the deputy asked, "Is there anything else you might have seen that would be pertinent?"

Will told him they saw little more after that since they were all crouched down to protect themselves. "We're not used to seeing anything like this," Will concluded. "All of us are professional desk-jockeys. None of us even owns a gun."

The deputy thanked them and told them traffic would be moving again as soon as the medical examiner confirmed the death of the victim.

CHAPTER 5

"Seven Mile Bridge is coming up soon," Will said. "By the way, there's a restaurant on the Gulf side called the Keys Fisheries. We've got to bring you back up to go to it one day while we're here. You sit on picnic tables out on the edge of the water and eat some of the freshest seafood in the Keys."

Before they knew it they had passed through Marathon and were close to beginning the drive on the bridge. To their left just before reaching the bridge was an old railroad car that was the distinguishing landmark on Knights Key, and home to a souvenir shop and shuttle for Pigeon Key.

"Interesting," Jimmy said, pointing to his right at a little island tucked away under the well worn concrete trestles of the old Seven Mile Bridge. It had seven white, wooden, tin-roofed cottages from yesteryear and was ringed with coconut palms. A ramp of massive railroad ties curved gently down to the island. A tiny, almost toy-looking, open-air train with a dozen or so eager passengers was headed up the ramp.

"That's Pigeon Key, and that train is called Henry," Betsy commented.

Pigeon Key was originally a work camp for Henry Flagler's railroad workers. Over four hundred people lived there during its heyday. It was a town – had a post office – then became a home for the bridge tenders. It has been used for a lot of things over the years – everything from a bar to a satellite campus of the University of Miami where their marine biology lab was once located. In fact, there are fish holding tanks still present on Pigeon Key.

"Wow! Look at that view beyond Pigeon Key! The scenery just keeps getting better and better," said Henri Sue.

"See that section of the old bridge that's been cut out? That was the old swing span that was designed so boats could get through. They removed it when the new bridge, the one we're on, was opened in '82. Did you ever see Arnold Schwarzenegger's movie *True Lies*?" asked Will.

"Oh sure! The one about missile strikes," said Jimmy.

Will continued, "That's it! That's the bridge they destroyed in the film – the old Seven Mile Bridge. The special effects experts replaced that span for the movie just so they could film it before it was destroyed again in the movie."

"You mean the authorities let the movie makers bomb it?" asked Jimmy.

"Naa! They bombed a model, but the special effects boys replaced the missing span because they wanted to film pre-destruction scenes on the actual bridge," said Will.

"Didn't they also film one of the James Bond movies on the old bridge?" asked Henri Sue.

"Oh sure!" Betsy said. "*License To Kill*...the one where James' buddy Felix Leiter gets tortured and his new wife gets killed by the scuz bag drug czar."

"I remember! Timothy Dalton played Bond in that one," added Jimmy.

Once again conversation dried up because they were so overwhelmed by the panoramic view of the Atlantic Ocean transitioning into the Gulf. The graceful feel of the precast box-girder bridge made each person feel like they were on an airport runway surrounded by water. The shoulders on the bridge were generously wide so it made the two lane bridge seem even more open and wider than it was. Pelicans and gulls soared. The different shades of green and blue water alternated with dancing whitecaps. Colored buoys from an occasional lobster trap were seen, as was an infrequent fisherman. Sporadic Australian pines grew straight out of the pavement at a few places on the old bridge. Birds lined the abandoned bridge in perfect formation like nature's soldiers. At the top of the bridge, they were sixty-five feet above Moser Channel, headed for Ohio Key and then to Bahia Honda. The old bridge and the new one had been launched from Marathon into the water at virtually the same place until the old bridge crossed Pigeon Key. Now the two bridges shot parallel to each other for the rest of the almost seven miles across the shimmering water.

"I'll never get tired of this drive," Betsy commented. "It's like no other."

"We're getting close to our final destination. Only fifteen miles or so to go," said Will.

"I'm ready to get there," Jimmy sighed.

The scenery was now mangrove-fringed with water going to the horizon. They saw more power boats and more fishermen. Soon the road turned four-lane as they approached the Bahia Honda Bridge. Will passed a slower moving truck towing a boat and an RV.

"Notice the car tags on both of those guys," Henri Sue commented. "The truck towing the Wellcraft is from Delaware, and the RV in front of him is from California. I'm glad that I didn't have to drive either of those things all that distance."

"I'd rather take poison," Will replied cryptically. "I'm glad Bahia Honda popped up when it did. I read somewhere that before this bridge was built its predecessor was laid right on top of the old railroad trestles. The article said that the angle was such at the peak, drivers felt like they were going down a roller coaster when they topped it."

"I also read that it was so narrow when cars passed others their close encounters would rip the cars' rear view side mirrors off, and if you met a truck, someone would have to back off the bridge to let the other vehicle by."

"That must have been exciting...especially at night," said Jimmy.

After a few miles there was a bend in the road, and they started seeing black chain-link fence on the shoulders.

"Look at the car's compass. It shows we're going north. It sure is easy to get disoriented down here," Will said. "And see the dual speed limit signs – forty-five in the daytime and thirty-five at night. They are enforced too. That's to protect the Key deer. This is the only place in the world where these little deer live. I'm sure you'll see one sometime before we leave."

"I just brought my fishing gear – I should have brought a deer rifle instead," Jimmy said jokingly.

"Only if you want to go to jail," Betsy replied. "Key deer are a protected species, and they're very serious about it. There's only three or four hundred of them left. You'd have an easier time not getting convicted here for killing a human being."

"Kill a lobster trap robber, and they'd throw you a party. Kill a Key deer, and you'll go to jail," Will added. "Dolphin Marina - next stop. Soon as we get over the Newfound Harbor area, we'll be there."

"Thank goodness," they all agreed. "We're tired of riding."

"According to the trip odometer we've been 274 miles," Will said.

CHAPTER 6

The mismatched glasses, mugs, goblets, and jelly glasses filled with wine clinked in the tepid night air.

The ceiling fan purred.

Terry Cassidy played his song about the Bat Tower on the boom box.

> *Down on the coast of Florida*
> *On an island called Sugarloaf Key*
> *Everybody was running for cover*
> *As mosquitoes had started to feed*
> *It was out of control…*

Guy snuffed out his cigar and raised his glass high, "A toast to good friends and to the fourth of July in the lower Keys. I'm glad the Dolphin Marina could take us all."

Will reached over and turned the music down a notch.

Henri Sue broke in, "And to have the opportunity to spend a few days with my goddaughter and her friend Laura Walsh."

Laura and her parents, Guy and Penny Walsh, completed the group. Guy, like Will, was in the financial services industry. Instead of working for a large wire-house like Will's longtime employer, Reynolds Smathers and Thompson, Guy owned his own boutique financial services firm. Technically, he and Will were competitors, but each respected the other's ability, intelligence and integrity. Their similar backgrounds gave them interests in common. This strengthened their ability to keep their perspective and be friends first and competitors a distant second.

Henry Sue continued, "We stay so busy at work that we don't see enough of any of you. Thank you for including Jimmy and me this weekend. Girls," she said as she smiled at Lexie and Laura, "you've grown up to be delightful young ladies."

She affectionately squeezed Lexie's hand.

"I can't believe that you're both in college. Makes me nostalgic for when my Jim and Charley were still in school," Henri Sue added.

Lexie and Laura grinned at each other, pleased but embarrassed, and murmured softly, "Thank you."

Jimmy added, "Also let's toast Miami's football season. They got a BCS bowl invitation last season and whipped the fire out of Nebraska. That Hurricane program is certainly back on the map. I bet they'll do it again this year."

The girls looked pleased again. Both were wearing tee shirts with the big orange and green "U" logo.

"This rib platter is heavy," Penny said. "Why don't you pass your plates to this end, and I'll serve from here. Just tell me how big a slab you want."

35

The assemblage had set up a table on the screen porch of one of the furnished efficiency apartments they had rented from Dolphin Marina on Little Torch Key. They had been fortunate enough to rent the Hibiscus Building for the holiday weekend. It had three apartments, one upstairs and two down. The upstairs apartment had two bedrooms, a large living room-dining room area, a big roomy kitchen and an oversized screen porch. This porch was where the group planned to eat. From the porch they could see across the pearock driveway to the Dolphin Marina office. Flanking the utilitarian combination office and bait shop was a large L-shaped boat dock and launch area. There were gas pumps by the docking area and bait tanks on the dock adjacent to the building. From seats on the waterfront beach a guest could see the Newfound Harbor Bridge connecting Big Pine Key to Little Torch. Passing under this bridge allowed boats access to the Gulf from the Atlantic and vice versa, and it was the Atlantic Ocean channel that led to Picnic Island and then on to Little Palm Island. Boats continuing south past Little Palm Island took divers and snorkelers to Looe Key, the popular federally protected underwater marine sanctuary, or fished the Atlantic waters.

Dolphin Marina was an ideal place for harried vacationers to snag a few days away from the realities of the hectic mainland. As slow as the lower Keys pace was, the pace at this Little Palm Island resort was even slower.

Little Palm Island, a five acre island only accessible by water, had at one time been Harry Truman's fishing camp and retreat. In those days there had been no running water or electricity. Only after the island was used as a set for the movie about the war exploits of John F. Kennedy, *PT 109*, did the island rate these amenities. Local historians say Joe Kennedy, JFK's father, used pressure to force the extending of utilities to the tiny virtually uninhabited island because his son, the President, could not sleep at night with noisy generators running. The island later evolved into the five-star resort that now attracted moneyed people worldwide. Its slogan was appropriately "Do Nothing."

Betsy and Penny had ordered the ingredients for the Independence Day feast, and the entire group had pitched in to bring the meal together. They decided to hold this festive meal on July third since they were planning to spend the day at Picnic Island on the fourth and afterward go see the fireworks on Lower Sugarloaf Key. The electric oven in Hibiscus 1 easily accommodated the fifteen pounds of ribs that had been bought at Murray's meat market. Betsy made potato salad. Will called Aurelia Garcia to make sure Five Brothers 2 grocery store on Ramrod Key was open and then ran over to get a loaf of Cuban bread. The girls got the rest of what was needed with a quick run across Newfound Harbor to the Winn Dixie on Big Pine. Guy and Jimmy had made a wine run to Little Torch Key's only restaurant, Parrotdise, to buy a split case of Chardonnay and Cabernet Sauvignon, which was sold under the Big Pecker brand with the parrot on the label. Now it was time to savor and enjoy and to be thankful for just being there.

CHAPTER 7

The morning after their festive event everyone got up in a lazy mood on July fourth. The cloudless azure sky made it look like it was going to be another flawless Keys summer day.

About that time Betsy asked Will, "Would you mind seeing if they have a *Citizen* or a *Herald*?"

Will returned a few minutes later with a *Citizen*.

The front page revealed the details of the shooting the Blacks and the Bynums had witnessed the day before.

Gunman Apprehended In US 1 Shooting

A shooting occurred just after 1:15 pm yesterday on the eastern edge of Key Colony on U.S. 1, tying up traffic for ten miles in each direction. According to a Monroe County Sheriff's Department spokesman, a 68-year-old white male from Michigan will be charged with the assault with a deadly weapon and the murder of Douglas Handleson. Handleson, the manager of Club Tropic Real Estate Sales in Monroe

County was shot by Harris Snubs, a self-avowed racist with a long criminal history of violent behavior. Snubs also shot and wounded a Club Tropic realtor and attempted an assault on a third employee of that firm. Four others received minor injuries from broken glass on a bus caught in the gunfire.

One witness to the shooting, Will Black from Vero Beach, Florida, said he saw three men running from the real estate office pursued by another man shooting at them. A group of road construction workers, led by Bubba Cooley, tackled Snubs and held him until deputies arrived. It happened so fast, according to Cooley, he and his men could not stop Snubs before he allegedly killed Handleson and wounded the Club Tropic salesmen. "I just want the victim's family to know we reacted as quick as possible to prevent others from being shot," said Cooley.

In the gunman's car officers found a notebook with a sales contract on a Club Tropic property that had closed last month. The notebook had a hand-written note that read, "You want my weapons – this is how you'll get them – one bullet at a time. I'm not going to let the Jews take over the world."

Douglas Handleson was declared dead at the scene by the Monroe County Medical Examiner. Snubs is being held in the Monroe County Detention Center without bond.

Betsy began to tremble as she finished reading the article to Will. "Do you realize how close we were to the possibility of being caught in that idiot's sick obsession with a gun?"

Will responded, "I wonder if the holocaust and all of the hate and violence associated with it will ever end?"

Soon they were each drinking a cup of coffee. Betsy read the paper to Will.

Coast Guard Returns Migrants

The Coast Guard returned eight Cuban migrants to Cuba, at Bahia de Cubanas on Sunday. They were stopped in two separate incidents last week, reports say.

On July 2, the Coast Guard stopped a rustic boat carrying three Cuban migrants 70 miles southwest of Key West. On July 1, another such boat, with five migrants aboard, was stopped 80 miles southwest of Key West. All eight Cubans were transferred to Knight Island and provided with food, water, shelter and any necessary medical attention.

"Boy," Will observed. "They just keep on coming, don't they?"

"Yes, they do," Betsy sighed and shook her head.

They were both silent as they stared at the water.

"Looks like God picked a perfect day to have a holiday," she continued.

"That he did," Will agreed.

Presently they saw Guy over by the dock and waved.

"I'm going to launch the boat in a little bit," Guy announced. "Weather looks perfect."

"That's what we decided," Will said back. "I'll help you."

Shortly thereafter they saw Penny coming back from Dolphin Marina's office waving the newspaper about the shooting. Will and Betsy walked over to join them. All four strolled down to the waterfront to watch the birds diving for fish.

"I thought all night about those Cuban illegals we saw last night. I wonder what will happen to them," Penny commented.

"I'm sure they had relatives waiting to pick them up or were taken to Miami by the authorities to be processed into the United States. Whether they did or not, the main thing as far as they are concerned is that they made it – 'wet foot, dry foot.' They're here to stay. A year from now they can apply for legal residency," Betsy added.

"It sickens me to think how people struggle to get to our great country and then there are creeps here that are so consumed with hate they can kill a fellow American with no remorse," said Will.

Guy continued, "It may be out of season for tourists or lobsters but not for Cubans seeking asylum. The human smugglers work year round, inadvertently encouraged by the U.S. government. It's an ever-growing problem. Not only do the smugglers make a handsome living, but it takes up valuable Coast Guard time and money and risks the lives of desperate people."

"I guess these people will risk anything to get away from Castro's tyranny," Will said.

"The Cuban Adjustment Act really has good intentions," Guy said. "It acknowledges that Castro runs a despicable regime that crushes individual liberty as it suppresses economic freedom. It's no wonder every year thousands of Cubans make the decision that they will brave any hardship or danger to escape. Since the Adjustment Act ensures that any Cuban who touches American soil has the right to claim refugee status, smugglers have a guaranteed lucrative market.".

"Even if they're here illegally?"

"Makes absolutely no difference...The refugees also get entitlements and benefits, and after one year they can petition to live permanently and legally in the United States."

"I guess those incentives make it worth the risk," said Jimmy.

"Well let me put it this way, Cubans are willing to spend anywhere from eight to ten thousand dollars each for a three hour trip by go-fast boats from Cuba to the U.S."

"Yep, as you hear so often, it's only ninety miles," said Penny.

"With a guaranteed welcome from Uncle Sam if they make it. That's why someone is trying it almost every day of the year," said Will.

Guy had everyone's attention. He resumed his explanation.

"These smugglers are smart, efficient, and ruthless. For about $250,000 they can buy a boat that can outrun a Coast Guard cutter. People call these 'go-fast' boats. They often hire one of their recent clients to pilot the boat on a Cuba run in exchange for forgiving what they owe the smuggler for their own recent passage over. If these people get caught they are subject to federal prosecution. The owner of the boat then reports his boat as being stolen. That way if the authorities stop the boat, they can quickly reclaim it. As soon as it is reclaimed they send it out again."

"You can do the math in your head," Betsy said. "It only takes 25 passengers to pay for the boat."

"Velly good math! Most of the time they try to come in through the Dry Tortugas since it's the closest destination from Cuba as the crow flies," Guy continued.

"The irony of the whole situation is on the one hand we have our government encouraging smuggling with this legislation, and on the other hand they are insisting the Coast Guard do everything possible to stop it."

"Kind of reminds you of Federal policy on tobacco, doesn't it? We tell everyone not to smoke while we subsidize the tobacco farmer," said Will.

"The smuggling runs are made in the absolute dead of night. The boats are overcrowded as hell...They'll put thirty people or more on a boat rated to carry eight to ten. The smugglers run these boats full speed without any running lights, life jackets, or any kind of safety gear. When the Coast Guard spots one of these 'go-fast' boats a desperate race ensues. The only way they have to stop the smugglers is to shoot out their motors. This isn't exactly easy when it is pitch dark on rolling seas and everyone's hauling ass at fifty or fifty-five miles an hour," Guy said.

"That must be exciting," said Jimmy.

"Suicidal is more like it. The smugglers know that the Coast Guard has been instructed not to hurt anyone if at all possible, so the smugglers make some of the refugees lie across the boat motors," said Will.

"I can't imagine. Everybody involved is nuts," Jimmy added.

"Or desperate..."

Guy continued, "When they get near the shore, they beach the boat at full speed. The passengers are liable to be thrown most anywhere. Sometimes they go overboard. Sometimes they get concussions or broken limbs. People die. Sometimes they let them out on sandbars and leave the poor devils to try to swim to shore by themselves or drown."

"I guess these interdictions at sea are as risky for the Coast Guard agents as they are for the refugees," said Jimmy.

"I'd say that's right. I wonder why the smugglers take such chances. Why should they care if these people make it or not?" asked Henri Sue.

"Because they don't get paid unless the refugees make it to shore."

"Ohhh!"

"Besides the danger, think about how much time the Coast Guard has to devote to halting this process. They could be spending that time on port security or combating terrorism."

"Or stopping drug smugglers."

"I guess that bunch we saw last night had it pretty easy, comparatively speaking. The boat we saw let them off right at the Dolphin Marina."

"I guess that's one way of looking at it. Can you imagine though leaving behind everything you own and starting all over in a strange country?"

"We don't know how lucky we Americans are."

"And we forget that people will risk their lives to get to this country and enjoy the freedoms we have."

CHAPTER 8

By mid morning everyone was up and ready to go for the day.

"I've got a plan. Let's divide the jobs up," Will suggested. "Why don't I run over to Five Brothers 2 and get some breakfast sandwiches and Cuban pastries so the girls won't have to cook. I can pick up some Cuban mix sandwiches and munchies while I'm there to take out on the boat. Y'all can get towels, sunscreen et cetera ready for the boat. Jimmy and Guy can put the boat in the water and get it ready to go."

"That works," said Betsy.

"Lexie and Laura…Fill the ice chest with drinks. You can get bags of ice out of the machine over near the office."

"With everyone pitching in, we should be able to get out to Picnic Island before noon and get a good spot. You know it's going to be crowded as hell."

"Plus the weather is drop-dead gorgeous," said Lexie.

By eleven Guy was piloting his boat out of the harbor at Dolphin Marina, and they were headed out to the channel to go to Picnic Island. The waters were still relatively free of other boats.

Guy and Penny owned a Boston Whaler 240 Outrage with a blue canvas T-top. They called it *The Float Aloan*. It was almost twenty-four feet long and had an eight-foot beam. They were running two 150-horse Mercurys on the boat. It was rated for twelve people. One thing Guy and Penny loved about this boat was its eighteen inch draft. This made it perfect to go into shallow waters like those in the Keys. They also loved the boat's storage capacity and how it handled in rough seas.

"Let's take a few minutes," Will suggested, "and go down a couple of canals adjacent to Dolphin Marina. I've been told that there are some really nice houses there."

Guy turned down the first canal. There was a wide assortment of houses. Some had wooden docks, others PVC, and many had concrete. Everyone seemed to have some kind of boat. A few of the older houses had been built on ground level, but most were elevated. There were two houses under construction. As they got to the bend in the canal a house came into view that had brightly painted lobster trap buoys hanging almost everywhere. About halfway down the canal Guy had to negotiate around a huge catamaran that protruded out into the water. On their left they saw a house with a tall observation deck that seemed at least three stories high. Another house had a tiki hut with a rustic nameplate that said *Soltero*.

"We know that name, don't we?" Betsy remarked.

"With all the Latinos down here in the Keys, that's probably a common name," Will said.

A blue-gray three-story house with a full length porch came up on their right. It had a wide stained wooden dock that ran the entire length of the property.

"That looks nice," Betsy said.

"Has a *For Sale* sign on it too," Jimmy commented.

After passing a few more houses, Guy put the boat in reverse and said, "We probably ought to get on out to Picnic Island."

When they had emerged from the canal, they were back in the channel. Within ten minutes they saw boats at anchor and knew they had arrived at their destination. The little island before them was not much more than a sandbar. It couldn't have been more than two acres. Boats were already anchored, some as much as one hundred yards away from the shore. There were fishing boats, speed boats, pontoon boats and personal water craft. The sandy bottom gently sloped out from the island, nowhere exceeding four feet in depth. Most areas were only two to three feet deep. Sponges clung to rocks and coral along the bottom.

People in bathing suits waded from one boat to another. Others hung out on their own boats eating fried chicken or sandwiches. Some boats were tied together caravan fashion. Other people roamed along the postage stamp sized beach. There were dogs on boats, dogs with life jackets, dogs swimming, dogs on floats, dogs chasing Frisbees, dogs roaming the beach. Most people had a beer or other beverage.

Guy found an acceptable spot, and soon they were securely anchored. Henri Sue commented on how many of the boats were flying American flags.

"After all, it is Independence Day," Penny said.

More and more boats were continuing to arrive. Within a short period of time some boats were anchored as close as five yards from one another.

Lexie and Laura had already climbed off the boat and were working their way toward land.

"They've got the right idea," Jimmy announced. "I'm going to get wet."

"I've got cold beer here," Will announced.

The Bynums and the Blacks started wading lazily from boat to boat, drinks in hand.

Soon they were laughing at some of the boat names they saw.

Salt Diet
Mental Floss
Passing Wind
Wand'rin Star
Pontoon Tang
When Pigs Fly
Hail Merry
Sanbar Hunter
Nauti-Buoy

"Look," Betsy said pointing. "*Why Knot.*"

"Why not?" Jimmy said and laughed.

"That boy's probably telling the truth," Will said, pointing at the *N 2 Deep*.

"Look there's *Da Boat*."

"Sure it's not de plane, de plane?"

"When you name a boat, you can let it all hang out," Will laughed again. "See *Wackie Jackie*. There's *Z-Cruise* and *A'natural*."

He pointed around them.

"I know where *A'natural's* mind is. There's *Pam*. How did a name that normal get out here along side of *Satur Daze* and *R U Wet Yet*?"

"We don't have room to talk. We're riding in the *Float Aloan*," said Henri Sue.

"Look there's a little barge anchored over by the island. Let's go see what is going on," said Betsy.

When they got close to the island, they could see that there was a poster thumb-tacked to the barge. It announced:

4th of July
FREE CONCERT
WETSTOCK 2
THE STRAY DOGS
PICNIC ISLAND

A generator was humming on the barge. There were two banks of Peavey speakers on it. The band was starting to set up microphones and to test their guitars.

Jimmy pointed and exclaimed, "Well, damnation, they're going to have a concert out here on this sandbar."

"Looks like we lucked into a bonus we didn't expect," Will replied.

"See those Peavey speakers?" Jimmy said, "I went to school in Meridian, Mississippi, with Hartley Peavey. He started making those things in his basement. Now he sells his products in virtually every developed country in the world."

"It's not a public company, is it?"

"Nope, still private. Never had to go public. Can you imagine?" said Will.

"I honestly can't. Peavey's got to be one of the richest men in Mississippi."

"Ya'll stay here and I'll go find Guy, Penny and the girls and tell them about the concert," Jimmy suggested.

"Oh, I'm sure they'll be able to hear it."

"But they won't know what it is. I'll be back in a few minutes."

Jimmy waded off in the knee-high water to find the rest of their group. More and more sun-tanned people were gathering, drinks and food in hand. He passed a swimming Dalmatian. Another dog was wearing a straw hat and had on sunglasses that matched those of his owner. One man was towing his boat by hand to a mooring spot closer to the band. As Jimmy waded by, the owners of the *Black Pearl*, who were sitting up to their necks in water next to their boat, toasted him with margaritas they had topped with paper umbrellas. Jimmy almost lost his footing at one point trying to avoid stepping on a sponge. One man wore a red, white and blue top hat. Baseball caps, wet T-shirts and tank tops were the apparel of choice. Often T-shirts advertised their favorite restaurant or bar – No Name Bar, Schooner Wharf Bar, The Hogfish Bar and Grill, Sloppy Joe's, Mangrove Mama's, Boondocks, The Green Parrot. The list went on and on. A definite festive atmosphere was starting to take hold. Jimmy didn't see any apparent drunken troublemakers, only people from all walks of life who had come to have a relaxing party in the sun.

"No wonder they call this Wetstock," he said to a stranger paddling along in an inner tube.

The stranger laughed and toasted him.

"Lord," Jimmy said aloud. "I haven't seen an inner tube in years. I wouldn't even know where to buy one any more."

As they waited for the Stray Dogs to crank up, Will started talking to an old hippie wearing a T-shirt with cut out arms and an old pair of cut-off jeans. The old faded T-shirt said KARMA in big letters.

"You ever heard The Stray Dogs before?" the old hippie asked.

"No, I haven't," Will said.

"You're in for a treat if you like good classic rock and roll," the old hippie added. "By the way, my name is Reuben Nolan."

He held out a wet calloused hand. Reuben's other hand clutched a Budweiser.

Will noted that Reuben appeared to be an escapee from ZZ Top. He looked kind of like Billy Gibbons, ZZ Top's lead guitarist, in a bathing suit. Reuben's scraggly beard extended halfway to his waist. No attempt had been made to trim or shape it. It just simply grew wild out of his face. More of the beard was grey than any other color. Will guessed that Reuben had already seen his fiftieth birthday, maybe even fifty fifth. Completing the outfit was a pair of tortoise shell sunglasses and an old, ragged, very wide floppy straw hat that bore a *Re-elect Bush-Cheney in 2004* campaign button.

"My name is Will Black. This is my wife Betsy and our friend Henri Sue," Will responded, shaking hands back. You live near here?" Will asked.

"Yeah, over in Buccaneer Estates, that's the neighborhood that abuts the Dolphin Marina," Reuben said.

"So that's what they call that area. The Dolphin Marina's where we're staying," Betsy chipped in. "We took our boat through some of the canals before we came out here this morning. There's some really nice homes in there. We probably saw yours."

"Depending on which canal you went down, you probably did," Reuben agreed.

"We saw a for-sale sign on one really nice one," Will said. "It was a three-story blue-gray house with a big porch facing the canal. Had an absolutely pristine stained dock."

"That's the LaRiccia house – Phil and Sherrie, Reuben said. "If you went down that canal you did go right by my house. You're right. That's a very well built house. It's not some modular piece of shit that was built just to be flipped in a hot real estate deal. Phil's son is a general contractor. He constructed that house for his mom and dad to live in and built it as solid as a brick shit house. It was one of the first houses built after ROGO was passed. We all thought Phil and Sherrie would end up dying in that house. I still can't believe they're moving. Someone said they have a daughter up on the mainland, and they want to move closer to her and their grandchildren…Plus I heard that Hurricane Georges scared the hell out of Sherrie, even though it was one of the few houses in Buccaneer Estates that didn't sustain any damage."

"What's ROGO?" Will asked.

"Rate of Growth Ordinance. ROGO was instituted to control runaway growth in the Keys. It makes it very difficult to build new houses. If you invest in real estate in Monroe County, you'll soon learn all about it."

"We'd really love to own a second home here. We've talked about it before," Betsy said. "Will, maybe we ought to go over and look at the LaRiccia house while we're down here. If it looks anywhere near as nice on the inside, it might be a real gem."

A chunky, middle-aged woman in a faded two-piece bathing suit appeared and Reuben introduced her. "This is my fiancé, Esther Avery."

Her disheveled hair had gray streaks she had made no effort to color and hide. Her face was tanned and weathered. She had a beer in a coozie in one hand, a cigarette in the other. Around her neck was a dolphin pendant with a bright red cut-stone eye.

"Did I hear you talking about Phil and Sherrie's house?" Esther asked. "We had the Buccaneer Estates fish fry there. It's really nice."

"So you've been in it?" Betsy asked.

"Sure have. It's got these high ceilings that make it feel twice as big as it is. Somebody's going to get a good buy on it before it's all over. It's been on the market for at least eight months. It hasn't been shown much because Phil keeps vacillating on whether he really wants to sell it. Sherrie wants to be near her grandchildren pretty bad so I'm sure she'll win. They live up in Vero Beach."

"Well, I'll be damned. That's where we're from," Will said.

"Maybe that's an omen," Reuben said with a laugh. "By the way, I'm gettin' ready to marry this woman."

He put his big hand around Esther's waist and squeezed gently. He held out Esther's coozie, which read:

REUBEN AND ESTHER – JULY 5, 2005
PICNIC ISLAND
LITTLE TORCH KEY, FLORIDA

"That's tomorrow," Henri Sue commented.

"You're all invited. This is going to be one helluva celebration of life," Reuben said.

"You're inviting us? We just met. What an honor," said Henri Sue.

"Starts at one o'clock," Reuben said. "Just bring your boat out here…As many people as you can get on it. Get here early. We're going to party all afternoon. I guarantee that you won't forget it."

"What if it rains?" asked Betsy.

"Harrumph! It wouldn't dare rain on Reuben and Esther's parade," Reuben said.

He and Esther high-fived each other and did a booty bump.

"Now it's time to boooogie! I hear the Stray Dogs cranking up. Rock and Roll!" Reuben said.

He belched and leaned over into his boat to get another Budweiser.

CHAPTER 9

By the latter part of the afternoon everyone in Will and Betsy's party was starting to feel sunburned, waterlogged and beered out. The Stray Dogs were still going strong playing loud classic rock and roll. The party was sure to extend until sundown, which wouldn't be until almost eight. Since they were going to see the fireworks that evening, this would be a good time to go back to the Dolphin Marina.

"This sun's about to sap all the energy out of me," Jimmy said.

"A little nap wouldn't hurt," Guy agreed. "Why don't we pull anchor?"

Soon everyone was aboard the boat except Will who used the bow line to tow the *Float Aloan* far enough away from the massive tangle of boats surrounding Picnic Island so they could safely crank the engine and ease away from the ongoing ocean picnic.

"That was fun," Henri Sue said. "I can't think of a better way to spend the Fourth."

"I can't wait to get back and rinse the salt off," Betsy said.

Within minutes they were back at Dolphin Marina, unloading the boat and gathering up their belongings.

"Why don't we plan on reassembling at six, and we'll make plans from there," Will suggested.

Betsy washed her hair, and she and Will then relaxed under the ceiling fan on their porch. Will stretched back on the chase lounge and closed his eyes.

"That was an interesting house for sale over in Buccaneer Estates, don't you think," Betsy said.

"I loved the way it looked from the back. Seemed to be a nice clean, wide canal too," Will said.

"The old hippie, Reuben, seemed to be impressed with it. He said the place was really well built."

"He was a piece of work, wasn't he?" said Betsy. "But, if you didn't look at Reuben too closely and just listened, the old boy seemed to have a lot of sense."

"There's more to that old boy than it seems," Will said. "I found out he used to be CEO of a company that was a major supplier to Harley-Davidson. He sold it and made a fortune."

"I think it might be a mistake to underestimate Esther too," Betsy replied. "She's not as free a spirit as she appears. She is a loan officer for the credit union in Key West."

"Keys originals," Will said, laughing. "That's what I love about this place. People don't always fit a preconceived mold."

"Always…try *never*," Betsy said.

"Why don't we get Lexie, jump in the car, and see what the front of that house looks like this afternoon. It's only a few blocks from here. We'll be back in nothing flat," said Will.

"I'm up for it...I've got my second wind now. Why? Are you interested in it?" asked Betsy.

"Well, we have talked about how we like it down here," Will said.

"I guess we've been married too long, I was thinking the same thing," Betsy said. "Doesn't cost anything to look! Let me put on a visor to disguise this wet hair."

Within a few minutes Will, Betsy and Lexie were driving down Buccaneer Road. It was only one street away from the Dolphin Marina. Wetlands dotted the right hand side as they got their first look at Buccaneer Estates. The street was typical Keys eclectic. Most houses had a pearock yard. Some houses were neat as a pin; others were overgrown with sand spurs and other weeds and brush. They made the mistake of driving all the way down Buccaneer Road to the dead end and turning left on the street they found there. It was so narrow they couldn't turn around and had to back their car to get out.

Will drove back down to Le Grand and took a right. One block later they saw the sign for Port Royal Road.

They turned right and soon they saw a house on the right with a *FOR SALE* sign in front of it.

"That's it," Betsy said. "I recognize the dock."

Behind a large clump of buttonwood trees, was the attractive three-story house they had seen from the canal. The pearock yard appeared neat and swept. There was parking for two cars beneath the house. It was not boxy like many houses in the Keys, but had staggered wings of various sizes and heights. On one side the house went up three stories. The exterior was constructed of horizontal siding. From the roof line up was a vinyl fish scale siding that gave the house a remotely Victorian feel, Lexie pointed out. A round louvered porthole had been added as decoration near the top.

"I wonder if that siding is wood or vinyl," Will said.

"I can't really tell. Notice it does have a metal roof... That's good," said Betsy.

The house had Bahama-style shutters hinged at the top of the windows, imparting a relaxed tropical feel. A staircase came up parallel to the house to a landing and then continued in the opposite direction until it ended with a second porch landing. The staircase posts were decorated with large round newels and the entire stairwell had been stained a dark walnut color. There were several coconut palms in the yard.

"I know we didn't come down here to buy a house, but I'd like to see more about this one...And I do think the timing is good," Betsy said. "Didn't Reuben say it had been on the market for a while?"

"Uh! Huh! Says Century 21 on the sign. Maybe we can call them in the morning," Will said.

He wrote down the Realtor's phone number and name."

"Nira Tocco – the southernmost Tocco Belle – that's cute."

"And catchy," Lexie said.

They rode down a few more houses to one that had a Harley with a sidecar in the yard.

"What do you want to bet that's where Reuben and Esther live," Betsy said.

"I'm sure you're right," Will said. "You want to go to their wedding tomorrow?"

"Do we have to?" Lexie whined.

Betsy laughed and said, "I think that it would be a mistake if we don't. You know it's got to be a total hoot. Oh look, there's the name Soltero on the mailbox."

"Look at all those Hispanics under his almond tree. Looks like a family reunion," Betsy continued.

"They certainly don't look like they belong here. I know they're not workers – this is a national holiday," said Will.

"Notice what's pulled up to his dock. Looks like one of those 'go-fast' boats," said Betsy.

"Doesn't look like it has a name. I thought everyone here named their boats," added Will.

The street dead-ended. Will pulled into the driveway of a house under construction and turned around.

"Let's see what Port Royal looks like back down toward Dolphin Marina," Betsy suggested.

They retraced their route on Port Royal. Suddenly, Will pointed and laughed.

"Do you see what I see?"

They stared at a rustic old house surrounded by lawn decorations. There were balls, fountains, a radiator, gnomes and dwarves, baby shoes, an old Radio Flyer, a Schwinn bicycle with no tires, a car bumper, chains and ropes, a television antenna, boulders, a metal dog sculpture, spheres, concrete statuary. Hundreds of items, all painted bright silver.

"I know it's rude to stare, but I've never seen anything quite like that. Let's go down one last street and then get back to the marina," said Betsy.

This street was also not without its surprises. Right next to a multi-million dollar home on open water was a house, in front of which were neatly lined-up concrete discs about twice the size of a hubcap. Each piece of concrete contained a hand-made happy face.

"And this is considered to be a prime neighborhood," said Betsy.

They all laughed.

Soon, Will, Betsy and Lexie were back at the Dolphin Marina excitedly telling their friends about their excursion and contemplating calling Nira Tocco the next morning. About six they all shoved off for Lower Sugarloaf Key to attend the Fourth of July fireworks exhibition.

By the time they got to the turnoff, there was a constant stream of cars steadily turning off the Overseas Highway. Will went through the tiny Lower Sugarloaf Airport until they saw a volunteer motioning them where to park. Leaving the parking area, they carried lawn chairs toward the sound of music.

After walking a couple of hundred yards, there was a temporary stage that had been erected in an open field. Lights had been mounted along a crossbar on the top. A banner with a Rotary emblem welcomed new arrivals to the festivities.

Mile Marker 24 had already started a set. There were 14 musicians on stage, including Howard Livingston, a pan player, a drummer, guitar players, a brass section and female backup singers. The chorus of the band's signature song could be heard as they approached.

I'm going back to the place I know
I'm going back to where the cold winds don't blow
I'm going back
Ain't gonna leave no more
I'm going back to Mile Marker 24

Lawn chairs and blankets covered the ground. There were wine and beer booths; food booths offering chicken and fish, burgers, French fries and hot dogs. There were areas for carnival-like games. Local business people had set up tables and were handing out marketing brochures and promotional items.

People mingled with the informal familiarity of a church picnic or a school PTA function. Flip-flops, shorts, and T-shirts were the dress of choice. Kids were allowed to run free, largely unsupervised, since parents were confident of their safety. Neighbors and friends exchanged greetings and introduced acquaintances. All the adults seemed to be drinking, but no drunks were in sight.

"Don't you love it," Henri Sue said, "A great American picnic – the scene looks so wholesome it could have been extracted from *The Music Man* or *State Fair.*"

They found a vacant spot and set up their chairs. The people sitting on the blanket next to them welcomed them as if they were old friends.

"This was a good idea," Guy agreed. "It kind of reminds me of Family Day at Saint Edwards except the crowd is much more interesting and eclectic. Anyone want a beer?"

"There's a sense of community here," Betsy said. "Can't you just feel it?"

"Definitely," Penny agreed.

Lexie and Laura wandered up toward the stage where Mile Market 24 was selling band souvenirs. Lexie bought a tank top; Laura bought a baseball cap and a CD for her father. In the meantime the guys were out foraging for beer and trying to get a look at the food booths.

They got back in time to hear the last song before their intermission.

Howard Livingston lamented
I know I should leave this island
But the tide keeps pulling me back like a long lost friend.

When the number had been completed the band took a break and joined the crowd.

"Do you know what I saw when we went to get the beer?" Will asked Betsy. "A Century 21 table."

"I wonder if Nira Tocco was working it," Betsy said.

"One way I know to find out. Why don't we mosey over that way during the break?"

Will led Betsy over to the Century 21 table, and there was Nira, an attractive middle-aged blonde with an engaging personality and helpful attitude. She and Howard Livingston were talking. Nira introduced him to Will and Betsy. When Will explained to her what they wanted, she instantly knew the house he was referring to.

Howard excused himself when they started talking business and said he had to get back to the stage.

"If you would like," Nira said. "I can set up an appointment with the owner as early as tomorrow. I've known Phil and Sherrie for years."

"Could you?" Betsy asked. "We're only going to be down here for a few days. We're staying at the Dolphin Marina in the Hibiscus building."

"I'll call you in the morning after I get it set up," Nira said.

Will and Betsy walked back to their seats. Mile Marker 24 was setting up an outboard motor for their next set. It was a 1952 five-horse Johnson. The motor was mounted on a stand and had been cut out so a blender could be attached to the top. With much fanfare a member of the band loaded the blender with margarita mix and ice as Howard entertained the crowd.

"Who's got the oldest Johnson here?"

Some members of the crowd started yelling back their birthdates.

"August 23, 1943!"

"October 8, 1939!"

Howard pointed at that man and teased, "That's a REALLY old Johnson!"

A band member began to pull the starter cord to crank the motor. The old outboard at first resisted.

Howard continued to tease the crowd.

"Well, ya gotta keep workin' those old Johnsons."

After about ten pulls, the antique outboard finally cranked with a "putt putt." The crowd roared its approval and soon margaritas were being distributed to anyone who came down to the front of the stage.

The second set was under way.

That's why I drive a red '69 Oldsmobile
I've got four on the floor and I can make that rubber squeal
I lay the ragtop down and I cruise into town
And turn all the pretty girls' heads
Cause there's something about an old Oldsmobile
Especially since it's red.

Everyone was having so much fun that they seemed to barely notice the impending sunset. Finally, the band stopped and a canned Merle Haggard song came on the PA system. An announcer thanked everyone for coming, recognized the sponsors, and announced the upcoming fireworks.

As soon as dusk turned to dark, patriotic music began to play as a spotlight-highlighted an extremely large American flag flying from a crane. Then the first fireworks were released. The sky exploded with color and music filled the air. There were stars and comets followed by a loud pop that sounded like a gunshot. There were single, double and triple rings of brightly colored stars. Barrages of Roman candles burst simultaneously in the clear, star studded sky. Fountain-shaped streams of spray colored sparks shot upward in a dramatic fan pattern. Sporadic popping and cracking brought oohs and aahs from the crowd. A waterfall of light cascaded. One rose without a tail then suddenly burst with a tremendous flash and report. This was followed by several fireworks that rocketed upward looking like palm trees. They suddenly burst into large trailing palm fronds. The raining sparks looked like falling coconuts. Strobes of colored stars flashed on and off. A shell broke into large stars which fell for a short distance and then burst into more aerial shells. The crowd gasped as rockets that looked like candles on a birthday cake burst, sending lights in every direction. Finally there was a grand finale that lit up the entire sky as if like daytime in every direction.

"Look," Betsy said pulling on Will's arm and pointing. In the distance they could see another fireworks show going off toward Marathon. When they faced the other way, they saw the grand finale of the distant fireworks show at Smathers Beach in Key West.

"I've never seen anything like this before," Will said. "This was truly cool as hell."

"Awesome!" said Lexie.

CHAPTER 10

The following morning Nira Tocco called Will and Betsy to confirm their appointment with the owner of the Port Royal Road home. She came by and picked them up.

After they got out of the car, Will stood out in the street and surveyed the house and its surroundings. They walked across the pearock yard. Nira introduced them to Phil and Sherrie LaRiccia.

"If I had a house this nice, I'd have a hard time convincing my wife to let me sell it," Will said with a laugh.

"It was a hard decision, but we're getting older and we thought maybe we should move back to the mainland where our grandchildren are," said Sherrie LaRiccia.

"You mind if I ask where that is?" Will asked.

"Vero Beach...our son's in business up there," said Phil.

"Small world," Will grinned. "That's where we are from."

The owners quickly went across the street to visit a neighbor and let Nira take over.

Nira led them up the front stairs. About midway up, there was a landing and the stairs turned and continued up to another landing and the front door.

"Awesome," Lexie said.

The Blacks walked through the front door into a large great room with a massive cathedral ceiling. Over half of the main floor was dominated by this great-room, dining room, kitchen combination. Exposed beams reminded them somewhat of the pattern on a British Union Jack. It was a three-bedroom, two-bath house with the master suite one level up from the rest of the house. The large porch they had seen from the canal was even more impressive up close. The dock was immaculate.

"Wow! I really like this," Betsy exclaimed.

"So do I!" Will agreed. "The high ceiling makes the whole room seem so big."

Lexie's favorite feature was the stacked washer and dryer in the compact utility closet.

They climbed another set of stairs to the third level. The master bedroom at the top of the stairs also had a cathedral ceiling. Outside the bedroom was another landing that gave a panoramic view of the great room below. Behind the master bedroom was a balcony that allowed them a full view of the canal.

"This is really cool," Lexie gushed.

Down another set of stairs off of the deck and they walked out onto the wide, long boat dock. The first level of the house had a large breezeway, an area to park cars under the house, and enclosed storage.

"Will, I really like this place," Betsy said as soon as they were alone.

They thanked Nira for her time and told her they'd get back to her. When Will and Betsy got back to the Dolphin Marina, the *Float Aloan* was ready to shove off for Reuben and Esther's wedding. Betsy reminded Will to grab a local newspaper.

"I can't wait to see this event," Penny said. "I've never been to a wedding on a sandbar."

"That makes two of us," Jimmy said.

"That makes eight of us," Guy chimed in.

The warm breeze was hitting them in the face and within a few minutes the *Float Aloan* was anchoring once again at Picnic Island. Probably 25 boats had arrived before them and the party was well under way. Radios and CD players were blaring. Beer and wine were flowing. The crowd was a mix of people who appeared to be in all age groups from all walks of life. Some were swimming; some were in their boats.

A boatload of Cubans anchored near the *Float Aloan*. Salsa music blared from their boat.

"I wonder how many of that bunch is legal," Will said wisecracking.

"I wouldn't say that too loud," Betsy responded.

Boats continued to arrive. Soon there must have been 40 or more grand total.

"Looks like the social event of the season," Guy said.

At one o'clock a boat horn blew. It was soon joined by others. Will looked toward Picnic Island and pointed so the rest of their group would notice.

Reuben Nolan emerged from the brush. He was wearing a black short-sleeved, short-legged wet suit. It had been painted with a white shirt and a formal tie. He doffed a top hat to the throng of boaters.

"Well, I'll be damned," Jimmy said.

"Holy shit," Will said.

Reuben removed his hat again and bowed.

From the brush not five feet away, Esther Avery emerged in a bikini over her chunky frame. Her face was covered with a veil that trailed down her back onto the sand. She waved and threw kisses. Both Reuben and Esther stood silently to savor the spotlight. They were greeted by loudly cheering family and friends.

When the boisterous cheering died down, a third figure emerged from the brush. He wore a red Speedo and carried a black book. Even from where they were anchored Will and Betsy could see his tattoos and body piercings. He too paused to enjoy the limelight and wave to familiar faces. The crowd roared its approval. Gays in adjoining boats threw him kisses and hugged one another. The Cubans turned up the salsa.

When the hubbub died down once more, the three stars of the show waded into the water. When they were all about knee deep, the man in the Speedo signaled for the crowd's attention. The Cubans turned down the loud music. It seemed that it was time for the ceremony to begin.

"We are here today to join this man and this woman in holy matrimony."

He continued the standard part of the marriage ritual until he came to the vows.

"Do you take this woman to be your lawfully wedded wife, to have and to hold from this day forward, for richer or poorer, in sickness and in health, to love and to cherish; from this day forward until death do you part?"

"Fuckin' A," Reuben yelled.

The gathering of boats cheered. Horns blew.

"Do you take this man to be your lawfully wedded husband, to have and to hold from this day forward, for richer or poorer, in sickness and in health, to love and to cherish; from this day forward until death do you part?"

"Hell, yeah!" Esther shouted.

The cheers became louder.

"I now pronounce you man and wife."

The crowd went nuts. Beer cans sailed. One hit the bride on her forehead.

"I ain't never…"Jimmy started. "Sure isn't Mississippi."

"You're right about that one, or Alabama either," Will said as he laughed and squeezed Jimmy on the shoulder.

A friend brought Reuben a large, black garbage bag out into the water.

"Whaaa?" Henri Sue questioned.

Momentarily, Reuben and Esther started reaching into the bag and throwing its contents to well-wishers. Guy brought a throw back when he returned to the boat. It was a baggie full of miniature liquor bottles.

"I guess it beats rice," Will said. "Let's take a swim."

Will and Betsy waded over to congratulate the newlyweds. It wasn't long before a wading cocktail waitress in a swim suit and bunny ears asked them if they would like a drink.

"What are our choices?" asked Will.

"We have a complete bar," the waitress responded.

"Well, in that case I'll take a Bacardi and diet Coke," Betsy said. "Do you want your regular, Will, a Jim Beam on the rocks?"

"That would be nice."

"Will Jack Black be OK?"

"You betcha!"

"Another waitress waded over with a platter of cheese and sausage slices on various crackers."

"This is really nice," Jimmy said as he laughed and chose some hors d'oeuvres.

"This is really bizarre," Henri Sue added.

"There's a pig roasting on the beach. Plates are on that folding table next to it," their waitress pointed. "When you're hungry, help yourself."

The party moved into high gear and lasted most of the afternoon. The music was a loud, competing medley of sounds. Mini parties developed, each seemingly self-sufficient.

As Betsy was getting a slice of roast pork, an attractive lady about Will and Betsy's age suddenly asked, "Are you the couple that I saw over at the LaRiccias this morning?"

"Yes, we were," Betsy said. "How did you know?"

"Are you thinking about buying it?"

"Well, we looked at it."

"Oh, excuse me. I should have introduced myself. I'm Irene Ware. This is my husband, Donald. We live across the canal from Phil and Sherrie. I saw you over there this morning from my dock."

"It's really nice to meet you. I hope I didn't seem rude. You just caught me by surprise. By the way, this is my husband Will."

They shook hands.

"We don't know if we're serious about it or not. We just saw it for the first time this morning. We are down for the holiday weekend from Vero Beach with some friends," said Betsy.

"Staying at the Dolphin Marina?"

"That's right. How did you know?" asked Will.

"Well, I figured you were either there or Parmer's. There's not a lot of choices on Little Torch," said Irene.

"And you saw us there?" asked Betsy.

"I make it a point to keep an eye on what goes on in the neighborhood when we're here. We live here most of the year and return to Titusville for a couple of months. My husband's retired from the Cape."

"You'd get a good house if you bought that one," Donald chimed in. "We watched it being built from the ground up. Sure hated to see that vacant lot go. But Phil and Sherrie's son did a good job. I know good work when I see it. I was an engineer before I retired."

"That's good to know. Quite honestly, we haven't even had time to talk about it since we were over there this morning, but our first impression was very good. Anyway, it was nice to meet you. Maybe we'll end up neighbors," said Betsy.

"I'd like that," said Irene.

Will and Betsy waded back into the water to find the rest of their party.

Nira saw them and waded over.

"I guess you're not used to seeing your realtor in a bathing suit drinking coconut rum," she said with a laugh. "I see you're getting acclimated. You're not even local yet, and already here you are attending one of the social events of the season."

"I'll have to admit I didn't expect to run into you here, but somehow all this seems very appropriate for the Keys," Will said. "By the way, we loved that house on Port Royal. We're sure we want to make an offer."

"I think you'd be getting a great house," Nira said. "That's a stick-built house, not a modular, but they're getting that much per square foot for modulars that have had no imagination at all built in them. Just cookie-cutter houses made in a factory. Stamped out – like the old tin toys we had as kids."

"You think they'll come down."

"I don't really think so. Other people have tried to lowball them and it just seemed to make them mad. I'll tell you something. A recent CMA I ran on a comparable house showed that the house is probably underpriced by seventy five to a hundred grand."

"So you think it's priced right," said Will.

73

"Nothing is priced right in the Keys, but I think it's priced about as right as you're going to find in this part of the world," Nira said.

"I truly don't think I'll find anything in our price range that I would like any better," Betsy said.

"I don't think I would either," Will added. "I say let's give it a try."

"I'll call you tomorrow," Nira said. "I don't think you would regret buying it."

About four, Reggie and Esther climbed aboard their thirty-foot Pursuit. Beer cans had been strung from the boat's outriggers. They made a quick circle to wave one last time to their guests. Then as soon as Reuben had the boat back in the channel, he took off like a shot back toward Little Torch Key with his new bride.

"One hell of a wedding," Will said. "Certainly different from ours…or anyone else we know. Maybe running into Nira here was God's way of sending us a message about the house on Port Royal," Betsy said. "Maybe it's his way of saying welcome to the lower Keys."

CHAPTER 11

Henri Sue was knocking on the door.

"Come on in. The door's not locked. We're decent," Betsy said.

Henri Sue opened the door and entered. Betsy was wrapping a towel around her wet hair. Will was in the bathroom shaving.

"Morning," Will yelled. "I'm just trying to get rid of this gorilla disguise. What's Jimmy doing?"

"He's over at the office getting Dolphin Marina baseball caps for Jim and Charlie."

"When's Jim get back from Iraq?" Betsy asked.

"September...I still can't believe my boy is a naval intelligence officer. I won't breathe easy until he is back on good old U.S. soil."

"Well, for better or worse at least he's doing what he wants to do. How many people go through the motions of life in quiet desperation doing something they hate?" said Will.

"It still doesn't make it any easier when the news reports mines and car bombings and every other kind of casualty and horrible death happening in Iraq. Speaking of death, have you seen the morning paper?" asked Henri Sue.

Henri Sue spread the paper she had brought with her on the kitchen table.

"Will, come here," Betsy called. "You need to see this."

Will dried his face and came into room.

He picked up the paper and scanned the article.

Man's Body Found In Keys With Suspicious Injuries

A 48 year-old man's body was found late Thursday, lying in mangroves in Big Spanish Channel off No Name Key, not far from the bridge near the rock quarry that abuts Bahia Shores. It was adjacent to a popular homeless hangout. The man's name has not been released by the Monroe County Sheriff's Department.

The man suffered "suspicious injuries" but detectives said they didn't know if the injuries were severe enough to cause his death. They declined to go into detail.

An autopsy will be performed.

An unidentified woman discovered the body about 10 AM Thursday. She told detectives she was the man's friend and had last seen him about noon along the bayside road Wednesday when they walked together across the street to a marina.

Detectives said although the body was found close to some homes, no one questioned there recalled hearing anything in regard to the death.

Two months earlier, Michael Simpson, a 58-year-old homeless man known as The Gypsy, was found dead in the same location from blunt force trauma. His death was ruled a homicide. Detectives are still searching for his killer and relatives.

"Holy shit," Will exclaimed. "That's close to where we were!"

"Um huh," Henri Sue said. "I thought this would get y'all's attention. Didn't you tell me that things like this rarely happen in the Keys? That you can count the murders each year on one hand...We are up to two in as many days."

"Yeah, I did. Now flip over to the next page. This is more the type of thing that you usually see."

Will pointed to the crime report column on page two of the *Citizen*.

Man Had Heroin In Diaper He Wore

Samuel Kopf III faces up to 40 years in prison after he was found cruising down U.S. 1 with more than 200 grams of heroin in the diaper he was wearing, federal officials said.

Kopf, 38, of Islamorada, was charged Friday by a federal grand jury. He got in trouble June 3 in Grassy Key when sheriff's deputies pulled over his car for a traffic violation, according to court documents.

The deputies and Drug Enforcement Agency special agents searched the car, and a drug sniffing dog alerted them to the passenger side.

The occupants were ordered out of the car, and patted down. During the pat-down, "officers felt a large hard object in the pants area on Kopf," according to a news release from the U.S. Attorney's office.

"Now, that's more like it," Will said with a laugh.

CHAPTER 12

Right after Henri Sue left, the phone rang. It was Nira Tocco.

"Good morning. Enjoy the wedding?" Nira asked.

"I didn't know weddings could be so much fun," Betsy said.

"Just another day in paradise," Nira responded. "Still want to make an offer on the Port Royal house?"

"Will and I have talked about nothing else since we saw it."

"Had breakfast yet?" Nira said. "If you haven't I'll pick you up and we'll talk about it over eggs."

"That would be great. We're both dressed so any time is good for us. We don't have a schedule since we're on vacation."

Nira picked Will and Betsy up in ten minutes.

"Ever heard of a place called The Cracked Egg?" Nira asked. "That's the place to go for breakfast in Big Pine. It will be an absolute mad house. It is every morning. Packed with tourists and locals. Don't worry about privacy.

Just don't say where the house is and no one will know or care what we're talking about. All they'll be talking about is fishing."

Nira drove them to a small wooden one-story building on U.S. 1. As she had predicted cars surrounded the building. Hungry customers poured inside. Satisfied ones exited. The inside of The Cracked Egg looked like an old-fashioned diner without the booths. Odd tables with old wooden chairs were everywhere. Waitresses negotiated the obstacle course with huge platters of food. The din of talkative diners seemed to rattle the walls of the old building. Fortunately, they quickly found a table.

"Three coffees?" she asked.

They each nodded and were instantly rewarded with hot coffee being poured into ceramic cups.

"I'll bring you some milk in a sec, darling," she said as she disappeared again.

The waitress quickly returned to take their orders bringing with her an aluminum cream pitcher.

"I felt like I just stepped back in time 50 years," Betsy said.

"I think that's part of the charm of this place," Nira agreed. "I really believe if the restaurant moved to larger, more modern quarters it wouldn't do as much business. When I lived up north there was a rundown restaurant in a questionable part of town. That hole-in-the-wall had been there forever. Like this place, you always had to wait for a table. The owner decided to move to a more modern building twice as big – guess what, his business went down the drain. So now that you've had all night to sleep on it, you want to move forward?"

"That's all we could think about last night," Betsy said. "I think the place is perfect for us. I would love to see it again though so I can get a better picture in my mind on how furniture is going to fit into it."

"I'll go outside and try to reach the LaRiccias on my cell phone. Be back in a moment," Nira said.

While Nira was gone a scruffy looking middle aged man took the table across the room. He was wearing an old cowboy hat and had on a tank top that said Dinken's Roofing. He ordered a Miller and a cup of coffee.

Will elbowed Betsy and nodded in the man's direction. Betsy smiled.

The waitress noticed and grinned back at them.

"Hell," she said. Some of these Conchs drink a beer every morning before they have their coffee."

A minute later Nira returned with a puzzled look.

"I don't think I've ever had this happen before," she said. "Sherrie LaRiccia said no. I told her you would only be in town for a few days. She said no anyway. She must really be having seller's remorse. She said she would have to clean up the house again, and she simply didn't have time to do it."

"I guess you can't call her a motivated seller," Will said. He turned to Betsy, "Are you comfortable going forward if we can't get in to look again?"

"I guess I'll have to be satisfied with the look we got. Will, I really do like the house."

As the food arrived, Nira said. "Let's enjoy a good meal and head back over to my office to work on an offer."

"I had thought about offering to introduce the LaRiccias to people in Vero Beach," Will smiled. "I guess that won't be necessary now."

CHAPTER 13

Will and Betsy made a full offer that was ultimately accepted. The closing was set for August 15. They were both excited about their new adventure.

Betsy was having lunch one day with her area president, Joe Lincoln, when an opportunity presented itself. He was a fan of the Keys. He and his family had been fishing and lobstering there for many years.

"Joe, Will and I are so excited about our new house in Little Torch Key. I'm going to finance it here through the bank."

"I envy you, Betsy," Lincoln said. "Diane and I have had some great times over the years in the Keys. We've often said when we get all the kids out of school we might do just what you're doing, get a second home down there. By the way, you've got to go to the Fisheries in Marathon. It juts right out into the water, and the food is so good. Have you looked at our employee web site lately?"

"You know I'm too busy to look at things like that. Why, what's on it of importance?"

"Only that we're looking for a new area president for Monroe County. The guy that has the job now is being promoted to Charlotte. You know you're qualified for that position, and I think you'd be good at it. Besides, if you and Will were down there, I'd have someone to fish with."

"Joe, I know you're being facetious, but I really might just talk to Will about applying for that position. Reynolds Smathers and Thompson has mentioned from time to time that they would love to have representation in the Keys, and Lexie's in college, which frees us from Vero Beach."

Betsy almost rattled with excitement. She thought about it again for a second, "You know this could really work!"

Joe looked mildly panicked, "I don't want to lose my number one lender."

Betsy smiled back at him, "Just look at it this way, lose a lender – gain a fishing partner."

CHAPTER 14

By mid August, Will and Betsy Black were the Blacks formerly from Vero Beach and now residents of 605 Port Royal Road, Little Torch Key, Florida.

As they sat arm in arm out on the dock, watching the sunset, recuperating from unpacking boxes, Will sighed, "I can't believe that in less than a month and a half, our lives have totally changed."

"It is hard to fathom, isn't it?" Betsy said. "I have to pinch myself to believe I'm now the area president of our Monroe County bank, that you are RST's newest branch manager, and we are sitting in our own house in Little Torch Key. When we came down here with Guy and Penny, Henri Sue and Jimmy, and the girls on the fourth, I sure didn't see all this in our future."

"Other than the trip down in the car with Red Stripe trying to sing while the dogs barked, it was not too much of a challenge," Betsy added.

Their red-throated conure, Red Stripe, usually repeated just about everything he heard. So Betsy decided it might be cool to take the time to teach Red Stripe a patriotic song like *America* while they drove down to the Keys. After many attempts of singing the lyrics to Red Stripe, he managed to sing

My country, 'tis of thee, sweet...

For some reason, he never could seem to master the rest of the first stanza, *land of liberty*. Will simply accused him of being a communist. Betsy decided to keep working with Red Stripe, who had been named by their daughter after the Jamaican beer of the same name. Lexie also thought his red throat looked more like a "red stripe" since it collared his neck.

"Well, other than that, things seem like they've almost gone too smoothly," Will said. "I keep waiting for something to go wrong. I'm sure glad we have three weeks to get everything straightened out before we have to hit the ground running."

"Welcome, neighbor!"

"Welcome, neighbor," the parrot, Red Stripe repeated.

Will and Betsy looked across the canal. Irene Ware was waving at them.

"I told you it was a good house. You're going to like it here in Buccaneer Estates. Very interesting and diverse group of people in this neighborhood."

"Who lives next door to us?" asked Will.

"People from North Carolina. They're rarely here. Come in a few times a year for holidays. Nice enough, just never around much. The one that's two down, well, it's a corporately owned house. He's one of the managers for Club Tropic. Jack and Joan Maselli. I'll tell you more about them when I have time. Their next-door neighbor is Ken something or other. We never see much of him or his roommate for that matter. He manages a restaurant and bar. Works late every night. The guy across from you is a retiree from FPL. They are here only during the season. I'll fill you in later, but right now I've got to get back in the house. I've got a cake that is almost ready to come out."

Will and Betsy watched as the splendid sub-tropical sun sank towards the coconut palms gently waving in the warm breeze. A pelican soared overhead and bobbed up and down when it landed on a flexible limb.

"Will!" Betsy suddenly jumped up and screamed.

Will looked to his left and laughed. A large green iguana with a striped tail was working its way down the dock. It had a ridge on its back and big prehistoric looking feet. Will threw a piece of pearock at it, and it disappeared into the water. Their dogs, Coco, Lucy, and Dexter up on the porch never even saw it.

"You better get used to those," he chided. "I understand they're as common as coral rocks in Monroe County."

The sun continued to sink until it made the palm trees glow with its aura. Then the sun began to be a half circle as it started to fall behind the houses across the canal.

"Gorgeous! Absolutely gorgeous!" Will said. "And just think we have to look at this every night."

"When we bought the house I didn't even think about this western exposure," Betsy responded dreamily. "We sure are fortunate."

"Yes, we are. Nothing like having a natural extravaganza in your back yard every day. I can't imagine what would disturb this reverie."

Will had turned the portable stereo on low. A soft ballad reinforced their mood.

> *And watch the sun go down*
> *Listen to the sea roll in*
> *I'll be thinkin' of you*
> *And how it might have been*
> *Listen to the nightbird cry*
> *Watch the sunset die*
> *Well, I hope you understand*
> *I just had to go back to the island*

Will and Betsy heard a car pull up but paid little attention. They heard a woman's voice in the background.

"I love your taste in music. Who's the singer?"

Will and Betsy turned toward the voice. A woman whom they guessed was in her late forties was walking toward them. She was dressed in Keys' casual – not sloppy Keys casual but neat, tasteful Keys casual.

"I'm Joan Maselli. You must be the new neighbors."

"Yes, I'm Will Black and this is my wife, Betsy. I'd invite you to have a drink except everything we own is in boxes. And to answer your question, the singer goes by the name of The Barefoot Man. We became familiar with him in Grand Cayman. He's singing an old Leon Russell tune."

"Interesting! Why don't you come down to my house for a drink. My husband, Jack, should be home any time. He would love to meet you."

"Sounds terrific! We don't want to be any trouble," Betsy said.

"No trouble at all. Just call it Keys hospitality."

"Give me a sec to take our parrot back in the house," Betsy said.

The Blacks followed Joan to her house, which was bright and clean but nothing like Will and Betsy's. Now they understood the term "modular home."

The rooms were basic and square. Standard ceiling heights, standard Mexican tile on the floor, standard kitchen layout. The rooms were small. The windows standard aluminum. It was a nondescript three-bedroom, two-bath home. The dock was half the length of Will and Betsy's. Now they were starting to understand why their house was something special. Their house had about the same square footage as Joan's, but it seemed so much bigger and certainly more imaginative and unique.

Right after Joan made Will and Betsy their first drink, Joan's husband came in from work.

"Jack, darling! These are our new neighbors, Will and Betsy Black. They bought the LaRiccia house. Want me to open you a beer?"

Will and Betsy exchanged pleasantries with Jack, and soon each couple was relating to the other particulars about their backgrounds. Jack seemed excited to learn that Betsy had recently been promoted to be the new area bank president for WB and Will would be opening a Keys branch office for Reynolds Smathers and Thompson.

The conversation turned to Jack's line of work. Jack jumped at the chance to tell them about Club Tropic.

"I'll have to say, I believe that I work for one of the most dynamic companies in the Keys. I'm the condominium sales manager. We're coming on strong. In a few years we are going to be the most dominant company in the Keys. And I'm in on the ground floor. When this thing goes public, Will, those of us who were fortunate enough to have believed in its potential and to put our efforts behind making them become a reality are going to be very well off. Condos are only a division of the company. We're taking over prime properties on the waterfront in Key West. We own restaurants, gift shops and hotels. We have properties in Key Largo, Islamorada and Marathon. We have a real estate rental agency named Blue Water Rentals that is on the way to being the largest rental agency in Monroe County. It handles not only condo rentals but seasonal rentals for home owners. It also controls a cleaning company so we have that captive business when renters move in or out. We can see where we will eventually take home listings and become the dominant realtor in the county. I'm not at liberty to comment on particulars, but there is a very well known company up north that is this close," he pinched his index finger and his thumb together– "to infusing millions of dollars into Club Tropic in a merger of equals. Once we're together, the mom-and-pop operations of this county better watch out. We're going to be unstoppable. We will have unbelievable buying power. We'll have promotional dollars. We'll have the market share that will make everyone else green with envy."

Jack looked almost out of breath from talking nonstop. He drank the rest of his beer in one chug.

Will and Betsy didn't know what to say. Will finally said, "It sounds like Club Tropic really has it all together."

Jack went to make them all another round of drinks.

"Did you say you were down here for the Fourth?" he asked.

"Yes," Betsy said. "We stayed at Dolphin Marina with some friends. We went out to Picnic Island and ended the day watching the fireworks on Lower Sugarloaf. What a day and perfect week! That's the week we found our new house."

Jack's tone became serious.

"If you were here for the Fourth, then I guess you read about that body the cops found in the mangroves near No Name Key. That was really strange."

"We did see the story in the *Citizen*, but never heard anything else about it," said Will.

"I knew the person who was killed," Jack continued. "His name was Aldo Colletti. He was a client of ours who had just moved here from New Jersey and had just purchased for cash two Club Tropic preconstruction condo units.

"The paper reported his death as accidental and even inferred he had a connection to the homeless community near there. The *Citizen* reported that he had been seen previously with a woman who claimed to be his friend. The newspaper report played down his injuries, but I know for a fact that he was brutally beaten to death. It was especially spooky since he was wearing the Club Tropic T-shirt that my assistant had given him the day before."

The discussion was starting to get uncomfortable so Will and Betsy thanked Jack and Joan for the information and the drinks but said they really needed to get back down to their own house and do some more unpacking before dark. They promised to have the Masellis over as soon as they got everything straightened out.

CHAPTER 15

Will tried without success to hold the large tropical painting straight while Betsy eyeballed it.

"Hold that picture. That's perfect. That's where I want to hang it," Betsy said after she stood back and sized up where Will was holding an acrylic of palm fronds.

The phone rang.

"Damn it to hell! I wonder who that could be," Will said. "It better not be someone trying to sell us a credit card. Hold the picture while I mark this place on the wall."

Betsy took the picture from him, set it down, and answered the phone.

"Mrs. Black, this is Estelle York. I am head of branch operations for WB in the state of Florida. We received a call this morning from the Key West branch that needs immediate attention. I realize that you are in the midst of a three-week leave to move to the Keys."

"Has the bank been robbed?" Betsy blurted out.

"Oh, heavens no, nothing like that! This is just a very unusual collateral situation that we need someone with your experience and authority to handle."

Betsy agreed to go to the bank. Ms. York said she would call the branch back to let them know Betsy was on her way and gave Betsy her contact information.

"What a bizarre request," Betsy said to Will as she hung up the phone. "I need to go to our Key West branch and deal with some problem."

"What happened?" Will asked.

"Branch operations calling here caught me by such surprise that I really didn't get any details."

Will and Betsy quickly threw on some business casual clothes and headed for Key West. When they pulled into the bank's parking lot, nothing appeared out of the ordinary. As Betsy and Will entered the branch, however, the problem was readily apparent. While customers and bank employees attended to their transactions on the perimeter of the lobby, the center of the lobby looked like a warehouse for a liquor distributor. There were Smirnoff boxes, Captain Morgan boxes, Jack Daniels boxes, Jose Cuervo boxes, Gordon's gin boxes. There was every brand of booze that either Will or Betsy had ever heard of and then boxes of exotics they were unfamiliar with. The boxes were piled head high. People looked like they were negotiating an obstacle course to get from one part of the lobby to the other.

Betsy and Will stopped dead in their tracks. They didn't know what to say.

Will finally broke into a big grin and wisecracked, "They sure do banking differently in the Keys."

Betsy gave him a sideways glance.

"Is this what banks give away in the Keys in lieu of toasters?" Will continued.

Betsy elbowed him lightly in the ribs.

"Working here wouldn't be a job; it would be heaven on earth. An all day happy hour," Will said.

"Will, enough, this is serious," Betsy said trying to look authoritative. Seconds later she couldn't help but smile.

They were approached by an attractive middle-aged lady who seemed to recognize them.

"Mrs. Black? My name is Margaret Anderson, your administrative assistant. I'm sorry to have to welcome you as the new area president with this situation. There was nothing I could do – this truck pulled up to the door before the bank closed yesterday, and the driver said Carson Crown asked them to put all these cases in the lobby," she said breathlessly.

"Who is Carson Crown?" Betsy asked.

"He is one of our loan officers. I tried to reach him by phone yesterday afternoon…but he usually turns his cell phone off when he is playing golf. I reached him last night about this and he said it was no big deal. Said he would take care of it this morning."

Angrily, Betsy asked, "So where is he?"

"Oh, he doesn't get in until around eleven on Wednesdays because he has a morning Rotary committee meeting."

"Did he offer an explanation for this?"

"No, he just said this was how we would be able to pay off John Peterson's loan. I had to let them in…I didn't know how to keep the delivery boy out...I'm sorry...I called branch operations in Jacksonville this morning...I..."

"Margaret, you did the right thing – Mr. Crown on the other hand..."

"One other thing, Mrs. Black, usually late in the afternoons...local drunks sometimes wander in the bank by mistake. Well, some did yesterday, and when they saw all this booze stacked in here, they called in their other buddies, and I had to call the police to get all the winos and freaks out so we could close the bank."

Will was having such a hard time keeping a straight face that he had turned beet red. Betsy glanced at him.

"My God, is there anything else I need to know," Betsy said.

"I don't know if he was kidding or not, but one of the police officers said it was illegal to have this much booze on the premises without a liquor license."

Will had to turn his back and grab a desk to try to muffle the unexpected snort that escaped. He turned back around when he felt like he had regained control. Neither the snort nor the grin that followed had gone unnoticed by Betsy, but she managed to keep her composure.

Slump shouldered and shaking her head in disbelief, Betsy asked Margaret to show her to her office and telephone.

"Margaret, do we have a file on Mr. Peterson?" Betsy asked.

Betsy reviewed the credit file on John Peterson. It revealed that Carson Crown had loaned Peterson the money to start a liquor store. Since banks rarely do loans for start up businesses, the equity in Peterson's home was used to secure the $100,000 prime equity line.

Betsy called the Key West Police Department to inquire on the legality of the bank's dilemma. She demanded that Margaret find Carson Crown.

Shortly before eleven, a large rotund balding man with a flushed face walked into Betsy's office. He turned on a broad grin. He stuck out his meaty hand and said, "Welcome to the Keys, Mrs. Black. My name is Carson Crown. Just call me CC. Margaret says you are looking for me."

Betsy gave Crown a stony look, "Well, Mr. Crown, you are right on target with that."

"We were not expecting you for another couple of weeks. What brings you into the bank?"

"I would think the storehouse of booze in the lobby could be an obvious clue to my presence, Mr. Crown," Betsy said angrily.

"Not Mr. Crown, just call me CC, Mrs. Black. Everyone does."

"And you, CC, can you tell me why this bank lobby is a warehouse for a company that is out of business?"

CC sucked in his gut and smiled. "This is no big deal – they shouldn't have called you in for this. I was going to take care of it."

Betsy was incredulous by now. "How?" she said.

"Well, I have to admit there is more to John's inventory that I expected. I was going to call some of the local bars and sell it to them at a discount and apply the proceeds to John's loan. I also might be able to move it off on Club Tropic. They're one of the big up and comers in the

Keys. People the bank needs to know. I'm plugged in with them. You know their head man is in Rotary with me."

"Mr. Crown, there is no bank policy or procedure that covers your actions," Betsy said. "You have no legal authority to take possession of Mr. Peterson's inventory. You have no license to sell liquor and neither does this bank."

Betsy continued, "Further more, Mr. Crown, you cannot store booze in this bank's lobby or building nor dispense it via sales or other means."

"Well, John said he used the proceeds of his line of credit to buy this inventory he couldn't sell," Crown said. "He knew I would have to sell it at a discount – he doesn't want to lose his home because his loan is delinquent."

"Mr. Crown, get out of my office," Betsy said as she struggled to maintain a civil composure. "Margaret, please get me the name and phone number for the bank's local attorney."

Will knew better than to laugh again. He just slipped out the door after Carson Crown left and tried to find a chair in the crowded lobby.

CHAPTER 16

"Skill takes you a long way in life, but I sure wouldn't rule out timing and luck," Betsy said as she and Will sat talking to Jason Pearson.

"Thank goodness your wife, Monika, works at the bank, and thank divine providence that you happened to come in the day the hooch was piled up in the lobby, and thank God Will started joking around with you when he did, and thank heavens you had a solution to the problem that I could sell to the bank's attorney."

Jason laughed, "That is a lot of things to have work out."

Will and Betsy's introduction to Jason Pearson, entrepreneur at large, had been very well-timed. In fact it had been divinely sent. Jason was a general contractor, salvage diver, landscape designer, tree surgeon and stump grinder, jackleg electrician and plumber, boat auctioneer, roofer, davit installer, nuisance animal trapper, interceptor of illegal aliens, part time fireman, volunteer sheriff's deputy, and, thank goodness for WB Bank, distressed merchandise selling agent.

Once the bank's attorneys had been satisfied that John Peterson did indeed own the liquor cache in question and that it was fully paid for and not the subject of any liens it did not take Jason long to empty the bank's lobby into some trailers he owned, enabling the bank to return to some semblance of normality and quit being the butt of jokes from one end of town to the other. It then took him less than forty eight hours to sell the merchandise to bars all over Duval Street. Betsy breathed a sigh of relief. Her first crisis as area president had been successfully resolved.

"Jason, is there anything you don't do?" Will asked kiddingly.

"I'd love to start a flying service if I had a plane. I do have my pilot's license," Jason said. "But I think Monika would get upset with me if I took on one more thing. When I started doing volunteer EMT work she drew the line."

"Gee, I wonder why?" Betsy said with a grin.

"But back to the subject at hand, we would really like to upgrade some things at this house. There's so many projects I really don't know where to start," Will said.

"You prioritize the projects, and we'll sure jump on them," Jason responded. "I usually use some of my buddies from the fire department when they're off. We will do a good job. We've done work all over Buccaneer Estates, even for some questionable people I'd rather avoid."

"By the way, did you get involved with that body found near No Name Key?" asked Betsy.

"No! Not directly, but I saw something strange that night that I haven't told anyone but Monika about."

"You've got my curiosity up," Betsy said.

"I was too tired to go to the fireworks that night. I had worked all afternoon."

"It was the Fourth. I don't know if anyone told you, but the Fourth is a national holiday," Will said cryptically and smiled.

"I know! I know! Monika has been reminding me ever since...but I manage these rental houses over in Big Pine. One of them called and said their AC wasn't cooling. I went over there thinking it was probably a breaker switch or something simple. I ended up killing the rest of the day before I solved the problem. Monika was pissed. She wanted to take Tyler to Bahia Honda, but what could I do? I couldn't leave these poor devils without AC in the middle of the summer. So after all was said and done I thought I'd make it up to Monika and Tyler by stopping by No Name Pub and picking up pizza on the way home."

"As I was going in, I noticed these two guys sitting at the picnic table outside the front door. They were in a major argument. Both of them were wearing Club Tropic shirts – one a golf shirt, the other a T-shirt. I figured they probably worked together. The guy in the T-shirt was waving his finger in the other one's face and yelling, "I will get what I want, asshole, and you're going to get it for me. Comprende?"

"I thought the jerk just sounded drunk. He had an almost empty draft on the table. I went on inside to get the pizza, and when I left they were still going at it outside. I heard the guy in the golf shirt say something about being reasonable. I went on home and didn't think anything about it. I figured they were arguing about some problem at work. Mentioned it to Monika who thought it was more amusing than important. Totally forgot about it, in fact, until the next day when I had to go over to the Club Tropic condo sales office. They called me because their toilet wouldn't stop running. At one of the sales desks I saw the same guy that had been wearing the golf shirt outside No Name. He had it on again...the one with the Club Tropic logo...Had a name tag that said Joey Giambi...Then this morning the *Keynoter* ran the picture of the man found floating off No Name on the Fourth. Sheriff's department finally released his identity. The article said he was from New Jersey. I swear he was the same SOB I saw threatening that guy at No Name the night of the Fourth...either that or the one I saw has got a twin brother."

"Have you told anyone?"

"I just saw it this morning. I've been busy since then putting on a roof down on Summerland all day," Jason said.

"You do need to tell someone," Betsy said.

"Surely this disagreement had to be a personal matter. I can't imagine that it had anything to do with Club Tropic. All we've heard since we moved here is what a top notch outfit Club Tropic is," Will said.

"Not everyone is in love with them," Jason said. "Many locals are afraid Club Tropic is going to make a cookie-cutter resort out of the Keys and force the mom-and-pop establishments out of business. Also, word I hear is that all may not be hunky dory there. I've heard from some of my buddies who are vendors to them they're slow pay, and they've quietly reduced staffing at some of their locations... letting attrition do the layoffs for them by just simply not hiring people to replace employees who have left. I also hear from some friends who are CT subs that there's some real quality control issues on many of their projects, like skimping on structural materials the buyer can't see and then cutsying up the units with inexpensive cosmetic bull-shit like crown molding and designer paint colors...the type of thing that makes a naive snowbird think he is really getting a high quality Florida home," Jason said.

"You mean snowing the snowbirds," Will said.

"Or anyone else who doesn't know a hell of a lot about what counts in construction," Jason agreed.

CHAPTER 17

"You've been saying you'd love to meet the neighbors. We're about to get our chance," Betsy said as she opened the mail. "Read this."

Will took the computer-generated invitation Betsy handed him. It was a homeowner's association barbeque to welcome new homeowners. It was going to be held at Marvin and Sue Cheney's house. There would be wine and beer. It would be Keys casual. The Cheneys were having it catered and had hired a local musician.

"Wow! Going all out for a homeowner's association function, but aren't the Cheneys the ones who own a hedge fund out of Connecticut? The ones we've been told have made a gazillion dollars and have a huge catamaran?" he asked.

"That's them," Betsy agreed. "The same ones who own two houses with the landscaped vacant lot in between. You remember, the ones with real grass instead of pearock. Should be a fun evening."

"You're right. This should be a great opportunity to meet some of our neighbors. And it's this Saturday night. Let's see if the Masellis want to walk down there with us."

Jack Maselli jumped at the chance to go to the party with the Blacks. He said he had heard at the office the Cheneys were doing some business with Club Tropic at a very high level and he had wanted for some time to get to know Marvin better.

Saturday night, the weather was perfect – hot but perfect. The Cheney house was over one street on open water. As Will and Betsy approached they could see the blue waters of the Atlantic form a perfect backdrop to the house. They could also see the large catamaran. Terry Cassidy was playing the guitar and singing.

Henry built the railroad
through the islands it would run
A wonder of the world
They said it could not be done
He and all his men they didn't stop to rest
Until the day they reached the little island of Key West

Food had been set up in a gazebo. Some people were waiting at the bar, others had already attacked the food table, others listened to the music as almost everyone carried on brisk conversations with neighbors that they had not seen in months.

"Looks like its going to be a fun evening," Joan Maselli said.

Soon the Blacks and the Masellis had split up. The Masellis were visiting with people they knew. Will and Betsy were talking to Don and Irene Ware, one of the few people there they knew by name. Don saw an old Navy buddy, and they began talking diving. Irene patiently introduced Will and Betsy to more people than they would later remember.

Then they were introduced to another new homeowner who seemed to be having the same memory challenge.

"I bet that's our hosts," Betsy said to Will.

Near the street where they could greet new arrivals was a distinguished looking late middle-aged couple. The man was over six feet; his hair looked prematurely gray-white. His shorts, golf shirt and boat shoes looked very Brooks Brothers. His wife, a slender, tanned woman, was wearing an expensive print sundress and dressy looking sandals. She looked like her life was one of personal trainers, manicurists and hair dressers. Both were sipping white wine out of stemmed glasses as they greeted people, made small talk, and then quickly sought out fresh faces to repeat the process. Will imagined that they would be very comfortable in a clubby atmosphere.

"I think you're right," Will said. "Let's not go over there right now. Let's wait until most people have arrived so they will have more time to talk to us."

"Good strategy," Betsy agreed.

The crowd of incoming people finally thinned, and Will and Betsy worked their way over to the Cheneys.

"I'm Will Black and this is my wife, Betsy," Will said, extending his hand.

"The two new financial wizards I've heard so much about. I'm Marvin Cheney and this is my wife, Sue. We thank you for coming.

"Have I heard correctly that you are the new area president for WB Bank?" he asked Betsy.

"As a matter of fact I am," Betsy said.

"Oh, where would any of us be were it not for our bankers," Marvin said quickly. "And do I hear correctly that you, Will, are bringing the services of Reynolds Smathers and Thompson to the Keys?"

"You heard correctly," Will said.

"We must be growing up and becoming more sophisticated down here in the lower Keys. I guess this is a sign we've been discovered," Marvin continued.

Sue stood patiently and sipped her wine.

"We have had a bit of success with investments and financial services I have to humbly admit," Marvin said. "We could not have done it without our bankers and brokers."

"What sector of financial services are you in?" Will asked.

"We have a small hedge fund in the Northeast - nothing major," Marvin said. "We manage about a billion and a half dollars. It's not large as investment pools of money go, but it's large to us. It has afforded us some of life's luxuries."

"What kind of investments do you make?" Will asked.

"A wide variety. The beauty of our format is that we have the freedom to seek out opportunities with a minimum of regulation and hindrances. We do not have a narrow objective like so many investment vehicles. Our objective

107

is simply to make money for ourselves and our clients. It is irrelevant to us whether our vehicle is real estate or securities."

He turned to Betsy, "Have you had the opportunity since your arrival at the bank to assess Club Tropic?"

"Actually, no," Betsy said. "I've heard the same things that everyone else has. They've bought everything that's not nailed down, and they're becoming a force to be reckoned with in the Keys."

"Do you bank them?" Marvin asked.

"No, we currently do not have a relationship with them."

"Would you be comfortable with becoming their banker?"

"It would be imprudent of me to respond, knowing as little as I do. I will say I can only be a bit nervous when a company seems to be expanding at the rate they are. The terms overextending and highly leveraged come to mind. Is your interest an academic one?"

"Very little I do is academic. Actually I have done a bit of business with them."

"Do you mind if I ask what kind of business?"

"Not at all! I am selling them some properties we developed. They offered us some very attractive prices – much higher than I thought these properties were worth based on the cash flow they were producing. They seemed to think there were opportunities to increase the cash flow substantially in ways that we could not achieve on our own. They made a pretty compelling case of why our sale to them was a win-win for everyone concerned."

"I hope it works out for you…and them," Betsy said.

"That's how I've made a lot of money over the years, being able to spot opportunities the more timid pass up," Marvin said, before turning to greet another guest who had been patiently waiting to get his attention.

CHAPTER 18

Jason Pearson and his crew had replaced questionable wood on the Blacks' dock, replaced the drywall screws holding it together with stainless screws, and applied a new coat of water sealer.

"That dock really looks good," Betsy said to Jason.

"Almost like brand new," Will agreed. "I can't believe how long it's been since this dock has been sealed."

"You need to try to keep it that way too," Jason said. "You've got something here that can't be replaced – a dock that runs the entire length of your property. You couldn't get a permit to build one like that now. Getting a permit to build a dock is a major challenge in the Keys. Getting one for this dock would be impossible. That's why most people just get a resurfacing permit or don't get a permit at all and just hope they don't get caught."

"I'm glad you got it finished. Some of our friends from Vero Beach are coming down to visit soon and I really wanted the house to look its best," Betsy said. "Guy and

Penny Walsh and our friend on the Vero Beach police force, Tom Mallette are coming down to dive and fish."

"Well, one thing's for sure...real estate is not a passive investment," Jason said. "You constantly have to do maintenance to protect your investment, especially here in this tropical climate. But it's worth it. Keys real estate has been a consistent money maker."

"I just made a good real estate investment," said Tim, Jason's EMT friend.

"Have you heard about the great opportunities Club Tropic is offering?"

"No, I don't guess I have," Will said.

"Wait'll you hear this deal," Tim continued. "I put $40,000 on a Leisure Bay Club Tropic unit in Islamorada. That's the old Mariner Landing condo. Club Tropic is rehabbing it. Anyway, I put up $40,000 at closing and 45 days later they returned $20,000 of my money to me in their leaseback program. Six months from now they will give me $20,000 more so I'll have my entire $40,000 back. This will cover my mortgage payments for the next two years while they finish the upgrades to the complex."

"How do they get their money back?" Betsy asked.

"They put the units in a rental pool. They'll make it back from that."

Will and Betsy looked at each other puzzled. Tim continued.

"On top of that," Tim went on, "Club Tropic's investment advisor sold me this unit preconstruction at $100 a square foot below market rates. He also showed me sales of other units to prove it. You know, you don't get opportunities like this very often in the Keys. My advisor told me that this will virtually guarantee I will make money. He said that real estate has gone up at over 20 percent a year and even if you cut that in half, which is a conservative worst-case scenario, I can't help but make money hand over fist."

Jason started to ask a question, but Tim barged ahead.

"Their leaseback program covers my mortgage for two years so I'll never be out of pocket any money. As they said, before that time is up the renovations will be complete, and people will see what a hot property it is. When that happens the units are going to sky-rocket, and I'll be able to cash in and make a windfall profit. I'm going to have to pay some taxes since I got the down-payment money out of my wife's retirement account, but hell, its going to be damn well worth it. I'm certainly not making that kind of money in the IRA. Not even close."

"Have you ever heard the old adage that if something seems too good to be true...," Will began.

"You haven't heard the rest of the story. It gets better," Tim was getting really excited now. "Since I went through Roger Packard at Interstate Bank, nice guy by the way, Club Tropic gave me my first year of condo association fees for nothing. That saved me another $1,200. I was worried to death that I wouldn't qualify for the loan. Good deals like this don't usually fall out of trees every day to common working people like me. Usually you have to be an insider... you know what they say, the rich get richer...and I've got to get serious about my future."

"So I take it you qualified?" Betsy asked.

"Not at first, but Roger took care of that too," Tim said. "I guess it's another one of these, 'it's not what you know but who you know'. I didn't have enough assets at first, but he showed me how to handle that. Then the computer model said my wife and I didn't make enough money, but he showed me how to fill that out too. Sometimes you just have to know how to fill out a form. For instance, I never would have known to call this a second home instead of an investment property. You know with the appreciation I'll get off of this when it gets reappraised six or eight months from now, I'll have the money to participate in another one of their investments. In a few years I won't be swinging a hammer anymore."

"But fudging on a loan application is fraud," Betsy told Tim.

"It's just smart business," Tim said. "The big boys do it all the time. How do you think they got where they are?"

Betsy had to walk away.

"Did you investigate any of the information the sales rep told you?" Will asked.

"Didn't have time to! He said if I was going to get in on this I had to do it right now. I'm telling you, this is a slam dunk."

"My God in heaven," was all Will could say as Tim walked away to answer his cell phone.

CHAPTER 19

Betsy began the process of getting to know her new employees with individual meetings. In these meetings she tried to determine the interests of her employees and their motivation levels. It was also important to understand their book of business, their pipeline of customers and prospects and their plans and goals to grow that business. She tried to identify the leaders and the followers. For the most part these meetings went very well. Betsy tried not to make the meetings adversarial but use them to learn what she and her staff could do to make each employee more effective. The meetings also gave Betsy a way to measure the morale of her organization and to let each employee get to know her and understand her expectations.

    Betsy was pleased with the outcome of the meetings. The employees embraced them on the constructive level she had hoped. She also learned a good bit about the people as individuals. She saved Carson Crown until the end on purpose. She just had to get herself in the mood to hear what she was sure would be a bucket of BS. She told Margaret to check and see if Carson would be available after lunch on Friday.

"I don't think that's going to work," Margaret said. "Friday is when Carson goes out to lunch at Pepe's with the Gator alums. He never makes it back until at least three o'clock."

"How do you know that?" Betsy asked.

"He has the orange blazer with a gator embroidered on the pocket he always brings to the bank to wear on Friday afternoons. After he gets back that's all he wants to talk about until he goes home, which I might add, is usually four o'clock."

"Well, I certainly wouldn't want to interrupt that. Why don't you see if you can schedule him on Thursday instead?"

"That won't work either. Thursday is Carson's Chamber of Commerce luncheon day."

"Wednesday?"

"That's when the Fantasy Fest committees meet."

Betsy was starting to get angry.

"Schedule Mr. Crown at eight o'clock on Monday morning. I guess that's the only time he doesn't have a meeting outside the bank. When does he have time to work?"

Margaret said nothing.

"Well!"

"CC won't be real happy with that," Margaret said. "He never comes in before nine."

"Well, he *will* Monday morning."

Betsy shook her head and walked in a disgusted manner back into her office.

Margaret just looked embarrassed.

On Monday morning Carson bounced into Betsy's office…ten minutes late.

"Sorry, buana," he said. "Traffic's always a bitch during rush hour. That's why I usually wait until a little later to come into the bank. Don't worry, though. I'm doing my job. I make sales calls early in the morning."

"Who do you call on first thing in the morning?"

"Oh, you know, retail type people. That way I can spend some time with them before their store opens. We can have coffee and break bread together. One on one. Mano-a-mano. The way selling ought to be done."

He grinned and winked at Betsy, positive he had shared an inside tip.

"Have any of them opened accounts recently?"

"No, but we've talked about it," he said. People don't change their banking relationships overnight, but sooner or later, the bank they're doing business with is going to do something to piss them off, and guess who they're going to think of? Good old CC! That's who they're going to think of. CC, the guy who's been breaking bread with them in the morning! Yep! You'll see. You just got to be patient. Sooner or later they all fall in your lap."

"But, what are you doing for business in the meantime?" Betsy asked.

"I've got the biggest prospect in the whole Keys, the blue chipper of blue chippers!"

"Who's that?"

"Well, Club Tropic, of course! There isn't a bank anywhere who wouldn't just die to get their business..."

He paused, then went on.

"But guess who has the inside track? I'll tell you who has the inside track. You're looking at him! Good old CC! Their CEO is in Rotary with me, and I'm telling you--If I'm lying, I'm dying--He makes a point to sit with me every week at Rotary. All we gotta do is make any kind of presentation that makes sense, and he's ours for the taking. This won't be a big deal; this will be a major deal. It will make you the fair-haired girl for all of WB! I've got an appointment set up with him for next Wednesday. You need to go with me so he can see that one of the real honchos wants his business. This will be the slam dunk of the year."

Carson jumped up and tried to high-five Betsy who just looked at him like he had lost his mind.

Thank God, we're alone and not in front of a sales meeting, she thought.

"Carson..." she began.

"CC, just call me CC," he interrupted.

"Carson," she continued, "let me do some research on Club Tropic and I'll get back to you."

Carson gave her a thumbs up as he left the office. Betsy never rose out of her chair.

CHAPTER 20

Betsy immediately told Margaret to get someone to assemble information on Club Tropic. By that afternoon, she was looking at the data they collected.

The info was very enlightening. A totally unknown Club Tropic had roared into the Keys in 2003 with what seemed to be an open checkbook. Purchases were made under the name of a private corporation named Club Tropic Hospitality. The source of their funds was a mystery. Their first purchase was a hotel resort in Key Largo that they named Deep Water Club Tropic. Club Tropic soon snapped up another resort in Islamorada they renamed Rum Reef Club Tropic. Within months they bought a second property in Islamorada, this one they retitled The Sporting League of Club Tropic. Within two years, nine condominiums and hotels in the Keys bore the Club Tropic logo. All of the properties had one thing in common. They consisted of older buildings that needed remodeling and updating. In the beginning these acquisitions were made on a low-key basis, with little publicity being given to the hospitality conglomerate being assembled. It evolved into one hell of a list – Royal Island Club Tropic, Leisure Bay Club Tropic, Sandy Beach Club Tropic, Leeward Cay Club Tropic. Other types of properties were not immune from Club Tropic's seductive grasp. Almost 200 single family homes soon came under their control. It was now apparent that Club Tropic had quietly become the largest owner of real estate and boat slips in the Keys. Club Tropic was suddenly a media phenomenon. Announcements were made that Club Tropic was starting to assemble a chain of independent restaurants and had plans to take over three of the oldest restaurants in the Key West Bight. There was a constant buzz among locals about Club Tropic and whether it would ultimately be good for the Keys. Billboards showed tanned, vibrant, wealthy young sophisticates at play in Club Tropic resorts. Similar image ads appeared in magazines. Club Tropic even became a court sponsor for the Sony-Ericsson tennis tournament.

Club Tropic activities were not confined to the Keys. More acquisitions were reported in Naples, Orlando, Sarasota, Clearwater, Vero Beach, Hollywood and Miami Beach.

The more Betsy read about Club Tropic, the more she was shocked and alarmed. She had never seen anything like it. These guys were buying too much too fast. It was like Club Tropic controlled a giant real estate magnet that was attracting everything it got near – a pac-man gobbling real estate. That, coupled with the story she and Will had heard about Club Tropic sales practices from Tim, the EMT man, made her stomach tighten. Her thoughts were bombarded with topics like money laundering and ponzi schemes and how that dumb-ass Carson Crown would be the very type of person who Club Tropic could take in if Club Tropic was not on the level.

Wednesday morning, Carson informed Betsy that their appointment with the Club Tropic CEO would be a luncheon at Little Palm Island.

"What?" Betsy exclaimed. "I thought this was supposed to be a business meeting."

"Don't worry, great white leader! He's treating us. He said this would be a nice quiet place for us to talk," Carson said. "Have you ever been there?"

"No, but that's not the point. It's not a matter of money. It's a matter of appropriateness," Betsy said. "And if he wished to meet with us in a restaurant, why didn't he choose one they own?"

"I guess because so many of their properties are in the middle of renovation," Carson said. "No worry! As always, CC has everything under control."

Betsy sighed, "What time do we need to be there?"

The boat ride from Dolphin Marina out to Little Palm Island was impressive. The boat was named *The Truman*. It was a thirty-six foot wooden vessel that reminded a passenger of the glory days when life was uncomplicated and elegant. When they arrived Betsy understood why it was classified as a five-star resort. She and Carson were greeted at the L-shaped dock, walked into a thatched-hut building and were escorted out onto a porch.

A special table had already been set up. Even though there were other diners in the building, there were none seated near their table. A fiftyish suave-looking man in a custom suit was already seated. The understated necktie he wore conveyed a subtle, expensive elegance. A silk handkerchief was tucked nattily in the suit pocket. He wore highly polished Italian leather shoes.

"Sol Schwartzman. It is a pleasure and an honor to meet you, Mrs. Black," the man said.

He smiled disarmingly and shook Betsy's hand, holding it a little too long.

"CC, it's good to see you. Thank you both for coming. I know it was a bit of a drive from Key West, but there is no place like Little Palm Island in the whole Keys. This is what we at Club Tropic aspire to be...and what Club Tropic will be."

Schwartzman's eyes conveyed sincerity and tried to make it seem to the individual he was addressing that this person was the most important person he had ever met. For some reason Betsy thought about getting caught in a Venus fly trap. He pulled back Betsy's chair which had been chosen to face the ocean.

He said, "Isn't this place gorgeous? Couldn't you stare at this ocean forever?"

Small talk continued. For once Carson did not dominate the conversation. It was expertly paced, controlled and guided by Sol Schwartzman. Soon their food orders were taken, and an exquisitely prepared lunch was brought to them.

"I hope it does not seem immodest, Mrs. Black, or may I call you Betsy, but we are in the process of assembling the most dynamic organization in the Florida Keys,"

121

Schwartzman said. "I don't want to take credit for this however. I have been fortunate enough to hire an incredible bank of talent. I may be the CEO, but they are the ones who make me look smart."

"How long have you been in Florida?" Betsy asked.

"I came down from New Jersey three years ago," he said. "We had had some successes there, but we wanted to be a part of a state with real momentum."

"You are a privately held company?" Betsy asked.

"Yes, we represent a number of very wealthy investors...names I'm not at liberty to disclose. They are low-key investors who wish to remain in the background."

"You have accomplished an awful lot in a short period of time," Betsy continued.

"It may seem like we're moving fast, but one has to take advantage of opportunities when they exist," he said. "We have been fortunate that a number of properties with the criteria we look for have been available and on the market recently. Not just getting properties but getting properties that we can utilize to bring value to our investors, that is what makes us successful. After all, our objective is to make above-average returns for our investors while minimizing their risk. If we accomplish these goals, we will have investors lining up to participate in future opportunities, and believe you me, we have targeted many such opportunities."

"Why did you want to meet with me?" Betsy asked.

"Mrs. Black...Betsy...my people report to me that WB is the most dynamic bank east of the Mississippi. You have the size, the services, the sophisticated systems that our company needs to grow and prosper. The purpose of our meeting today is to see where we can find the common ground to establish a relationship that will be good for both of us.

"I can tell you without violating any confidences that Club Tropic is just in its embryo stage. It may seem like we have accomplished a lot in a short period of time, but our upcoming efforts will pale these early successes. We will soon see a merger by a public corporation with our company that will bring an additional cash infusion of approximately fifty million dollars. This will give us additional liquidity to take advantage of many other long-term opportunities we have identified that are every bit as attractive as some of the ones reported by the press. You and your bank will want to be a part of our story.

"Our most immediate need is an operating line of credit of say $25 million – if necessary, we could collateralize that line with some of our assets. I will gladly provide you with whatever information you need. We would like to move forward to finalize this line and our banking relationship with all due haste. My CFO, Barry Silverman, will be at your disposal. Make no doubt about it, we are growing. Our revenues are up 127 percent year-to-date. We anticipate the rate of growth will not abate in the coming year. The income your bank will sustain by satisfying our needs for a wide variety of your services can become enormous. Once again not to seem immodest, Betsy, within a short time we could easily become your largest customer, not to mention we would introduce all of our investors to WB as our preferred lender. But enough - let's finish our lunch and enjoy this magnificent atmosphere. Have you had a chance to walk around the property? It would be an honor for me to be your guide."

After The Truman delivered them back to Dolphin Marina, Betsy climbed back into Carson's car for the return ride to Key West. As Carson pulled out onto the Overseas Highway, he pounded the steering wheel in excitement.

"Whooowee! What did I tell you? Would old CC steer you wrong? This is an absolute gold mine, and it's just waiting to be mined. Can CC pick 'em? I'm telling you there's so much money rolling out of Club Tropic you will be able to just pick it up out of the streets. Every banker in town will be green with envy. And did you see the suit that guy was wearing? It had to cost more than every suit I own. Damn! He's smooth as peanut butter, and he's all ours. You know why he's all ours? Because CC knows how to smell money and knows how to prospect it. Our year is made, boss lady! I can see that bonus money now! What are you going to do with yours?"

"You better watch where you're going," Betsy said. "I'd like to get back to Key West in one piece. Don't start counting that bonus yet. We've got a lot of due diligence to do before we decide we want to do business with these guys. I'll tell you right now, I have my reservations."

"Come on now, this is a no-brainer," Carson said. "It's going to be like shooting fish in a barrel. You just wait and see."

CHAPTER 21

It was another gorgeous summer day in the Keys. Will and Betsy worked feverishly to get the Grady-White ready to take out. Betsy hooked up the GPS system and tested it.

"I am looking forward to the next few days," Will said as he buttoned the cushions on the boat. "Not only are we going to have a barrel of fun, but it's really going to be nice to see some of our old Vero Beach buddies."

"We haven't seen Guy and Penny since we moved down here," Betsy agreed. "It's going to be a nice diversion to see Tom Mallette too. I was just sitting here thinking, we never even knew him until the Dave Tressler affair, but he's become a pretty good friend. He's a good contact to have."

"I'll never forget the Tressler situation as long as I live. I wonder if Guy and Penny have been keeping up with his widow, Connie?" Will said.

"I'm sure we'll have plenty of time to talk about it when they get here," Betsy continued. "I'll call Dolphin Marina later to see if they've checked in yet. I'm not sure when to expect them since they are trailering their boat. Let's plan on taking everyone to Parrotdise for dinner. That's the simplest thing."

The next morning was a good day for boating. Will and Betsy made arrangements to meet Guy and Penny at Looe Key around noon. Everyone was looking forward to a relaxing afternoon of sun and fun.

Betsy untied the boat, and Will eased away from the dock. Irene waved at them as they left. She and Don were going to Picnic Island. Irene and Betsy made tentative plans to maybe meet there later in the day. As Will guided the boat gently down the canal, Betsy tapped him on the shoulder and motioned for him to look. Standing on a dock a few doors down was a Cuban woman and a child.

Will did a double take. The woman looked very familiar. He put it out of his mind momentarily as he concentrated on keeping the boat in the deep part of the canal to avoid the big catamaran that as usual, was docked on the other side. After the woman and child were out of sight, Will turned to Betsy and smiled.

"You do know who I think that was?" he asked.

"I know who I think it was, but tell me anyway."

"That's the Cuban woman that I helped over at the Dolphin Marina when we were down here for the Fourth of July. I wonder what she's doing here."

"I thought she looked familiar. Maybe she's working at that house," Betsy replied.

"I don't think she's living there," Will said. "This is not exactly a neighborhood for indigent Cuban refugees."

"I don't know – with all the benefits the government hands out to new arrivals," Betsy said with a laugh.

Will added, "Let's check it out later."

Will guided the boat out into the channel and pushed the throttle forward. Soon they were cruising about thirty miles an hour towards Little Palm Island. Betsy pointed out to him the deck where she and Carson had had lunch with Sol Schwartzman. She described to Will the parts of the island she had seen, and they made plans to go there for lunch themselves one day. The Truman passed them like they were sitting still. Within a few minutes they had passed Little Palm and headed out to sea. Thirty minutes later they arrived at Looe Key. Will circled the perimeter of the marine sanctuary, looking for their friends. Betsy saw Penny waving at them. Betsy motioned for Will to guide the boat toward the *Float Aloan*. Within minutes they were both tied off to the same buoy.

"Man, oh, man," Tom Mallette said, "You just don't know how long I've been looking forward to this."

He grabbed his snorkel and fins and slipped gently into the blue-green water. The rest of the group was not far behind. The hues of greens and blues were almost too pretty to be real. They looked like professional pictures one might see in a tourist brochure. Will and Betsy swam northeast and saw a formidable stand of Elkhorn coral. A grouper lazily swam nearby. When they surfaced Will and Betsy could see Penny waving to them from the south. They swam toward her and soon they were staring down on a massive star coral. Angel fish and parrot fish finished the picture-perfect scene. Tom pointed at a barracuda swimming toward them.

Looe Key is one of the most spectacular reefs in the Keys. It was named for the H.M.S. Looe, which sank there in 1744. Water depths at the five mile long Y-shaped reef went down to thirty-five feet. Remains of the ship can still be found between two fingers of living coral about 200 yards from one of the markers. The ballast and anchor can be found camouflaged with centuries of coral growth. The waters surrounding the reef protect a diverse marine community.

Will surfaced and looked around. Dive flags could be seen in every direction. He cleared his mask and submerged again. Betsy joined him. Will pointed to a ray about ten feet away. Coral alternated with patches of sand. They held their breath and dived down to get a closer look.

After a half hour, Will motioned to Betsy that he was going to get out of the water for a while. He climbed up on the boat and Betsy handed her equipment up to him. Soon Tom joined them on the boat, and they sat on the bow sipping beer.

"Somebody grab this fin," Will heard Guy say. Tom walked to the stern and leaned over to take Guy's fins from him. Guy and Penny climbed up the ladder into the boat.

"You know, as warm as it was in the water," Penny commented, "It's kind of chilly when the wind hits your wet body."

"It sure feels good though," Will said. "Just look around and breathe this salt air. It's truly paradise found. There's some sandwiches in the cooler. Anyone hungry? I'm starved."

After lunch they were back in the water again. A curious school of barracuda checked them out while they watched in return. On their next sojourn to the boat they talked about going out to swim around the Adolphus Busch which was sunk another three miles west. The two-hundred-foot freighter had been sunk in one hundred feet of water to create an artificial reef. One of its main attractions was the many giant jewfish which sometimes weighed more than four hundred pounds. It was finally decided that because of the depth there would be little to see without scuba gear so the group packed up and headed back to Picnic Island.

CHAPTER 22

It was after five when Will pulled into their dock. After unloading the boat Tom, Guy and Penny headed for the Dolphin Marina. Guy said he was going to take a nap.

"Boy, that sun really takes the starch out of you," he said.

Arrangements were made to reconvene at Will and Betsy's house at seven.

"Want to walk the dogs around the neighborhood before we have to clean up?" Betsy asked after their friends left.

"Let's go down the street where we saw that Cuban woman this morning," Will said.

"You really think she was the same one you saw at the Dolphin Marina on the weekend of the fourth?" Betsy asked.

"I'm positive," Will replied.

Soon they had the dogs leashed and headed down Port Royal. Lucy tugged and pulled on the leash, coughing each time she almost choked herself. She was determined she would sniff and explore absolutely everything she saw on both sides of the street. She would pause momentarily as something caught her attention but would then dart after the next thing she saw. An iguana scurried through the weeds on a vacant lot. Will thought Lucy might break the leash as she tried to lunge for it. Coco and Dexter were content slowly sniffing around.

Betsy looked at a mailbox in front of the house. It was the same house where they had seen the Cuban woman that morning. It read "A. Soltero."

"That name must be a coincidence," Will remarked. "Surely the good old Adolfo we know in Vero Beach isn't trafficking Cuban refugees?"

"I wouldn't take bets on it. He was always, shall we say, entrepreneurial," Betsy replied. "We've got a homeowners association guide, let's check it out when we get back to the house and see if he's in it."

"Entrepreneurial! You are the grand mistress of understatement, my dear. Try the adjective opportunistic," Will said and laughed.

"We both know he's just a pragmatic businessman with a keen sense of timing," Betsy said with a wink.

When they returned home, Will checked the homeowners' directory. It only listed those homeowners who chose to pay dues and belong to the homeowner's association.

"Soltero's house is not listed," he told Betsy. "I'm not surprised. If it is *our* Adolfo, he's definitely the type of person who would want to keep a low profile."

Will and Betsy's guests arrived about ten minutes after seven. Will mixed a round of drinks for everyone, and they all adjourned to the porch. Betsy set out some crackers with cream cheese and Pickapeppa.

Tom commented, "Boy, this tastes good."

"We got this recipe in Jamaica. Pickapeppa is a Jamaican sauce. We even went through their plant in Shooter's Hill."

"That must have been interesting," Tom said.

"It was, but I guess the most interesting thing was how the plant tour got set up. One of our wealthy neighbors, John Smythe, made the arrangements. Nicest most unassuming guy you'd ever want to meet. We didn't know it at the time, but the source of his wealth was using his export business to smuggle pot. John had had free rein for years because his brother was a government official. He then laundered the money by building elaborate guest villas which he rented to tourists. His were always the largest, most modern villas to be found in Discovery Bay – five and six bedroom houses with all the amenities. We never suspected a thing. The only reason we found out about his sideline was that we were told by a local who was a good friend. We had asked our friend why Mr. Smythe continued to overbuild the neighborhood time after time and never seemed concerned when his villas were only rented sporadically. That's when Henry told us the rest of the story," said Will.

"Corruption has always been a major issue in the Caribbean," Betsy continued. "And don't get me wrong, I don't mean to pick on Jamaica. It's a third world problem."

"You mean places like Colombia?" Will said and smiled. "Remember the Colombians we met in Vero Beach?"

"Uh huh! We never have been able to pin anything on them," Tom said.

"That leads me to a new story. When we came down for July Fourth, we accidently witnessed a boatload of Cubans being unloaded from a go-fast boat at Dolphin Marina. Guy, Jimmy, and I were having a drink out by their dock, when the boat suddenly roared in, unloaded the Cubans, and immediately hauled ass back to open water. The Cubans scattered in the dark, but one woman with a child tripped and fell. We ran over and helped her up, and then she disappeared into the darkness with the others."

"They come ashore every day," Tom sighed, shaking his head.

"I know they do, but here's the part of this tale I think you'll find intriguing. I saw that same Cuban woman standing on a dock down the street as we were leaving for Looe Key this morning. Betsy and I walked the dogs by that house this afternoon after we got back. You'll never guess the name on the mailbox."

"I'm sure I can't," Tom said.

"A. Soltero," Will said, having trouble keeping the emotion out of his voice.

"Well, I'll be damned. You're right. That is fascinating. I'd love to know more. Give me the address, and I'll make a phone call to an old friend who works at the Monroe County Sheriff's Department," Tom said.

133

CHAPTER 23

The following morning Will was reviewing some client files when Tom Mallette called from Dolphin Marina.

"I just had breakfast with Guy and Penny. What's the game plan for the day? You guys want to go out on the boat again?" Tom asked.

"The water's pretty rough out there today," Will said. "The wind is blowing between twenty five and thirty. I really don't think you'd enjoy it. We could go into Key West, maybe go to Crane Point, or possibly Pigeon Key, Bahia Honda or we could just hang out here," Will suggested.

"Your call."

"Well then, why don't y'all come over here sometime before lunch, and we'll see what the group wants to do. It's your vacation. We can go to any of these places whenever we want."

"Oh, by the way, I called my friend Doug Morgan who's a sheriff's deputy. He lives on Big Pine. He said he is familiar with Soltero's address. The house was recently purchased by a Colombian company. Doug said there've been no suspicious activities going on there, but he also admitted the sheriff's department hadn't given the place a whole lot of thought. He said he'll put the house back on his radar screen," Tom said.

"Why don't you ask him to run by our house while you're here? You can introduce us. Besides that, I'm sure you'd like a chance to visit with him," Will suggested.

"Good idea. I'll see what I can do. Let me go now and see if the Walshes have any preferences," Tom said as he hung up the phone.

"Who was that?" Betsy said as she walked in the room. "The dogs are itching to go for a walk. Want to come?"

"Mallette, and sure I'll go with you. Let me get some shoes on. I'll tell you while we're walking."

They had barely started when a black Mercedes rounded the corner headed in their direction.

The car pulled into the driveway next to the Soltero mailbox and out stepped Adolfo Soltero, their acquaintance from Vero Beach. Al was wearing expensive chinos and a golf shirt. He smiled when he immediately recognized Will and Betsy and walked over with his manicured hand extended.

"Well, I'll be damned," Will mumbled.

"Now isn't this a pleasant surprise," Soltero said, smiling.

"Yes, it is." Will said back. "You're the last person I ever expected to see here. You remember my wife, Betsy."

"Of course! Who could forget one of the loveliest and most intelligent women in Florida. How is the world of high finance?" Soltero asked. "It is a pleasure to see both of you again. I heard you had moved to the Keys, but I never thought I'd be fortunate enough to run into you here."

"Actually we live right here on Port Royal Road. We've seen the mailbox with your name on it, but we never dreamed it could be referring to you."

"As they say, it is truly a small world. Now that we both know we're fortunate to live on the same street, we will surely have to renew our friendship," Soltero said. "Now if you will be so gracious to excuse me, I have an immediate matter I need to deal with. Great to see you both again."

With that, he turned and walked from the Mercedes to his house. Will and Betsy waved and turned back toward their own home.

"Wait'll the group hears about this," Betsy said. "Are we lucky at selecting real estate?"

Later that morning Will looked off the side of the porch and saw Guy's car pull into their driveway.

A sheriff's department patrol car then pulled in behind Guy. Will and Betsy went down to meet their guests.

"Will and Betsy Black," Tom said. "I'd like to introduce you to Doug Morgan. We've been to a lot of seminars together on how to rid the world of evil people."

"My pleasure," Will said as he shook hands with the deputy. "From what I've seen of the crime rate in Monroe County you've learned your lessons well. Let's go up the back stairs into the house. Anyone like something to drink?"

When they got in the house, Will could wait no longer to tell the group about his and Betsy's brief meeting with Adolfo Soltero.

"The house was purchased within the last year," the deputy began. "It's owned by a Superior Holdings. We have had no reason to pay any special attention to him. He's never asked the first thing of us. He's done nothing to bring notice to himself."

"He does seem to have his own security service," Will said, referring to Al's tough looking driver.

"Tom, do you want to tell Doug how we know Soltero?" Guy asked.

"The people here," Tom began, "helped me resolve a series of situations in Vero Beach after Hurricane Clarice. This is when we first became acquainted with Adolfo Soltero. He was never implicated in a formal case in Indian River County. To my knowledge he has never been arrested. He merely came to our attention as a party of interest. I'm not at liberty to discuss all the particulars of this case even with a fellow law enforcement officer."

Doug Morgan nodded.

"Will, Guy and Penny are securities brokers. Will works for Reynolds, Smathers & Thompson. Guy and Penny have an independent shop. Betsy, as you probably know, is a banker for WB. She is president of their bank in Key West.

"Adolfo Soltero owns a company named Superior Holdings," Tom continued. "Superior is in a variety of businesses, most involving real estate. Macadamia Partners, one of its divisions, raises money from investors to farm macadamia nuts in Costa Rica. Another division, Spoonbill Partners, develops condos. Señor Soltero also owns a used car lot and convenience store west of Vero Beach."

"Sounds like a successful entrepreneur. So why did he attract your attention?" Doug asked.

"We suspect that he might possibly be engaged in other activities as well. First, we're not so sure that he was following the letter of the law in his investor solicitations for Macadamia and Spoonbill. Second, we suspect but haven't been able to prove that he uses illegal aliens at times to smuggle art objects into the country. Third, we suspect that he might possibly be involved in money laundering, illegal gambling and loan sharking."

"This is getting more and more riveting," the deputy said. "Go on."

"Soltero also has some associates who look equally shady. They are Colombian as well. There's an Omar Perillo. He actually runs the car lot west of Vero Beach. Our observations lead us to believe that he is either part owner or very high up in all of Soltero's companies. I also had reason to suspect that he may have participated in a homicide in Vero Beach."

"Sounds like two sure 'nuff sugar boogas," Doug said.

"We think they may be the more law abiding ones in the organization. There's a third person named Miguel Valdes who we suspect may be the muscle in the organization."

"Do you think they are connected to one of the Colombian drug cartels?" Doug asked.

"I have no proof, but I wouldn't doubt it," Tom said. "They seem to have access to some serious big money. I don't think any of these guys are Sunday school teachers."

"Before we moved to Little Torch Key," Will chimed in, "this last Fourth of July actually, Guy and I happened to see some illegal Cubans being let off of a go-fast boat at the Dolphin Marina. I helped one Cuban woman get up after she fell in the parking lot and skinned her knee."

"Not a day goes by that Cubans don't try to slip into the Keys somewhere," Doug said.

"Well, I saw that same woman yesterday morning standing on Soltero's dock."

"And we know it's the same Soltero," Betsy added, "because we talked to him this morning. He seemed very cordial and glad to see us."

"This tale keeps getting better and better," the deputy said. "Now let me tell you what little we know about your Mr. Soltero – almost nothing. To our knowledge he has been an exemplary citizen. He is not a full timer. This must be a second home because he is not here all the time. Until now I've no reason to think of him in any light other than a good one, but you've given me plenty to consider."

The deputy finally shook hands and said goodbye. He and Tom walked to the street and talked before Doug finally got in his car and drove off.

When Tom got back to the house he said, "Doug says this neighborhood has been on their watch list from time to time because of your neighbors, the Blanchards. Jake Blanchard owns the house on the corner of Port Royal to the north of you - the one that's surrounded by vacant lots. He owns the lots too. Ike Blanchard is suspected of being one of the biggest drug smugglers in the Keys. He may be working

139

for one of the Colombian drug cartels. The Blanchards own Hades boats..."

"I know them," Guy interrupted. "The boats that are advertised as being 'Hot As Hades'."

"That's them. What we call go-fast boats," Tom continued.

"They suspect Blanchard may be using Hades to launder money for a very big pot-smuggling operation."

"Wow! Right here in little old Buccaneer Estates," said Will.

"On our street!" added Betsy. "As I said earlier, we sure have an eye for real estate."

"DEA hasn't been able to build an airtight case, but even if they do they'll have trouble seizing the property. The house and lots are formally owned by some of their relatives who have not been implicated in the smuggling/laundering operation despite the Feds being pretty sure where the money to buy them came from. Not surprisingly all Keys properties owned by any members of the Blanchard family are free and clear of encumbrances. There isn't a dime in mortgages on any of their Keys properties according to what Doug told me."

CHAPTER 24

After Doug Morgan left, the group decided to drive into Key West. Before Will could pull out on U.S. 1 he had to wait for a convoy of motorcycles to pass.

"I forgot this was biker Poker Run weekend," Betsy said.

"What's that? " Penny asked.

"It's a charity event sponsored by one of the Harley dealers in Miami and the Rotary Club," Betsy said. "The paper said there will probably be more than 10,000 bikers in town. They ride down from Miami and party all weekend. They buy poker hands all the way down, and the winning hands will get to play poker in Key West for a custom Harley. The profits all go to charity. The Diabetes Research Institute is the biggest beneficiary."

"Not the rough-and-tumble Hell's Angel image you usually associate with bikers," Penny replied.

"No, I don't think it's that way at all," Betsy said. "Many of the participants are businessmen and other professionals just out to have a fun weekend."

"Bottom line is there's going to be a lot of people on Duval Street," Will said.

When they finally arrived at a parking lot on Greene Street, Thomas, the parking lot attendant they knew was nowhere to be seen. Will pulled in, and they all got out of the car. Suddenly a grizzled, weather-beaten man in a torn T-shirt appeared from behind some lobster traps and yelled at him, "Hey, Mister, you can't park here without paying."

The man and his dog approached Will and Betsy, and then broke out in a toothless grin as he recognized them.

Will smiled back and stuck out his hand, "Who the hell am I supposed to pay if you're not here to take my money?" he chided.

"Christ, can't a guy go take a whiz every once in a while?" Thomas said.

"How much is the tariff today, Thomas?" Will asked.

"For most people $100, but for you $10 will do," Thomas said.

The group began walking, first through the Conch Republic Seafood Company, then over to the Schooner Wharf Bar where Michael McCloud, a long-standing Key West entertainer, was playing *Tourist Town Bar*. He drawled

> *We got bimbos and bozos and bikers and boozers.*
> *We get daytime drunks and three time losers.*
> *We get a room full of rednecks and we get these fancy dressed fellas*
> *And we get busloads of blue hairs and dirt bags and sailors...*

Some bikers cheered and hoisted their beer in a salute. After listening to the song and having a beer themselves, the group strolled on down past the Waterfront Market and had a late lunch at Turtle Kraals.

"Club Tropic's trying to get the lease on many of the restaurants in this area," Betsy said.

After lunch Will and Betsy walked their guests over to Caroline Street to show them B O's Fish Wagon before they strolled over to Duval Street.

Will poked his head in Sloppy Joe's and saw that their favorite bartender, Fred, was working the back bar. Fred saw them come in and waved. Bikers roamed in and out. Raven Cooper played her guitar on stage.

"So what's new?" Will asked after introducing Fred to their guests.

"Business is good." A customer with a bandana gave Fred a big tip. Fred rang the bell behind the bar in appreciation. "Did you hear about the dead man at No Name Key?" he asked.

"Another one?" Will responded. "There was a death there in July. What happened this time?"

"That rock quarry out on No Name...the drag line operator was scooping up a load of rocks...a body came up with the rocks. Apparently it had been there a day or two...in nasty shape," Fred said. "My buddy, Jeffrey Deal, a deputy with the Monroe County Sheriff's Department told me about it."

"No shit!" Will said.

"Disgusting," Penny added.

"They've been able to identify the body. Had on a Club Tropic golf shirt. Turns out he was one of their salesmen – guy named Joey Giambi."

"The last body found at No Name was one of their high rolling investors from New Jersey," Betsy said.

"I'd forgotten about that. I remember now - the week of the fourth," Fred said. "Word is that this one came from New Jersey too, and he wasn't slated for sainthood."

"I didn't see the story on this one in today's *Citizen*," Will said.

"Apparently none of the papers have this story yet," Fred continued. "According to Jeffrey, Giambi only escaped going to prison a few years ago in New Jersey by hauling ass just in the nick of time and in the process, stiffing a bail bondsman. In fact some of his competitors are serving hard time. They were running a seventy five million dollar construction and fraud ring through a company called Garden State Check Cashing."

"What exactly were they doing?" Tom asked.

"According to Deputy Deal, Garden State let numerous construction companies write them checks on phony subcontractors and then cashed them. Garden State pocketed a three to five percent commission fee and gave the cash to the construction firms which then paid employees and other expenses without fulfilling their tax obligations."

"Nothing like a tablespoon of fraud with your tax evasion," Guy commented.

"The officers were charged with conspiracy and filing false currency transaction reports. Head knocker was a guy named Juan Strazzuli."

"What the hell is that? Sounds like an Italian who got lost and ended up in Central America," said Will.

"You know what they say – you can pick your friends, but you can't choose your family. Giambi was running a similar operation called Quick Buck Cash Flow Financing, but it was a lot smaller. The Feds got onto him first. He worked a deal to get off lighter with a relative slap on the wrist by dumping the other thieves in the creek. The agents wanted the big fish bad enough to let Giambi cut a deal for reduced time."

"Garden State," Fred continued, "concealed the names of the various construction firms by listing various shell companies on the transaction reports. My buddy Jeffrey said they were doing this to help facilitate criminal activities, and we're not talking pikersville either. He said according to their investigation they filed more than six hundred million in financial transactions with the IRS over a two year period."

"There's other motivations as well," Guy said. "They were avoiding paying Social Security and Medicare taxes."

"Plus," Betsy added, "dealing in cash makes it easier to pay illegal aliens to work."

"Looks like your glasses are empty. You need another round?" Fred asked. "Looking into his past apparently this Joey Giambi liked getting his picture taken with celebrities. Do you remember Jim McGreevey? Giambi's picture was shown in a New Jersey paper with him."

"Name rings a bell – vaguely," Penny said.

"Sure! I remember...He was governor of New Jersey," said Will.

"Bingo! Good memory," Fred said. "He was the one who resigned after admitting to a homosexual affair with the Israeli man he had appointed to be his homeland security adviser."

"Club Tropic can really pick 'em, can't they?" Will said.

Everyone laughed.

"If you think that's funny, just walk down Duval Street and look at the utility pole."

They all looked perplexed.

"Down near Fast Buck Freddie's…across the street," Fred pointed. "Cops picked up a woman last night who had decorated her face and legs with fingernail polish…and…when they got there she was decorating the light pole in a similar manner while yelling obscenities at the pedestrians. She told the police it was her right because of freedom of speech to glue objects to the utility pole and screamed at them when they started removing her work. She glued postcards, condoms, lighters and mints to the pole with the same red nail polish. When I came to work the nail polish was still on the pole."

"That definitely calls for another round of drinks. Police work sure is different here than it is in Vero Beach," Tom said as he laughed.

CHAPTER 25

Will's phone rang.

"What are you doing Tuesday, after work, big boy?" Betsy asked teasingly.

"Is this a proposition or do you need a date?" Will responded.

"A date would be nice," Betsy said. "The Lower Keys Chamber of Commerce has a function. I really need to be there to represent the bank. It will give us a chance to meet some of the people in the business community."

"You mean we're going to get to know someone other than bartenders and waitresses?" Will asked.

"Smart ass! This cocktail party is for new people in town and better yet, it's the installation of new officers. You even know one of them."

"Oh, yeah – who?" Will asked.

"Carson Crown is the incoming vice president."

"I'm counting the minutes," Will said sarcastically.

"I knew you'd take it like a trooper, said Betsy."

Tuesday arrived. Will drove into town to pick up Betsy. The Chamber party was at El Masón de Pépe's on Mallory Square. They decided to walk over. As they got to the restaurant, they saw their friend Rolando Rojas setting up the sound system for his band.

"Rolando," Will greeted. "Are you playing for the Chamber function tonight?"

"You reserve Pépe's, you reserve me," Rolando said and smiled.

"Perfect place for a late afternoon cocktail party, with that magnificent Key West sunset as a backdrop," Will said to Rolando. "Doesn't get any better than this."

Jack and Joan Maselli, Will and Betsy's neighbors, walked in. They all ordered a drink. Rolando began to play a self-penned song, *Toda la Noche*.

"How are things, neighbor?" Jack asked.

"We're really starting to get settled in and feel a part of the lower Keys," Betsy said.

"It doesn't take long, we were the same way," Jack said. "The first week we were here Joan was invited to go to the United Way kickoff party. I got a call inviting us to come to a Hotel and Lodging Association meeting. It's just that kind of place once you cross over from being a tourist to being a local."

"I'm still trying to get used to some of the locals," Betsy said with a laugh. "I walked out of my office a few weeks ago to use the copy machine. In the teller line in the lobby was a clown in full regalia, and behind him was a guy dressed like a pirate, complete with earring, bandana and knapsack. And behind him was an obese retiree in a tank top."

"Gross!" Joan said.

"I'm not finished yet. Behind fatso was a college kid in a Kappa Alpha T-shirt."

"Diversity...Thy name is Key West."

"You know the most disturbing part of the whole thing," Betsy concluded. "It almost seemed normal. Then after I started to return to my office, a six foot plus drag queen held the door open for the clown."

"Yes, I love Key West," Jack said. "Well, my story isn't that exotic, but it's still exciting. Club Tropic has a major new investor."

"Tell us more," Betsy said.

Suddenly Carson Crown drunkenly slapped Jack on the back, causing him to spill his drink on Will.

"Ever had a coldbeer bought just for you by a double vice president?" Carson interrupted. "Hell, I'm about to be a vice president twice – once at WB and now here with the chamber. Sheeit! Most people are lucky to pull it off once. Waiter, this man needs a coldbeer. Put it on my tab. His credit ain't good here as long as CC's in the room."

Jack tried to be polite. "Good to see you, Carson," Jack said.

Betsy was getting pissed. "*Associate vice president* at the bank," Betsy reminded Carson. "And this isn't your tab. The bank is paying for this little shindig."

Carson didn't hear her. He was waving at someone across the room so enthusiastically that he tipped some beer on Betsy's patent leather pumps.

"I didn't know coldbeer was one word until I met Carson," Will said snidely.

Carson turned back around, and put his arm around Jack. "Your boss is going to make old CC into a hoss at WB. We're going to deliver banking services for Club Tropic that will make your head spin."

Betsy was getting angrier. "Carson," she said. "We are still considering these matters, and any banking transactions should never be discussed at a cocktail party."

"We both know that's just a formality with blue chippers like these boys." He saw a UF alum and his wife talking to another couple. "Go Gators!" he yelled in Will's ear.

"Gotta go now! I've got some swamp talk to talk – contacts to make – damn, I'm good. This is gonna be our year," he said as he moved away. "Don't forget – CC's running an open tab, so y'all drink up while it's free."

He staggered toward the other couple. Betsy seethed. Will knew when she was close to blowing and tried to cover for her by changing the subject.

"Carson's a piece of work, isn't he? Now you were saying about a new investor," he said.

"Oh, yeah!" Jack said. "Where was I? We're about to get a major vote of confidence from one of the world's great investors. I can't give you a name at this point. He's a billionaire from Colombia.

"We are told he's approved one of his companies to invest at least fifteen million in Club Tropic, and if he likes what he sees – and he will – he'll put in more. I know this may sound like a drop in the bucket for a billionaire, but they don't get to be billionaires by throwing their money away. They get there by spotting opportunities and then moving decisively."

"That's very impressive," Will said. "Congrats."

"And there's other things pending too. As I told you over at our house when you moved in, this is an exciting place to work. Oh, may I be excused? I see someone over there I've been playing phone tag with for three days." He and Joan moved away.

Will and Betsy heard a familiar voice from across the room. "Ever had a coldbeer bought just for you by a double vice president?"

Betsy gritted her teeth.

"Well, this is an unexpected pleasure." said Adolfo Soltero, smiling broadly. "I see the 'A' list got invited to this party."

They exchanged greetings and talked about what a perfect night it was for an outdoor function.

"So what brings you down to the Keys?" Will asked.

"Business opportunities. I sense there is a lot of untapped potential in Monroe County on many fronts. But you need to be here to get your arms around them," Soltero replied.

"I understand the importance of learning a local market. Betsy and I both have had to do the same thing," Will said.

They talked further and finally decided that when the chamber cocktail party was over they would meet for dinner at El Siboney, a Cuban restaurant in Key West.

"Have you ever experienced paella valenciana?" Soltero asked.

They admitted they hadn't.

"It is a special dish that one must call ahead to order. I will take care of it with my cell phone. You are in for an experience."

As they eased toward the exit, Will and Betsy heard over the din of the crowd, "Ever had a coldbeer bought just for you by a double vice president?"

CHAPTER 26

El Siboney was on the corner of Catherine and Margaret in Old Town Key West. They each took separate cars and arrived within moments of each other. El Siboney was a low slung one story red brick building with a shingle roof. Parking places came right up to the front door. A narrow pearock covered flower bed with small palm trees ran alongside the building. To the left of the entrance attached to a building was a sign saying "El Siboney Restaurant, Cuban Food, Paella, Seafood." Almost every parking space was taken.

Soltero graciously held open the door for Will and Betsy to enter. A smiling olive-complexioned man greeted Soltero and they exchanged pleasantries in Spanish.

"Pardon me," Soltero said, "I have not introduced you to my friends from Vero Beach, Will and Betsy Black. Will and Betsy, our host Julio de la Cruz. The Blacks are now residents of the lower Keys. Julio, Monroe County has been fortunate enough to attract not only one of the premier bankers but one of the foremost stock brokers in Florida.

Mrs. Black is president of WB bank in Monroe County – she is a good person for you to know. Mr. Black is the manager of the new Reynolds Smathers & Thompson office. I am honored to be the one to introduce them to your extraordinary establishment – one of the well kept secrets of Key West."

De la Cruz laughed, "I am indeed honored, but don't keep El Siboney *too* big a secret. We'll go out of business."

"Would I show my ignorance if I asked what Siboney means in Spanish?" Will asked as they shook hands.

"Not at all," responded their host. "You will note that our logo is an Indian."

"Yes, I noticed the Indian head in full headdress on the wall as well as a full length figure," Betsy said. "I wondered about that since this is a Cuban restaurant."

"Siboney is an alternate spelling for Ciboney with a 'C'," de la Cruz said. The Ciboney Indians occupied Florida and the Caribbean for more than thirteen thousand years. They were great fishermen who took their name from the sacred stone of the sea, the Ciboney. Many were found in Cuba. Much of the population died of smallpox after being exposed to the Spanish. Others intermarried with either the Spanish or Africans creating a Creole people."

The restaurant buzzed with activity as de la Cruz led Will and Betsy to an empty table. "I have been informed that you ordered paella – an excellent choice," he said.

A waitress appeared, and Soltero suggested they order a pitcher of sangria.

"To my friends," Soltero toasted after the wine was poured.

Soon a huge steaming pan of paella arrived at their table. "My God, we're going to eat all that?" Will said. "It looks delicious. What are the ingredients?"

"Many of the most heavenly foods on the planet," Soltero answered. "Pork loin, chicken breasts, scallops, squid, grouper, clams and mussels. There is also onion, pepper, tomato, other ingredients – all cooked with chicken stock, rice, and spices. Enjoy."

After a few minutes of silence as each savored the paella, Soltero asked, "Please, tell me, what do you know about Club Tropic?"

"I know they have barged into the Keys like a water spout sweeping up everything in their wake. I hear about them everywhere I go," Will said.

"Yes, I read the news stories too, but I'm talking about the substance not the hype," Soltero continued.

"We have been approached by them to establish a banking relationship," Betsy contributed. "Our underwriters are still examining the information they have provided. I have not heard back from our underwriters which indicates they have reached no conclusions yet. Not to be impolite but you understand we have privacy policies on what I am able to disclose. Would it be out of line for me to ask why you are interested in information about them?"

"You are not impolite. I respect the bank's discretion," Soltero said. "Confidentially – Club Tropic has offered me an investment opportunity."

"To buy into one their real estate packages? What I have been told about some of their sales presentations would

155

make me want to conduct a thorough due diligence," Will said.

"Actually, they approached me and some of my associates about possibly loaning them money. The terms they proposed sounded rather attractive on the surface," Soltero said.

"I know you are a sophisticated investor," Betsy said, "but I must caution you about assuming the role of a banker. At WB we have a large and experienced staff to evaluate proposals daily, and we also have the size to enable us to diversify our risks…and even with these advantages we still make mistakes."

"I appreciate your concern," Soltero said.

"One last comment, and please don't think I'm being condescending. Why would Club Tropic attempt to borrow funds from you unless conventional sources of capital were unavailable to them?" Betsy asked.

Soltero smiled.

CHAPTER 27

It seemed like an excellent Saturday to catch up on house chores, and it appeared everyone was outside working. A cool front had blown in the night before and there was a slight breeze blowing. There was just enough wind to discourage fishermen and boaters but more importantly, it discouraged the mosquitoes and no-see-ums. Canal visibility was limited because of the high tide and the ripples on the water. Will had put the boat in the water earlier that morning to get it out of his way.

Donald Ware was fiddling with an obstinate bilge pump. Irene was washing out an ice chest with the hose. Jack Maselli was trimming his coconut palm, putting the cuttings in garbage cans. Will was spraying Roundup on some stubborn weeds, while Jason Pearson changed out the worn ball bearings on the Blacks' davits. Betsy had left earlier to go grocery shopping.

Despite the breeze, the weekend warriors were soon starting to get sweaty. Jack was the first to decide it was time for a beer break and a swim.

"I've about had enough of this crap. I'm going in the house, get a beer and take a little swim in the canal. Anybody want to join me?"

"I'm game," Donald called back. "Maybe after I cool off, I can get this son of a bitch pump working."

"I don't know why you don't just go buy a new one. They don't cost that much," Irene said.

"There's nothing wrong with this one," Donald grumbled to his wife.

"I'm ready any time you are," Will said. "I'm about finished here anyway."

"You boys jump in, and I'll throw you a beer. I think you've earned it," Irene told them.

"Don't pay any attention to me," Jason said. "I really need to get finished with this. I promised the wife we'd go to Bahia Honda this afternoon."

Donald dived into the canal first. Will followed.

"Lord, this water feels good," Donald said. "Watch your step though. I saw a man of war in here the other day."

They both swam toward Jack's house just as he emerged with a beer in his hand. Will's foot kicked something solid as he got near Jack's dock which caused him to stumble into something spongier. He put his face near the water to see what it was.

"What the hell!" he yelled at the top of his lungs. "Come here!"

Donald swam toward him. Jason and Jack came running.

"Shit!" Jason yelled. "That's a body!"

Jason grabbed his cell phone and called the sheriff's dispatcher.

"We have a possible 31 at 605 Port Royal Road. We need a car now," he said.

"Get out of the water, guys. Leave the body alone until the deputy gets here," he said to Donald and Will.

Within minutes a patrol car rolled in, and Jason, an experienced EMT, jumped into the canal. He pushed the body toward the surface while the deputy and Donald pulled it onto Jack's dock as Red Stripe shrieked his advice from the porch. It was heavy and hard to lift. As the soggy carcass came up, Will saw why. The arms and legs had each been weighted with a concrete block. The man's face had been blown away. Two crabs clung grotesquely to the raw facial meat. The body was fully clothed – a short sleeve white shirt, long pants and wingtips. Irene stared silently from across the canal. Jack ran to the far end of the dock and blew his breakfast into the mangroves. The dogs started barking, creating an eerie soundtrack.

About that time Betsy rolled into the driveway. After seeing the patrol car in the driveway and the crowd, she panicked, thinking someone had had an accident. She ran down to the dock and saw the body as Donald and the patrolman were laying it out. Other vehicles arrived, including an ambulance. The ID team arrived. A forensic photographer snapped pictures. Yellow tape was stretched out. The medical examiner kneeled next to the body for a closer look. In their house Betsy could see Lucy jumping up and down like a pogo stick behind the sliding doors. Coco and Dexter continued to bark incessantly, setting Red Stripe off again.

Within a couple of hours the hordes of people – and the body -- were gone.

"Well, so much for taking the family to the beach. I'll make it up to them tomorrow," Jason said. "I guess I might as well go over to the sheriff's substation on Cudjoe and find out what's going on; I'll finish the davits this afternoon."

After Jason left, Jack, Joan, Donald and Irene came over at Betsy's invitation to make sandwiches for lunch. Jack still looked shaken.

"I never dreamed when I got out of bed this morning I'd be swimming with a dead body," Will said. "I'm glad I had wet-shoes on."

"Oh, it's no big deal," Donald commented. "When I was in the Navy…"

Irene rolled her eyes.

Before Donald could continue, Jack who had been silent, jumped up, coming out of the almost catatonic state he had been in since they had discovered the body.

"I know who that was," Jack suddenly shouted. "That was Myron Levitt in our accounting department. God help us! Another Club Tropic employee dead, and this one definitely didn't die by accident. But why did he end up at the foot of my dock?"

Joan turned white. Jack looked like he wanted to throw up again.

"Jack, you need to call the sheriff's office with that information," Betsy said.

After Jack reported his recognition of the victim, the investigator told him he would confirm the victim's ID and call back. Jack hung up and shoved aside his uneaten ham sandwich. He was still shaken.

"Someone's trying to send me a message, but what... and why? I haven't done anything to anybody," Jack said.

"Why don't you both stay over here for a while, calm down and think about things. Maybe you'll come up with some answers," Betsy suggested. "You want another beer?"

Jack didn't seem to hear her.

Jason dropped by about an hour later.

"Well, we know who the victim was," he said.

"So do we," Jack said. "Myron Levitt in Club Tropic's accounting department. He was part of the nucleus group who came down from New Jersey."

Jason looked a little disappointed he had been upstaged. "I'm sorry," he said. "Did you know him well?"

"Primarily through office scuttlebutt. He has always been rumored to be part of Sol Schwartzman's inner circle," Jack said. "We talked occasionally at sales meetings and Christmas parties. Now that I think about it, he did do me a few favors from time to time."

"But you didn't know his background?" Jason said.

Jack shook his head.

"Levitt was a convicted felon," Jason said. "Served four years. He was involved in a massive tax scheme involving illegal aliens. He was the executive vice president of a New Jersey company named Levitt-Rosenblum International."

"Jason now had everyone's attention. He continued, "He was charged in a twenty-one count indictment with conspiracy to defraud the United States, evading federal employment taxes and harboring illegal immigrants for profit."

"Whoooee!" Will said. "Federal counts. That's not good."

"Just before the indictment was handed down," Jason went on, "more than 300 undocumented workers from Mexico, Honduras, Guatemala and Haiti were rounded up on 73 LRI sites across the nation. They were detained pending deportation proceedings.

"LRI's attorneys negotiated a plea agreement for the president, pleading guilty to charges of conspiring to defraud the government and harboring illegal immigrants. Levitt negotiated the same agreement for himself.

"Boy, as I have said before, Club Tropic sure knows how to pick 'em," Will said.

"LRI built one hell of a business undercutting their competition by building their labor force with illegal workers," Jason said. "It worked because these illegals were willing to be paid with cash, could be fired without legal recourse, and were highly unlikely to report the irregular nature of their employment."

"I swear, guys, I knew nothing about Myron's background," Jack said, wringing his hands. "What kind of company do I work for?"

"I wish we were back in New Jersey," Joan said.

CHAPTER 28

As long as the boat was in the water, Will and Betsy decided to take it for a late afternoon spin.

"Do you think Jack was really as shocked by the body as he appeared to be?" Will asked Betsy as he opened up the throttle.

"I sure do," she said. "I don't think you can pretend to be that scared. If someone wanted to put the fear of God into him, they succeeded. Have you ever seen anyone look so terrified?"

Will guided the boat into the channel, and opened it up to 25 MPH. The cool wind was refreshing. Soon the summer stickiness of the shore was left behind.

"We're going to have a stunning sunset tonight," Will said. "By the way, Jason came back while you were upstairs. He said the sheriff's department is not going to release the details of Levitt's killing to the press for the time being. They don't want it in the paper that there has been a mob style killing in the Keys."

"I wonder how long they can keep a lid on those facts," Betsy said.

An hour later Will and Betsy returned to their dock. Jack Maselli saw them come down the canal.

"You feel any better?" Will asked after the boat was tied off.

"Not really," Jack answered. "Would you two mind if I used you as a sounding board?"

"You know we don't mind, and you know we'll keep it confidential," Betsy said.

They pulled up lawn chairs and sat down. Jack had a manila folder of papers. He looked uncomfortable.

"As you know," he began, "I'm the condo sales manager for Club Tropic here in the Keys. You also know Club Tropic has developments in other cities in Florida and is starting to develop sites out of state as well."

Will nodded.

"Recently, Club Tropic has hired a national sales manager, Carmine Scarpetti, to coordinate sales for our many locations. I now answer to him. He has started dictating the agenda at my sales meetings. I am not comfortable with some of the tactics he's demanding I foist on the sales force. I made the mistake recently of making my feelings known to Carmine. He said, "Either sell the goddamned things my way, or don't let the door hit you or your salesmen in the fucking ass."

"He said he could find another peon with real gonads to fill my shoes in five minutes…and he punched me in the chest with his forefinger."

"Sounds like the sales manager from hell," Will said. "What was it you found objectionable?"

"Several things. Here's one handout he gave me to use as a pro forma for a sales presentation," Jack said, pulling out a piece of paper.

> <u>Example – 20% appreciation</u>
> Original purchase price: $500,000 (@ $400 square foot=1250)
> Appreciation year 1: $100,000 (20% of $500,000)=$600,000
> Purchased @ $400/ square foot
> Appraised/ worth $450-500/ square foot
> Appreciation year 2: $120,000 (20% of $600,000)=$720,000
> Recap: Purchase for $500K, worth $720,000 includes 2 years appreciation of $220,000
> Total value $720,000=44% increase in value in 2 years
> Less 7% at time sold ($35,000) realtor fees etc. est.
> Profit after 2 years: $185,000

"That's some pretty aggressive projections," Will said.

Jack nodded.

"Carmine told me to make my salesmen memorize these numbers so they could rattle them off without any hesitation, and for me to instruct my people they can paraphrase it if necessary, just be sure to never, never leave the illustration with the prospect in writing," Jack said. "We are to tell the prospect these are conservative, realistic estimates, but as a worst case scenario even if you cut these numbers in half – everyone was still going to get rich."

"I can certainly see why you have a problem with that...talk about overselling," Betsy said.

"Wait'll you see this prospecting letter," Jack said.

Dear :

We have the unique ability to enable you to purchase property with little money out of pocket.

With over 6,000 people moving to Florida every week, there really is no end in sight as to when prices will stop rising on housing, especially waterfront. Monroe County is rising 27%, Hillsborough is rising 23%, and Lee County at 44%. You can't find any printed material which has "bubble" and "resorts" in the same paragraph.

Your ability to become part of our group is dependant upon future openings and the result of a simple screening process.

I don't want to appear too good to be true, but the figures speak for themselves. After taking a look, decide to invest <u>AT YOUR OWN RISK.</u>

We want you as a customer for life. **While performing your due diligence, please refrain from obtaining information from our retail sales staff or web pages.** *There are entirely different price levels between the retail and the investor levels and policies in place preventing overlap.*

Current availability, first come first serve, is as follows:

Tavernier 600-800K, $35K membership, 14 available, condo-hotel

IGC Acad. 1.049-1.3M, $35K membership, 5 available, townhouse

Sarasota 250-550K, $15-25 membership, 450 available, condo

Marathon 310-380K, $35K membership, boat slips

Orlando 180-300K, $15K membership, 80 available

Your next step is to make a decision. Should you be interested you may call my office for more information. ***I am an investor, just like you. I am taking the risk just like you.***

Feel free to contact my office should you have any further questions at 239-539-2582. *I believe in striking while the iron is hot.*

Good luck with your investing and call me when you are ready to move forward.

Regards,

Carmine Scarpetti
National Sales Manager and Director of Investor Relations

"Carmine has started to blanket the area with mass mailings of this letter," Jack said. "He says he expects the sales force to close 75 percent of the prospects it brings in. We are to use the first illustration I showed you as proof of Club Tropic's investment acumen. He also said if we don't have the balls to close those percentages he will bring in his old sales force from New Jersey and get it done – no excuses are acceptable."

"I can see why you might not sleep at night," Will said.

Jack whipped out one more memo.

INTERSTATE BANK
ZIPPY CHEATS AND TRICKS
If you get a "refer" and if you DO NOT get
Stated Income / Stated Asset findings
Never Fear!! Zippy can be adjusted (just ever so slightly)
Try these steps next time you use Zippy! You just might get the findings you need!!

*Always select "Alternate Docs" in the documentation drop down
*Borrower(s) MUST have a mid credit score of 700
*First time homebuyers require a 720 score
*NO BK'S OR FORECLOSURES, EVER!! Regardless of time
*Salaried borrowers must have 2 years time on job with current employer
*Self employed must be in existence for 2 years (verified with biz license)
*NO non-occupant co borrowers
*Max LTV/CLTV is 100%
Try these handy steps to get SISA findings

1. In the income section of your 1003, make sure you input all income in base income. DO NOT break it down by overtime, commissions or bonus.
2. NO GIFT FUNDS! If your borrower is getting a gift, add it to a bank account along with the rest of the assets. Be

sure to remove any mention of gift funds on the rest of your 1003.
3. If you do not get Stated/Stated, try resubmitting with slightly higher income. Inch it up $500 to see if you can get the findings you want. Do the same for assets.
It's super easy! Give it a try!
If you get stuck, call me...I am happy to help!
Roger Packard, Loan Originator 305-874-2265

"That's illegal," gasped Betsy. "They're falsifying a loan application. That's mortgage fraud plain and simple. You will be prosecuted by the federal authorities when they catch you."

"And you wonder why I'm a nervous wreck," Jack said. "Carmine told us to use Roger Packard at Interstate Bank to make sure there's no slipups. He also told us to tell the lenders to label purchases as second homes instead of investment properties no matter what."

"Why?" Betsy asked. "How can he justify that?"

"Because with the Club Tropic lease-back agreement you have possession of the property two weeks out of the year," Jack said.

"That's a stretch," Betsy said.

"No shit!" Jack replied.

"No shit! No shit!" Red Stripe repeated.

"That's enough from the peanut gallery," Betsy said.

Jack didn't even smile.

CHAPTER 29

WB Underwriting got back to Betsy with their decision. After giving the matter of Club Tropic data and the limited data on the related companies a very comprehensive analysis, the bank had decided it was not interested in initiating a banking relationship with Club Tropic, particularly one that involves making loans to an already highly leveraged company.

Betsy sighed when she got the news even though it was fully expected. She concurred, but she was reluctant to have Carson Crown be the messenger. She was going to have to do this herself, and she anticipated Club Tropic CEO Sol Schwartzman probably might not receive the rejection graciously.

She decided to tell Carson first. She told Margaret to ask him to come up to her office.

When he arrived, she asked, "How are things going, Carson?"

"Boss lady, exceedingly well," he said. "If it got any better, I absolutely couldn't stand it."

Betsy smiled as she wondered how many times she had heard Carson use that exact same line. She silently grinned again as she thought of "coldbeer." Carson interpreted her smile as approval and grinned from ear to ear.

"Sit down, Carson, I am about to ruin your day," Betsy said.

Carson sat down, leaning back in a leisurely manner, with his legs extended and his fingers intertwined behind his head. The front legs of the chair were off the ground.

"The bank has decided we do not wish to establish a banking relationship with or loan money to Club Tropic at this time," Betsy said.

"Whaaat!" Carson said, tipping his chair forward. "You are not serious."

"Very serious," Betsy said.

"You…you…you're all conspiring to ruin my career," Carson said.

"Carson, you know this has nothing to do with you. This is a business decision."

"But I won't make my goals," he said. His face had turned red.

"Then you'll just have to quit sandbagging and work a little harder. The year's not over by a long shot."

"You're still mad over that liquor store deal, aren't you?" Carson said. "This is your chance to get even."

"Carson, that's a juvenile statement. This has nothing to do with anything else that's happened. We just don't want to be Club Tropic's bank. By the way, I'll take care of calling Sol Schwartzman and telling him."

"I'll never be able to face Sol again at Rotary," Carson said as he stumbled out of Betsy's office.

Betsy had Margaret call Sol Schwartzman and set a time for her to visit him at his office. There would be no lunches this time; it would be a short, to-the-point business meeting.

Margaret set up a meeting with Mr. Schwartzman that afternoon.

Betsy perceived that Schwartzman sensed her purpose was to deliver bad news because he kept her sitting in the lobby for thirty minutes before she was finally escorted to his office.

Betsy made a few pleasantries and then quickly got to the purpose of her visit. "Our underwriters have closely reviewed the financials you and your staff provided us. There are items they do not feel comfortable with and have recommended WB decline Club Tropic's loan request at this time," she said. "Based on the information you have provided, the amount of leverage exceeds our internal guidelines. If you would give us the financial data on all of Club Tropic's related firms, perhaps our conclusion would be different. However, since we do not have sufficient data to establish the cash flows of these multiple firms or assess the aggregate assets and liabilities of inter companies and their transactions, we are limited to this decision. I'm sorry things have not worked out. But, for example, if...."

Before Betsy could list or discuss some of the other concerns of WB's underwriting group, Schwartzman gave her a frightening, if not calculating, icy look.

Betsy did not anticipate Schwartzman would be pleased with the rejection, but she was unprepared for the explosion that followed. There was a look of veiled hate in his eyes. Betsy said nothing, waiting for him to organize his thoughts. She didn't have to wait long.

"Mrs. Black, your bank's short-sightedness and small thinking has just cost you the largest customer your bank would ever have in Monroe County. I guess I shouldn't have expected anything more of your bank's limited vision from a bunch of salaried, unimaginative grunts who would have trouble picking up dollar bills off the streets without assistance, not to mention trying to select the right-colored socks. It's obvious they certainly don't have the wherewithal or initiative to bank a conglomerate like Club Tropic. That's why they work for a bank. I guess it is good I found out now how mediocre and shortsighted your bank is and didn't put myself in a position of relying on them in the future for something truly critical."

He continued, "We have an investor coming aboard soon who will make it completely unnecessary for us to have to provide you with additional financial data or grovel before your organization again. The capital this investor will bring to us will dwarf anything you can ever imagine. Mrs. Black, you will soon know just how badly you've blown it, but it will be too late. We will have made other arrangements, and no matter how hard you try, you will never, never ever have an opportunity to have even a checking account relationship with this company again. Am I making myself crystal clear?"

"Mr. Schwartzman, the facts portrayed by the financial statements presented to us currently…"

Schwartzman interrupted, pointing his finger at Betsy, "I have one final thing to say to you, and this meeting is over. I will not have you compromise my personal reputation or the reputation of this company by breathing a word of this declination. If one word leaks out from you or from that buffoon, Carson Crown, or anyone else in your bank about this matter, I will make you pay. If you ever repeat this conversation, I will deny that it ever took place. Do you understand me? Now, if you will pardon me, Mrs. Black, I must get back to work. I have allocated all the time for you that I can allow today…or any other day. Rebecca, will you show Mrs. Black out?"

Sol Schwartzman did not bother to stand.

CHAPTER 30

Will was having a good day. The Dow was up 65 points. He had just rolled 200 muni bonds with a point in them for a client. Half a million in stock certificates had been booked in that morning into an estate account. The stocks were to be sold. He had already been told by the heir that what was left of the money after estate taxes would stay at RST.

Will poured himself a cup of coffee in the kitchen and took the *Key West Citizen* back to his desk. He smiled as he read about an altercation at a bar on Duval Street. One combatant named Ray Kohl claimed to have gone into the bar to pay a man named Leonard King money he owed him. King allegedly asked Kohl to go outside and started punching him. During the fight King put Kohl in a headlock and removed his false teeth. "You ain't gettin' these back," King announced. Police charged King with felony robbery and battery causing bodily injury. While the battery charge was a misdemeanor, the robbery charge was a felony carrying a sentence of two to eight years.

He flipped to the editorial page. There were several letters to the editor expressing fear that Club Tropic would ultimately take over enough downtown Key West businesses, which would be detrimental to most small businessmen, and Key West would lose some of its eclectic funkiness and charm to corporate standardization and homogenization. Will wondered about the validity of this paranoia.

He glanced up and looked out the window. A middle-aged man in a blue golf shirt and shorts parked a white Vespa scooter in the parking lot outside and entered the building. He asked for the person in charge. Will walked to the lobby and held out his hand. He had learned long ago that clients with money came in all shapes and sizes.

"I'm Will Black. May I help you?"

"I think we can help each other," the man said. "Can I come in? Do you mind if I shut the door?"

The man wore his dark hair in a flat-top that accentuated his receding hairline. He was stocky and strong looking. His face was pock-marked probably from acne scars. He looked like he could handle manual labor.

"My name is Mark Michael Moore," he said. "My friends call me Mark. Mr. Black, this is your lucky day. I am here to make your office a lot of money."

"How do you propose to do that, Mr. Moore?"

"By becoming a financial analyst and an investment advisor. I have spent several years evaluating financial statements and learning to monitor financial strengths as well as financial weakness. I am confident now that I would do quite well in the capacity of an investment advisor. I will make the clients a lot of money in the stock market. I will double their money in twelve months – easily."

"Mr. Moore, I think you have unrealistic expectations," Will said.

"My goals are very realistic and attainable," he said. "I have a bachelor of science degree and a degree in accounting. All I will need from you to succeed is stringent security precautions, and I do know security. Once the security measures are in place, I'll take care of the rest. Rapid advances are being made in intercept equipment. Eavesdropping has become very easy. Intercepting can occur on telephones, computers, or with microphones planted in rooms."

Will was aghast. "Where did you gain your security knowledge – in the military?"

"Mr. Black, my background was with Wackenhut Security. I was a permanent guard. Even though I'm no longer under contract to them, I am still obligated to be silent around an outsider. I'm sure you understand and respect my position."

Moore plowed ahead.

"Every aspect of what I do must be secure – secure telephone lines, secure computer lines, secure work areas. It is necessary that I have the highest levels of security or else trouble could develop. Various entities could gain access to the trading account information and determine our investment position, hedge the investment position, and therefore cause the loss of money. I have selected Network Associates to provide network security and management. You will need to contact them at the phone number I give

177

you to review matters with them so we will be able to assure security."

"Mr. Moore…"

"These are the things I will need. First, I will need to establish a trading account for myself. It will not be in my Social Security number, but I must be able to place stock trades and receive checks and to be able to cash checks from the aforementioned trading account. There must be total confidentiality."

"Mr. Moore…"

"I will need Standard and Poor stock reports. I will also need the phones I use to gather information or place stock trades to be equipped with voice-alteration equipment."

Mr. Moore…"

"I will administer random lie detector tests to all individuals I become involved with. There must be extra security measures concerning the establishment of trading account numbers. I will draw up a contract for my services. I will receive a seven percent commission on all profits generated. I will expect payment on a frequent basis.

"Mr. Black, I urge you to seriously consider my proposal rather than have me implement it elsewhere. I will stop back by your office at a later date and discuss this proposal and work out the particulars of implementation."

Will was speechless.

Mark Moore rose to leave. He handed Will two pieces of paper.

"I have taken the liberty of making a copy of my driver's license and Social Security card for you. The second sheet of paper has my fingerprints."

Will finally got a word in. "Mr. Moore, we will have to get back to you."

Moore spun on his heels and was gone. The last Will saw of him was Moore putting off down the street on the Vespa scooter. Will laughed at the license plate: SUPR INVSTR.

"This guy would feel right at home working for Club Tropic. He's scary," Will said to his secretary.

CHAPTER 31

Betsy was emptying her in-box before Margaret could add to it. Her phone rang. It was Will calling to tell her about Mark Michael Moore and to see if she was going to have to work late.

"If you see a white Vespa with the tag SUPR INVSTR pull up in front of the bank put a *closed until further notice* sign on the door," he suggested.

"You know I can't do that," Betsy said. "Are you trying to tell me that MMM is not the white knight savior of the financial services industry?"

"Black night is more like it – and I'm spelling that N-I-G-H-T. I think this guy slinks around at night, bugs houses and peeps in windows. He might be funny if he weren't so squirrely."

"Speaking of squirrels, I need to jump. Margaret just slipped me a note saying Al Soltero is out in the lobby," Betsy said.

"I wonder what he wants," Will said. "Be sure and thank him for that delicious dinner the other night."

"I will. Love you. I won't be late," Betsy said.

Soltero greeted her with, "Mrs. Black, you look especially lovely today. I think the Keys must agree with you. I had to come to the bank today, so I thought as long as I am here I would come by and thank you for being such exquisite company at El Siboney. I hope I'm not interrupting anything," Soltero said. He looked very suave in his freshly laundered shirt, pressed chinos, expensive Italian loafers and silk socks. He smelled of expensive cologne.

"Not at all, Mr. Soltero. May I offer you some coffee?"

"No, thank you. And please call me Al. All my friends do."

"Then you must call me Betsy."

"Betsy, I have had business dealings that have taken me abroad since I had the pleasure of having dinner with you and your husband, so I'm slightly out of touch with local affairs. Have you heard anything new about Club Tropic?"

"Actually there have been some public announcements, Al. I was aware of the possibility of some of these developments when we had dinner, but as I'm sure you understand I have been restricted in the information I could impart until they chose to make the announcements public."

Soltero nodded. Betsy continued.

"Are the names Jorge Carlos and Centennial Partners familiar to you?" Betsy asked.

"Yes, they are one and the same," Soltero replied.

"Centennial is a hedge fund. Club Tropic issued a press release saying that Mr. Carlos has agreed to invest one hundred million of Centennial capital in their company and that they anticipate a larger commitment prior to year end."

"He is capable of honoring a commitment of that magnitude," Soltero said.

"I thought Centennial rang a bell when I first read the story. I asked my husband to see if RST's research department could tell me more about them. As it turned out there were reasons why the name was familiar.

"Both Carlos and Centennial had some problems with the SEC several years ago…By the way, this is not proprietary inside information. This is public record…They paid out over $200 million, $50 million of which came directly out of Carlos' pocket, in a fraud settlement with the SEC. Centennial was using what is known as 'fraudulent market timing' where Centennial executives hid their company's identity through a series of shell companies over the course of at least five years."

"It seems that Will's research was extremely thorough," Soltero said.

"Will tells me that shell companies and complex tiers of ownership are common and legal on Wall Street, but they must be transparently registered. Needless to say, as a banker I did not get warm and fuzzy feelings at the prospect of Club Tropic climbing into bed with someone with this questionable background."

"That is understandable," Soltero replied.

"A subsequent announcement Club Tropic has made concerned a possible merger."

Soltero arched his eyebrows.

"There is a company named Club Tropic Hospitality, which is incorporated in Delaware. It took in $70 million in an IPO last year. They are still sitting on the entire bundle of cash and looking for a permanent place to employ it. CT's press release says the merger should be consummated early next year and the combined companies will be called Club Tropic Inc. It will trade over the counter. Is your continued interest because you are still considering Club Tropic as an investment opportunity?"

"Yes, I am. This information has certainly given me additional matters to investigate and think about. Please thank Will for investigating Centennial. I hope you have a pleasant day."

Later that afternoon Betsy brought Will up to date on her meeting with Soltero. Will listened and said, "You know, my dear, Al can be a major bullshitter. Smooth as axle grease – but all in all, still a major bullshitter. He tells you he's been out of town since we had dinner. That's not entirely true. Remember the day last week I got in late from the office? When I passed by the Blanchard house, I saw him sitting on their dock with some people I didn't recognize, seemingly engaged in a serious discussion."

"I didn't even know they knew each other," Betsy said.

"I think there's lots of things we don't know about our newfound Colombian friend," Will added.

CHAPTER 32

"I had a visitor today," Betsy said as she was cutting an onion for dinner.

"Oh, yeah, who was that?" Will asked.

"My buddy the police chief, Walter Wanderley," Betsy said.

"Came by to drink coffee again?" You must make good java at the bank. What was today's tidbit?" Will said. "He's turned into a pretty good inside source on local affairs."

"That's for certain, and he's really a nice guy. That's why I just sit there and listen. Walter tells me that the Bight Board is having second thoughts about transferring some of the waterfront restaurant leases to Club Tropic."

"I assume, as usual, this is not public information yet," Will said.

"You got that right," Betsy said. "It will be announced in a couple of days. With what's happened to some people who have connections to Club Tropic, the board is just not as comfortable as they want to be. Those restaurants are a prime tourist attraction that must be run as such until the lease expires in 2019 to protect the integrity of the waterfront, and the city wants to make damned sure they are in noncontroversial, strong hands. They are too visible to risk having something come back and bite the board members in the ass. They're not saying no; they are just saying they want to consider the matter further."

"As long as you brought the subject up, did the chief say anything about the murder in our canal?" Will asked.

"Just that law enforcement is not saying anything until they can get a handle on what's going on. He told me they don't have a clue at this moment."

"I wouldn't repeat this outside of the house, but trouble sure seems to follow our friend Soltero," Will said.

Betsy nodded. Coco suddenly started barking and rushed the door. The door bell rang a second later.

Jack Maselli came in. "Hope I'm not interrupting dinner," he said.

"No, just happy hour. We welcome the company," Will said. "Your usual?" He mixed Jack a drink.

"Heard anything else about Myron Levitt?" Jack asked.

"Funny, we were just talking about that," Betsy said. "Nothing – you?"

"I get the creeps every time I look off my dock, but no, I've been too busy to even ask anyone until this second," Jack said. "Carmine's had the heat on me something terrible. It's balls to the wall – excuse me, Betsy – sales goals."

"What do you mean?" Will asked Jack.

"Well, sales have slowed down," Jack continued. "Staff morale is shit since all these dead people have popped up. Schwartzman told Carmine to give us an ultimatum –sell or else. He even reminded me that my house does belong to the corporation, and I live here at their pleasure. I hate to have to be a prick or a liar with my guys. They're really a good group. They just want to make a living. Carmine now told us to promise prospects a gondola traveled canal and a world class fitness center at Rum Reef Club Tropic. I've seen the plans for that place. I didn't see either one of those items in the plans or drawings."

"Maybe the plans have changed," Betsy said.

"That's a big change – multi-million dollar change – at a time when our budgets are tight? I don't think so. I would have heard something about it before now. I would have seen engineers sniffing around – something."

"I don't know what to tell you," Will said.

"I just don't know how much more of this I can take," Jack said. "Joan can tell you, I haven't gotten a good night's sleep in a week. I don't care what this job pays, I don't know if it's worth it."

"It sure as hell isn't worth going to jail over," Will said.

CHAPTER 33

Before the weekend the Bight Board announced publicly its intention to review further its previous decision to allow Club Tropic to take over some of the Key West waterfront restaurant leases. Within a day Sol Schwartzman countered with an announcement giving additional facts about the mysterious Colombian who had previously been reported to be infusing capital into Club Tropic and putting an even more positive spin on the story than the first press release had provided.

CLUB TROPIC ATTRACTS HIGH PROFILE BACKER

Florida Keys meet Jorge Carlos. Mr. Carlos, international financier, may soon come to know us as well. His riches will own a meaningful piece of Club Tropic, the most dynamic real estate force in the Keys. According to a Club Tropic press release, this shrewd investor will increase his exposure substantially to Club Tropic through his Centennial hedge fund over the next few months. Carlos, a native of Colombia, is listed in Forbes magazine's list of the richest men in North America. His net worth is estimated to be $1.5 billion.

In the Sunday paper another story broke.

CLUB TROPIC TO CLOSE THREE RESTAURANTS

Club Tropic on Friday said it will close three restaurants on some of its Florida Keys properties. This unexpected announcement will result in the layoffs of eighty-five employees. Doug Brown, spokesman for Club Tropic, blamed the layoffs and restaurant closures on the sluggish real estate market and slow tourist season. Brown maintains that the restaurants will reopen when the season picks up again. Brown says restaurant closures are common in Florida Keys when tourism is slow.

Club Tropic countered this story once again.

CLUB TROPIC ENTERS INTO JOINT VENTURE WITH RUM AND VODKA DISTILLER

"Heavens to Betsy, my dear," Will said. "There's so much going on at Club Tropic I have trouble trying to keep the stories straight."

"I know! Thank God I'm only an observer. For every negative story that comes out, Club Tropic seems to have a positive one. It's almost like Schwartzman is saving his trump cards and whipping them out when he needs to. I am *so* glad I don't have to police them – joint venture on rum and vodka – how far afield can you get? Talk about diversification," Betsy said. "And of course guess who was in my office trying to say 'I told you so today'?"

"Three guesses and the first two don't count. He walks; he talks; he crawls on his belly like a reptile. The greatest banker since Little Egypt, I presume, Sir CC?"

"Uh huh! Every time I saw him today he rubbed his index fingers back and forth on each other. Would killing Carson be considered justifiable homicide?" Betsy asked.

"Just be patient. Your day will come."

"Not soon enough for me."

"How 'bout a coldbeer?"

If Betsy's looks could kill.

CHAPTER 34

Will was watching the news on WFOR when the phone rang. Betsy was e-mailing Lexie.

The announcer, a woman with a pageboy hairdo, said:

Club Tropic LLC revealed today a merger that will infuse the company with $50 million is on schedule for the early part of next year. Club Tropic LLC has extensive real estate interests in the Florida Keys. When this merger is completed Club Tropic will become a public company and operate as Club Tropic Inc.

Will hit the mute button on the remote and picked up the phone.

The conversation was a short one. Jack Maselli wanted them to come over to his house - immediately. He said it was important.

"I wonder what's going on now," Betsy said. "Let me just finish this e-mail to Lexie and slip on some flip flops," Betsy said. "While I'm doing that, lock the sliders."

When Will and Betsy arrived at Jack's house they saw an unfamiliar gray SUV in the driveway. Jack introduced them to Percy Driskoll.

"Until today Percy was the assistant hotel manager for Royal Island Club Tropic," Jack began.

"I hope you didn't get laid off...," Will began.

"No, I quit," Percy said.

"The reason I asked you both to come over here is I want a witness to what Percy has just confided in me," Jack said. "Since you are both respected financial professionals who are knowledgeable of fiduciary responsibilities, I am confident that you will be both trustworthy and discreet. I don't think I have misjudged you."

Will and Betsy looked at each other questioningly.

"My boss is a dead man," Percy began.

"I don't understand," Betsy said.

"Yesterday some strangers...scary looking swarthy types...came to see my boss...the hotel manager," Percy said, wringing his hands. "The door wasn't completely closed. It's warped and pops open sometimes. One of the men kept calling him Paul Miles. His name is Terry Hayes not Paul Miles. I wasn't snooping. I just had to use the copy machine – the copier is right next to Mr. Hayes' office. I heard them also use Myron Levitt's name. Myron used to work in our accounting office. He's dead."

"We know," Will said.

"They said something about Mr. Hayes better keep a lid on the Levitt affair, and there better only be routine records in Myron's office. But they kept calling Mr. Hayes Paul Miles. At first I thought I had heard wrong, and they were talking to each other...maybe one of them was Paul Miles... until the big guy pointed his finger in Mr. Hayes' face and said, 'I mean it Paul, and you better not fuck this up, you disgusting little homo pervert son of a bitch, or I'll cut your dick off and stuff it down your throat."

Will and Betsy looked at each other. Jack turned white.

"I know they went through my desk last night and my computer was already turned on this morning," said Percy, looking pale and desperate.

"How do you know?" Betsy asked.

"I just know. I'm very organized. I know how I left my desk when I went home, and I always turn my computer off every night before I leave. When I took the mail into Mr. Hayes' office this morning, he wasn't there and his files had been shredded...It was almost like he had never existed. And I just know I might be next because I know too much. I decided I'm not going back to that office. I can find another job. I just wanted to tell Jack so someone would know if something does happen to me. I don't want to disappear without a trace."

Percy wrung his hands and started crying. His eyes had a terrified, haunted look.

"I don't want to die. You've got to help me," he said.

He slipped a small brown envelope into Will's hand.

"What's this?" Will asked.

"Just keep it safe. I'll call you when I want it back," Percy Driskoll said.

"But if something happens to me, this key will lead to information the authorities will find of interest."

Will glanced in the envelope. It contained a key with a paper disk attached to it. On the disk was scrawled in pencil "toolbox".

CHAPTER 35

"Betsy," Will called across the house. "Where'd you put my sunglasses?"

"They're right where you left them," she replied.

"I know I left them right here on the counter," he said. He turned to look and accidentally kneed a partially opened drawer. "Ouch! I wish you'd close these things."

"I did – you know I never leave drawers open. I'm kind of phobic about that."

"It didn't open itself," Will said.

"As long as we're griping, I wish you wouldn't jumble up the silver in the kitchen drawer."

"I haven't been in the kitchen drawer."

"Well, someone has."

"Maybe we've had an invasion of house goblins," Will said.

"Cute, but seriously, something's not right."

"I noticed the mat at the door was bunched up. I just assumed the dogs had done that," Will mused.

"No, some of my cosmetics have been moved around on the bathroom counter."

"Do you think we've had an uninvited guest?" Will asked.

"Sure do. Some things have been moved around in the fridge too. I know where I keep stuff," said Betsy.

"That's scary as hell. I'm sure it wasn't a thief. Nothing appears to be missing."

"No – someone was looking for something, and they weren't as careful as they should have been. It was a perfect day to search the place. The dogs weren't here today. I left them at the vet for their shots. When I got home, Red Stripe was all upset and screeched about a key. *Find a key, find a key, asshole.* I didn't think anything of it at the time."

"I don't know if they were looking for Percy's key, but if they were, they were disappointed. It's locked in my filing cabinet at the office."

"You should find a better place," Betsy said. "They'll probably search there next. I've got a feeling that key is important to somebody. I wonder what lengths they'll go to in order to get it. In fact, give me the key and I'll take it to the bank. With all of our security, no one can just pop in and search desk drawers or filing cabinets."

"Good idea," Will added. "I will get it out of my office tomorrow."

"Did you check out the doors to see how our *visitors* got in?" Betsy asked.

"No, but I will do that right now," said Will.

"Even though there does not appear to be anything missing, we need to call Doug Morgan at the sheriff's

195

department about this incident, and I will just let Walter know tomorrow to keep him in the loop. In the meantime, maybe we should talk to our parrot more often to find out what goes on here in our absence," Betsy said.

CHAPTER 36

Margaret Anderson came into Betsy's office and motioned for her to hang up the phone.

"Chief Wanderley is out here, and I don't think he wants to drink coffee today. He's got someone with him."

"Betsy, meet Lee Diaz. He's with the FBI," Chief Wanderley started out.

"Is there something wrong, Walter?" Betsy asked.

"May we talk in private?" The chief looked at Margaret, who immediately excused herself and closed Betsy's door.

"We have an anonymous tip that a bomb may be planted in your car," agent Diaz said.

Betsy was momentarily speechless. She felt a sudden knot in her throat.

"My God!" said Betsy "What about the bank, the employees, our customers?"

"I don't want to start a panic here at the bank," agent Diaz continued. "May I have your permission to evacuate the bank and then check your car? Whenever something like this happens you should be concerned, but I also want you to realize that most of these tips turn out to be bogus. But we just can't take any chances. You never know when the danger could turn out to be real."

Betsy fished in her purse for her car keys and handed them to Wanderley.

"Why would someone want to put a bomb in my car?" she asked.

"Don't jump to conclusions yet. Maybe no one did. It might just be a crank call. We'll talk about it after I've checked everything out," Diaz said. "What does your car look like, and where is it parked?"

"It is the bronze Hummer H2 in the bank's parking lot."

"We can clear the bank's parking lot to isolate your car. The bank customers and employees need to leave the premises immediately," Diaz said.

"I will have our security guard and bank officers ask everyone to leave the bank by telling them we are having a fire drill," Betsy said, "but you will need to direct them away from the bank and the bank's parking lot."

Betsy asked Margaret to bring the security guard and the platform officers into her office for instructions from FBI Agent Diaz.

After everyone left her office, Betsy called Will and told him what was going on before she left her office and the bank. He was as aghast as Betsy had been. Who would want to kill one of them?

About thirty minutes later all employees and customers were allowed back in the bank and the two men reentered Betsy's office and closed the door again.

"We need to talk, Betsy," Wanderley said.

"You mean you found something?" Betsy asked.

"Yes, we did, but don't worry; we disconnected it. The bomb was attached magnetically to the underside of your car. We have also gone through the entire building and drive-ups – all bank property is clear of any explosives."

Betsy gripped her desk pen so hard her knuckles turned white.

Diaz continued, "The bomb in your car was a fairly common type of bomb. It has what we call a tilt fuse. The tilt fuse was enclosed in a small plastic tube. One end of the tube was filled with mercury. The other end was wired with the ends of an open circuit to an electrical firing system. If you had driven the car, the tilt fuse would tip from the car's motion so that the mercury would flow to the top of the tube and close the circuit, setting off the bomb. This one was not terribly sophisticated since it did not have a timer attached to it. But don't worry; we got rid of it. I'm just glad we got the tip. The device may not have been very sophisticated, but it was powerful. The bomb squad has dismantled it and taken it away."

"But who? And why? I'm just a banker..." Betsy stammered.

"That's the next thing I want to talk to you about," Diaz said. "Who would want to kill you? Or scare you? You know it's entirely possible that the tipster was the bomber. Maybe he just wanted to make a statement. Maybe he didn't want you dead. It seems awfully convenient that we got the anonymous phone call when we did."

Betsy's first thought was the frightening look of veiled hate she had seen on Sol Schwartzman's face. This was not the first time she had declined a loan, but it certainly was the most violent reaction she had ever experienced. Although he had threatened her, she had not and would not disclose the declination.

Instead, Betsy told Diaz and Wanderley about the conversation she and Will had had with Percy Driskoll and the subsequent search someone had made of their home. Diaz suggested she call Jack Maselli and see if he had been in touch with Driskoll.

After making the call, Betsy said, "Jack just told me he has tried without luck to get hold of Driskoll at both his house and on his cell phone. It's like Percy Driskoll has vanished," she said.

Diaz and Wanderley asked for Jack's telephone number and said they could contact Maselli about Percy Driskoll's phone numbers and address and initiate their own investigation.

"In the meantime, we will have a patrol car parked in the bank parking lot for the rest of the day and police patrolling this bank just as a precaution," said Walter. "You should take your car home tonight and get a ride into your office until we can get to the bottom of this mess."

After Diaz and Wanderley left, Betsy called Will again.

"Walter and the FBI agent just left here. There was a bomb under my car. I'm still shaking. When they were in the office, I felt kind of safe and detached, but now that they're gone, it's starting to sink in. I could have been killed; bank personnel and customers might have been hurt or killed."

"Uh huh. My stomach's been doing flip-flops. That's all I've been able to think about since you called. Thank God they found it. Let's not tell Lexie. I don't want to upset her," Will said.

"I need to get away from here for a while. Got any lunch plans?" Betsy continued.

"I'll be there to get you in fifteen minutes."

"Good. I'm still not ready to get in my car yet. Even though I know it's clean."

"Did you say anything to them about Driskoll's key?"

"No. I thought we should see if they can find him, but I did tell them about Percy Driskoll's expressions of fear."

"Good. Let's just keep this key affair under our hats for the time being."

"Bring it with you and I'll secure it here at the bank," Betsy said.

"OK," Will said. "I tell you what. Let's go to the Hogfish on Stock Island. That'll be a good change of atmosphere."

"And I've got another idea. Jack said Percy Driskoll lives on Stock Island. Let's see if we can find his house. I already checked and found out he's in the phone book."

The Hogfish Bar and Grill on Front Street on Stock Island was a ramshackle open air building adjacent to the docks. The unique restaurant has great food but is somewhat difficult to find. Its sign announced "Free Beer Tomorrow…"

Will always got a kick out of the high-heel sneakers that hung over one doorway.

As they walked in, Will poked Betsy playfully and sang

> *Put on your high-heel sneakers, lordy*
> *Wear your wig-hat on your head*
> *Ya know you're looking mighty fine, baby*
> *I'm pretty sure you're gonna knock 'em dead*

"Let's not discuss the *dead* word," said Betsy.

Will and Betsy found a picnic table out on the dock and ordered fried hogfish sliders and two iced teas.

After lunch they found Driskoll's rental house. It was a small frame house with a weed-choked yard. The house needed painting. The roof looked worn and old. There was no car in the unpaved driveway. Several days newspapers littered the yard. Will opened the mailbox. There was a hefty accumulation of mail.

Will and Betsy walked up on the small porch. Will rang the bell as Betsy peeked in a front window. An air conditioner hung from another front window.

"The air conditioner isn't running," Betsy said.

Will opened the screen door and twisted the door knob. To his surprise the door opened. He knocked and, when no one responded, entered the living room.

The house had a damp, mildewy smell. Old newspapers littered the beat-up coffee table.

"The TV is still here. If he's gone, he's traveling light," Will said.

They walked into the outdated kitchen. The sink was half full of dishes and glasses. Will opened the refrigerator and saw spoiled food. They went into the bedroom. The bed was unmade. They opened the closet. It was empty, as was a chest-of-drawers. She opened Percy's desk drawer and noticed a pile of business cards held together with a rubber band. She flipped through them. Near the top was a card for Adolfo Soltero.

"Will, look what I found," Betsy called out.

"I wonder what their connection is to each other," Will said as he pocketed the card.

"That'll take a little thinking about," Betsy replied. "Found something else of interest. Here's a card for a place called the Storage Mart on Big Coppitt Key."

"Percy's key does not belong to that" Will said.

"I wonder if he has his personal property in storage there," Betsy said.

"It's a possibility."

They went into the bathroom. The toilet and shower had a foul musty odor. After opening the medicine cabinet door, they found it empty.

"I don't think Percy lives here anymore," Will said.

Betsy agreed, "It's like Percy Driskoll has disappeared into thin air."

"Just like he was afraid he'd do," Will said.

They left Percy's house and drove back to Highway 1. Betsy noticed Will kept glancing in his rear-view mirror.

"That black Mercedes behind us – I'm pretty sure I saw that car parked down the block from Driskoll's house," Will said.

"Pull over, Will," said Betsy. "If the car passes by, we can get the license number."

203

As expected, the black Mercedes passed Will and Betsy's parked car. They both saw the car tag: NEW JERSEY.

Betsy wrote down the car tag details as the Mercedes silently sped away.

CHAPTER 37

Several days later, Will and Betsy returned to Stock Island. This time, Will turned off of US 1 onto College Road and followed it around until they saw the Lower Keys Medical Center and then the Tennessee Williams Theatre. The Theater was a multi-faceted modern looking building with round concrete support columns. The different levels almost looked like they were stacked on one another. It had an open feel that resulted from the large glass panels used liberally as exterior walls.

Will and Betsy were representing their companies at an appreciation cocktail party which was being given for contributors to the theater. The bank was a corporate sponsor, having underwritten one of the plays for the current season, *Say Goodnight, Gracie,* a tribute to George Burns and Gracie Allen. Reynolds Smathers and Thompson had bought a full-page ad in the playbill.

Waitresses circulated with champagne and wine and had trays of various hors d'oeuvres. Will and Betsy were greeted warmly by the executive director the moment they walked in. The room was buzzing with hundreds of conversations. Some people had on sport coats and blazers. Others were in shirt sleeves and shorts.

Betsy felt a slight jostle from someone trying to get by them. She turned to apologize and found herself facing Club Tropic CEO Sol Schwartzman. He was dressed in a custom suit and Italian tassel loafers. He smiled and extended his hand to Will and Betsy.

Accompanying Sol was a woman with piled-up blonde hair who appeared much younger than he. She attracted the attention of most of the men in the room as she followed Schwartzman, hips swishing as she walked on spike heels. From a distance Betsy noticed that the hem of the woman's sequined black jersey dress was cut just a tad too high; her top was cut a tad too low, revealing perfectly sculptured cleavage. When she got closer Betsy took note of the extensive makeup and ostentatious jewelry.

"Mr. and Mrs. Black, how nice to see you again," he said warmly. "I hope things have been going well for you."

"Exceedingly well. And you?" Betsy responded icily. "And who is your beautiful escort?"

"I apologize," Sol said. "This is my wife Victoria."

"Pleased to meet you, I'm sure," Victoria said in a New Jersey accent as she finished her glass of champagne and quickly snagged another one from the passing waitress.

"There's been a lot of excitement at Club Tropic these days," Sol said. "We have been presented with several electrifying diversification options."

"I'm pleased to hear that," Will said. "There never seems to be any shortage of developments at Club Tropic."

"We have been approached to join forces with one of the most eminently regarded high elevation winter training academies west of the Mississippi. We will aid in the formation of a division that will specialize in sports training, education, health and fitness issues..."

"Honey, would you get me some more champagne," Victoria interrupted and drained her second glass. Schwartzman gave her a dirty look but said nothing and snapped his fingers at a passing waitress.

"Club Tropic will become the "in house" real estate development partner for this division. We will manage a 300 room, four-star resort that will provide lodging and dining for the academy's student body. It will be called Club Tropic's Peaceful Valley of Colorado. This will soon be one of the premier skiing and snowboarding training schools in the world."

"Wow! Congratulations," Will said.

Victoria looked bored.

"Pleasant Valley, Colorado, is just one project," Schwartzman continued. "Club Tropic will also soon be the sole purveyor of a new technology that will clean up old coal mines. The potential here is staggering."

"Once again, our congratulations to your organization," Betsy said. She turned to Victoria and asked, "Do you help Sol with the business?"

"I used to," Victoria giggled and said, "That's how Sol and I met. I was his personal assistant."

Will and Betsy exchanged subtle glances.

207

Sol didn't notice and continued, "These endeavors will take a little time to put together, but you will soon be reading about a third new venture. This may seem more mundane, but it's going to be a cash cow. We are starting an air service at the Marathon airport."

"A vodka on the rocks sure would be good," Victoria said.

"I read about the vodka/rum deal. You haven't exaggerated about sensational announcements," Will added.

"I'm telling you, my adrenalin starts pumping every day before I even get to the office. I sure wish we could put to bed some of the unfortunate stories that have surfaced recently about some of our former associates," Schwartzman said. "These were personal matters that regrettably were reported in such a way to tarnish the good name of our corporation and make it more challenging for us to convey the positives on what's really happening of consequence at Club Tropic. But isn't that just the way with the media, concentrating and dwelling on the sensational half-truths just to sell newspapers, tabloid journalism, even here in the Keys. It makes me see red."

Will and Betsy nodded.

"Honey...," Victoria said.

"Not now. I'm talking business," Sol interrupted.

Will waited to see if Victoria would finish her thought and finally ventured a comment, "I read about the restaurants closing."

"That's strictly a brief, temporary situation, not a big deal and an example of fallacious reporting," Schwartzman continued sharply. "This is a dead time, dead slow. It costs more to keep these restaurants open this time of year than the restaurants make. We're simply doing what any astute businessman would do – taking the necessary steps to run a cost-effective business. I assure you, it's strictly a seasonal thing."

"Honey, I see the waitress," Victoria said.

Schwartzman grimaced but continued, "By the way, Mr. Black, as everyone now knows, the merger of Club Tropic LLC and Club Tropic Hospitality will leave us a public company. We're going to need a good investment banker as we continue to grow. I could end up your largest account. I look forward to possibly discussing these issues with you more when that time comes. I'm sure it could become a mutually profitable relationship."

He abruptly ended the conversation saying, "I hope you have a pleasant evening. If you will excuse me, I see someone that I would like to say hello to."

He shook hands with Will and Betsy, grabbed his wife by the elbow and disappeared into the crowd.

"Listening to Schwartzman makes me feel like I have high blood pressure, but he's certainly acting more gracious than the last time I met with him," Betsy whispered. "He must be on his meds tonight. Last time I met with him he scared the hell out of me."

"Or sampling his new rum brand. If there's anything left to sell after his wife takes inventory. She is one piece of work. I understand your fears. Quite frankly, my dear, he scares the shit out of me too," Will whispered back.

CHAPTER 38

On Saturday morning Will and Betsy were on the porch enjoying their morning coffee. The air was crisp and fresh. A pelican lazily circled. Life seemed to be moving in slow motion. Betsy read the *Citizen* while Will read the new *Keynoter* he had picked up at the Chevron station by Looe Key Tiki Bar.

"I guess I shouldn't have expected anything but the most upbeat spin on Club Tropic from Sol Schwartzman," Will said.

"Uh huh," Betsy murmured. "I'm certainly not surprised that he attributes any negative publicity to media bias and persecution. I really don't understand why Club Tropic doesn't just stick to its knitting. Their bread and butter is real estate, not restaurants, booze, air services, coal mines, sports academies and God knows what else."

"I guess they want to be a conglomerate like Berkshire Hathaway."

"They'll probably end up more like Gulf and Western," Betsy said.

"I read they even have a dive shop and are taking people on snorkeling trips," Will said. "By the way, listen to this story."

GOD RESPONDS TO LAWSUIT

A Key West man who filed a lawsuit against God has gotten something he might not have expected – a response.

One of two court filings from "God" came Friday under otherworldly circumstances, according to Jim Friend, a spokesman for the Monroe County Circuit Court.

"This one miraculously appeared on the counter. It just all of a sudden was there – poof!" Friend said.

Ernie Chastain of Key West, a self proclaimed agnostic, sued God last week, seeking a permanent injunction against the Almighty for making terroristic threats, inspiring fear and causing "widespread death, destruction, and terrorization of millions upon millions of the Earth's inhabitants."

God in his response argued the defendant is immune from some earthly laws and the court lacked jurisdiction.

"I don't think I can top that one," Betsy said, "but this Key weird story is worth reading out loud anyway."

WHAT A WAY TO FLUNK A DRIVING TEST

A Marathon woman trying to get her driver's license is probably going to need some more practice.

The Monroe County Tax Collectors Office in Marathon says 24-year-old Preethi Akriti Patel was pulling into a space behind the driver's license office after finishing her road test Friday morning. That's when the driver's license spokesman says she accidentally hit the accelerator instead of the brake and ran into the building.

The instructor was taken to Fishermen's Hospital with minor injuries. Patel was not injured, and the building did not appear to be damaged.

Patel was issued a citation for an improper stop. She did not receive a driver's license.

Will laughed. Red Stripe said shrilly, "Key weird! Key weird!"

"Everybody up there decent?" came a sudden voice from below.

"As decent as we can get," Will called out.

Jason Pearson came up the back steps.

"There's some fresh coffee in the kitchen," Betsy said.

"Sounds good. I think I'll take you up on that, but I can't stay long," Jason said. "Marvin Cheney hired me to clean up some construction debris at one of his building sites. Since I had to run by his house and get the key to the padlock on the gate, I thought I'd stop by to see you."

"I haven't laid eyes on Marvin since we went to that homeowner's party at his house," Will said.

As they drank their coffee Betsy told Jason she had some projects for him. He promised to check back in later that day.

After lunch Will and Betsy still had not heard back from Jason. They tried calling several times, but he didn't answer his cell phone.

"That's not like Jason," Will commented. "Normally if Jason tells you he's coming back, he does."

"And he almost always answers his cell phone," Betsy agreed. "He must have run into something unexpected over at Cheney's construction site."

Just before sunset, the house phone rang, and Will answered. It was Jason.

"Sorry I didn't get back to you. I had a bit of excitement to deal with after I saw you this morning," he said.

"Was there more debris than you thought there'd be?" Will asked.

"You might say that. When I was moving the dirt with the Bobcat, I uncovered a body – a white male," said Jason. "The person had been strangled with a wire garrote. It was still stretched around his neck. It had been pulled so tight it almost cut his head off. His eyes were bulging out."

"You have got to be kidding! Did you find out who it was?" Will asked squeamishly.

"Does the name Percy Driskoll mean anything to you?"

"As a matter of fact it does. We met him once. He worked for Club Tropic," Will said without further elaboration.

"He was the assistant manager at Royal Island Club Tropic until recently," Jason said. "When I pushed a big mound of dirt with the Bobcat an arm fell out. I didn't uncover it further once I saw what it was. It was obvious from the odor the person had been dead for a few days. It was all I could do to keep the birds off the body once I had exposed it. Afterward I spent the rest of the day with the investigators. I had no idea who it was until they told me it was Driskoll. The investigator found his wallet in his pocket. I didn't know him."

Will still remained silent about any further knowledge of Driskoll.

Jason continued, "The investigator called Marvin Cheney since he owns the property. Did you know he recently forced Club Tropic to cede control of three of his former properties back to him?"

"No, I didn't," Will admitted.

"I found out when he called me to do some maintenance work over at Sandy Beach. Three Club Tropic resorts were originally developed and built by Cheney – Leisure Bay Club Tropic, Royal Island Club Tropic and Sandy Beach Club Tropic were all financed by Cheney's hedge fund. Cheney still holds controlling interest in all three projects. He eventually planned on selling them 100 percent to Club Tropic," Jason said.

"So what happened?" Will asked.

"All Cheney told me was that he had planned for these to be some of the premier properties in the Keys, and he felt that they needed to be reinvigorated. He said he will still be a joint-venture partner with Club Tropic, but he will bring in some of his key people to manage the resorts."

"Hmmmh!" Will murmured.

"He was also upset about an affordable housing snafu at Leisure Bay Club Tropic. The officials in Marathon are livid because Club Tropic has been operating without fulfilling its onsite affordable housing requirement. They had promised the city they would set aside one building to be used as a dormitory for employees. Instead they converted the building into a conference center."

"That's not good," Will said.

"Club Tropic claimed that the problem stemmed from a lack of communication between two of its divisions. To get them all out of hot water, Cheney has now had to promise Marathon officials not only that he will honor the original agreement at Leisure Bay, but he will also convert some townhouse units they own elsewhere in Marathon into ten more affordable units. He *was* extremely P.O.'ed. He told me he informed Sol Schwartzman emphatically of his displeasure," Jason said.

"But you should have seen his face when he came over and saw the body. At first Cheney looked scared, but then he said something to himself he didn't think I overheard."

"What was that?" Will asked.

"He said, 'If that cocksucker thinks he can send me a message and watch me tremble, he picked the wrong person to fuck with. I'll chop off his nuts and stuff them up his ass.' He didn't say who he was talking about, but I'm pretty sure I know."

"I think I know too," Will said.

"Lordy! Lordy! Is there no end to bad things happening to people connected to Club Tropic?" Jason said.

"I wish I had an answer for you," Will said. "I really do."

"Thank the good Lord Betsy's bank is not caught in the middle of this mess," Will said.

After learning of Driskoll's death, Will and Betsy considered telling Chief Wanderley about the business card they had found at Percy's house for the Storage Mart on Big Coppitt and the key Percy left to his toolbox for the authorities in the event something happened to him. They decided Betsy would call Walter with this information on Monday morning.

CHAPTER 39

The following weekend Will spotted Jack Maselli cleaning his boat. When Jack finished, he started swinging it back towards the water on the davits. Will went over to help. When the boat was back in the canal they sat and dangled their legs off the dock.

"I've had the week from hell," Jack began.

"Mine hasn't been too killing great either," Will agreed. "The Dow was down three days this week. Thank God we managed to eke out a gain on Friday."

"Did you hear what happened over at Club Tropic's new air service in Marathon a couple of days ago?" Jack asked. "We're renting hangar space to Mosquito Control. We had a trespasser."

"Steal anything?" Will asked.

"No, though he tore up some fencing to get to the hangar. He climbed in one of their helicopters and refused to speak to anyone."

"Weird," Will said.

"You ain't kidding. Whenever one of our people approached him, he grunted and wrote them a response on his shorts. He even wrote his name and address. Despite seeming friendly enough, he refused to speak. All the fool wanted to do was shake hands with everyone."

"Was he on drugs?" Will asked.

"It doesn't appear so. I think he's just nuts," Jack said. "It gets worse. Every time someone tried to talk to him, he would salute like the person speaking to him was an officer. Then he tore the tanks off one helicopter. He also removed the chemical sprayers from one helicopter and attached them to another."

"You're right. This is getting stranger by the moment," Will agreed.

"At first he refused to leave the hangar," Jack continued. "Then one of our employees refused to shake hands with him and told him to get the hell out of the hangar. All of a sudden, as docile as you please, the asshole walked out of the hangar. Two of Schwartzman's thugs caught hold of him by the arms. It's a good thing the sheriff's deputies showed up, or I'm sure Schwartzman's boys would have beat the shit out of the guy. The deputies escorted him to the patrol car without any further incidents."

"So where's he now – jail?"

"No, strangely enough, Mosquito Control and Club Tropic chose not to press charges."

Will shrugged quizzically.

"I guess you know Percy Driskoll turned up?" Jack said, trying to appear calm.

"Yeah – I heard!" Will said. "I sure never thought that time I met him at your house he'd be dead now. No wonder he was hyperventilating that day we met him. I don't think I've ever seen anyone so scared."

"My gut's been in a knot ever since," Jack said.

"I haven't said anything to anyone, but Betsy and I went by his rental house on Stock Island a few days later. It looked then like he'd chosen to run. There was out-of-date food in the fridge and old newspapers in the yard. His clothes were gone. The door wasn't even locked."

"I'm starting to feel as paranoid as Percy. I'm not sure I want to work at Club Tropic anymore," Jack said.

"Nobody's threatened you have they?" Will asked.

"No, nothing like that, but I keep having nightmares like I'm in a fishbowl with spear gunners circling." Jack said. "And I do keep getting sales ultimatums. Schwartzman calls them goals, but you'd have to be an idiot not to get the message."

"Every time Betsy and I run into Schwartzman all he can do is gush on how well things are going," Will said. "We have sure wondered about the business fit of some of the ventures he brags about. The pieces just don't seem to come together right. Seems like he's buying anything and everything. Since we're talking off the record, you don't think some of these ventures are to launder money, do you?" Will asked.

"Oh shit! Don't even think anything like that. I can come up with enough things to worry about without you adding something new," Jack said.

"By the way, is any headway being made on who killed Driskoll?" Will said.

"If they have, no one's said anything to me about it," Jack said. "Just like there hasn't been any progress made on any of the other deaths either. You heard anything?"

"I haven't heard the first word," Will said.

"I know you get tired of hearing me vent. If you don't want to hear it, just tell me to shut up, but now a new issue has emerged at the office," Jack said.

"What now?" Will asked.

"There's a group of disgruntled investors accusing us of selling securities without a license. You're familiar with our immediate leaseback program?"

"Somewhat," Will said.

"Let's pretend you wanted to buy a condo unit, and the down-stroke at closing was fifty grand. Forty-five days after you closed you'd get twenty-five grand back from our leaseback program. In six more months you'd get the other twenty-five grand back. This is supposed to cover your mortgage while the complex is being rehabbed and upgraded," Jack continued.

"OK, so where does the money come from?" Will asked.

"Purportedly from the rental pool they put your unit into," Jack said. "But now there's an investor group saying that this arrangement makes the deal an illegal security. They're saying that we must file the offering with the SEC and have our sales reps licensed as securities brokers.

"Schwartzman maintains that this investment should be treated like a mortgage, and mortgages are not securities.

The attorney for the investor group has also alleged that our salesmen have been making two other misstatements proving their point that we are selling an unregistered security. First, he says we have promised buyers we would take care of everything," Jack said.

"What's wrong with that?" Will asked.

"The point is essentially this. There's a central management scheme for the projects. This structure means returns are generated from the efforts of others; this means you are investing in something and letting someone else handle it. Therefore, it should be classified as a security."

"I can see their point. When someone buys 100 shares of General Electric, they are expecting GE's management to run the company. They have no say-so in GE despite being an owner. Can you imagine if a stockholder went in and tried to make management decisions at GE? They'd run his ass off as a nut case," Will said. "What's the other point?"

"That Club Tropic never explicitly offered the buyer the opportunity to live in the unit they purchase," Jack said.

"In a way, I can see that point too. I certainly could never get to use any of GE's property even if I am a stockholder. Can you imagine if I decided I owned five feet on their Pittsburgh property, and I wanted to pitch a tent on it?"

Jack smiled.

"Carmine Scarpetti, our national sales manager, has been screaming and yelling at sales meetings that the leaseback program is a type of inducement and does not make an investment a security. On one hand, he is insisting that my salesmen keep their sales numbers up, yet my men are reluctant to do anything or say anything that could be construed as criminal activity. You can't blame them. These are decent, hardworking people with families to support. He told the salesmen in no uncertain terms at the last sales meeting that as long as the sales department is separated from the property management department, they are safe. 'Do business as usual as if your job depended on it,' he demanded. 'Because it does.' Morale is nonexistent. They all know goddamned good and well, Scarpetti would hang them out to dry if it came down to protecting his own ass. Carmine reminded me in private after the meeting just to make damned sure no one left us vulnerable by putting any of these points in writing, or it would be my ass. He also made it clear that we better not try to use this - trumped up shit, as he called it - as an excuse not to do our jobs and get the order. He said if he catches anyone sandbagging, he'll personally kick their ass off the property."

He stopped and caught his breath and stared into space. He finally looked at Will and said, "This job sucks! Sol Schwartzman sucks! Carmine Scarpetti sucks! Club Tropic sucks! Why can't life in paradise be pleasant and easy?"

CHAPTER 40

Will was heating up the grill to cook a steak as Betsy relaxed in the hammock watching the sun set. The clouds were radiant and pink. One of the clouds looked like a hound dog. C.W. Colt was playing on the house stereo.

I'm a Key Western cowboy
Key Western cowboy
Key Western cowboy, without a horse.

In the distance they could see Fat Albert, the white helium-filled blimp that was tethered on the bayside high above Cudjoe Key. It lazily floated in the late afternoon sunlight about five thousand feet up as if it didn't have a care in the world. Fat Albert enabled technicians to track low-flying planes, drug boats and human traffickers, as well as monitor weather patterns approaching the islands. Will felt the tenseness of the day escape as he sipped a bourbon in the chaise lounge. Betsy offered to refresh their drinks.

"Did you ever hear about the time Fat Albert escaped and went to Cuba?" Will asked lazily.

"That's a new story," Betsy admitted. "Where'd you hear that?"

"Mr. Blackman, the old Conch who lives out at Geiger Key, was in the office the other day. He told me. I guess the story's true."

"This ought to be good," Betsy said.

"The yarn began one day in August when Fat Albert picked up a line of summer thunderstorms. The commander at the base on Cudjoe ordered his men to lower the blimp, but as they were doing it, lightning struck a transformer. This caused the clutch on the winch to disengage with a jerk. The emergency generator kicked in causing the clutch to grip. The gears started grinding until they were stripped. They tried to stop it with the emergency brake, but the reel was spinning so fast it fried the brake," Will said.

"The crew must have been freaking out," Betsy said.

"I'm sure they had to be, but if they weren't, they were about to," Will continued. "About that time there was another bolt of lightning. This time it ran down the cable, and blew apart what was left of the machinery. The cable suddenly snapped. Fat Albert was then totally out of control, dragging its cable as it blew south."

"Will, you're not making this up?" Betsy said.

"Would I lie to the woman I love?" Will said with a laugh. "Besides, my imagination isn't that good. But you ain't heard nothing yet, I'm only on chapter two of this tale. Now where was I?"

"Fat Albert was out of control."

"Oh, yeah! The cable was dragging just off the ground and kept wrapping around tree trunks and stripping the trees clean. Then it hit power lines on US 1 and ripped them off their poles. It finally exited into the water on the Atlantic side of Cudjoe Key. Then the real excitement started."

Will giggled, "There was a Cuban fisherman anchored to the reef..."

"Oh, no!"

"Oh, yes! He tried to pull anchor when he saw the thunderstorm coming, but his anchor stuck. When he looked up, Fat Albert was heading straight for him. He managed to cut his anchor line, but the cable blew across his boat and the frayed end of the cable got wedged between the transom and the engine. Every time a gust of wind hit the blimp, the transom would come out of the water. The storm settled down, the sun came out, and began heating the helium in Fat Albert. The blimp started rising and took the boat with it. First thing you know the poor bastard was dangling in mid air, hanging onto the boat for dear life."

"I can just see it," Betsy said. "Sounds like a scene out of the movies."

"You're right," Will paused to sip his Jim Beam before continuing.

"Well, back at the base the commander became increasingly afraid that Albert would blow all the way to Cuba, and Castro would get his hands on some of our sophisticated equipment so he ordered the Boca Chica Air Station to shoot Fat Albert down."

"With the boat hanging from it?"

"They didn't know about the boat until the jets got within visual range. By that time Fat Albert had climbed to 10,000 feet, and they knew if they blew it out of the sky, the poor SOB in the boat was dead meat so the pilots were ordered to shoot little holes in it instead and let it descend gradually. They figured it would take a little under two hours for the blimp to fall, but further calculations were run, they found this put it about fifteen miles off of Cuba."

"And you think we have bad days," Betsy said.

Will laughed and continued, "About this time two Cuban MIGs showed up and the Boca Chica jets started running low on fuel. So they returned to their base and hoped our Coast Guard cutter could intercept Albert. The cutter managed to get under Albert and it set down on the deck. The Cuban fisherman was able to remove the cable from his boat but then for some reason, instead of letting the Coast Guard men rescue him, he immediately cranked his motor and then headed toward Cuba, probably to visit his family."

"That's the wildest story I ever heard," Betsy said. "You win today's tall tale award. It is head and shoulders above what I was going to tell you...The grill's smoking. It must be hot."

"Then hold your story one momento while I put the steaks on," said Will.

Will got comfortable on the chaise lounge again once the steaks were on the grill.

"Shoot. I'm listening."

"We were having our weekly sales meeting this morning," Betsy said. "Carson was doing his usual alibiing about being behind on his goals. Of course, it's still the entire bank's fault since they declined involvement with Club Tropic. You know, he's always the man of vision who's the victim of our shortsightedness and ultra-conservatism. He's too dumb to know it, but he keeps digging his hole deeper and deeper with me. One of these days CC's going to just fall in the hole and never be seen again. I don't know why he can't just do his work," Betsy started. "And I swear, I think he knows every crank and screwball in Key West."

"Oh, Betsy, you're just exaggerating because you're frustrated. Get on with the story."

"Before I do, I'll give you an example of a Carsonism. Carson's been talking for weeks about prospecting Dr. Glaser, the podiatrist over on Eaton. Well, according to my friend, the police chief, Glaser got hauled off to jail today. He was charged with battery on a law enforcement officer," Betsy said.

"Whaaa!"

"His ex-wife appeared at his office this morning when the waiting room was full of patients and started a commotion. The receptionist called 911. When the Key West police got there, she clobbered a cop and ripped off his shoulder microphone. The second cop tried to put her in handcuffs, but she pulled away and tried to claw him. At that point, one of the officers tasered her. Dr. Glaser jumped on the officer's back, and the second cop tasered him too. Both Glaser and his ex ended up in jail."

"You've got to be kidding. Maybe old CC is snake-bit after all," Will said.

"So this is CC's latest and greatest big prospect! What a joke! Anyway, what made me think of Carson was I got a call late today from Joe Miller, our president in Palm Beach County. This is what I was leading up to," Betsy said. "Joe tells me a lawsuit was filed last week in Palm Beach County against Club Tropic. The suit is alleging several things. First, that Club Tropic has captive lenders who have been falsifying loan applications, and second, they have appraisers who have been making appraisals based on fictitious comparable sales. In addition, it accuses Club Tropic of encouraging prospective owners to use preferred lenders as a way of controlling the process and preventing investors from obtaining information from unbiased, independent sources. The suit also maintains that Club Tropic promised higher investment returns if buyers would agree to use one of these inside loan originators," Betsy said.

"That's heavy stuff."

"According to Joe, the suit goes on to say that Club Tropic pre-selected brokers to help them pull off closings. Loan officers of the captive lenders frequently falsified incomes and other financial information about the applicants as well as skewing the nature of the purchase by declaring it to be a second home. It says these people were paid bonus commissions to encourage buyers to lie on their applications. The suit maintains that loan originators talked people into leaving vital information blank on the forms thus allowing them to fill the forms in as needed."

"This Club Tropic cesspool just keeps getting dirtier and stinkier," Will said.

"You haven't heard it all yet. On the second major issue, the suit also alleges that some of the sales comparables were on transactions in which Sol Schwartzman sold properties to his wife and vice versa, and that they were based on numbers furnished by appraisers who were from out of the state and had no idea of what comparable properties in Florida were selling for. Club Tropic discouraged people from using their own local real estate agents, who might have told them the truth about values."

"Do you think the wheels are starting to come off the CT car?" Will asked. "We've heard accusations like this before."

"If they're not, the lug nuts are sure getting loose," Betsy said. "Don't tell Jack; he'll have the final breakdown for certain."

"I'm sure he already knows. I certainly hope he's not one of the culprits. I really do like Joan and Jack."

"I do too. I feel for Tim, Jason's EMT buddy. He's just a young, gullible guy who doesn't have much money he can afford to lose."

You tell Carson?" Will asked.

"I will tomorrow. On second thought, I don't think I'll bother."

"I'm starting to feel sorry for a lot of people, and I'm getting the feeling I'm going to feel sorry for a whole lot more of them before this affair is all over. But I'll tell you who I'll never feel sorry for – the gaping asshole who put a bomb under your car. I hope he fries in fucking hell," Will said. "Dinner's served. Steaks are ready."

"Gaping asshole! Fucking hell!" Red Stripe repeated.

"You tell 'em, buddy," Will said and picked up the platter of steaks.

CHAPTER 41

Will's private line rang. It was Betsy.

"Have you checked your e-mails lately?" she asked.

"Not in the last half hour or so – I've been working on some new account documents for Henry Walker," said Will.

"I just forwarded you one," Betsy said.

Will clicked on his Microsoft Outlook and saw the e-mail Betsy was referring to and opened it.

Mom

Did you arrange an appointment for me to look at a condo over in south Miami with a company named Club Tropic? I just got a call from a woman to confirm that I would be there at 3 tomorrow. I don't understand. You know I have a lease on the duplex Laura and I are renting until the end of the school year. They said I was supposed to meet with someone named Mr. Scarpetti.

Love ya,
Lexie

"Did you make any appointment I don't know about?" Betsy asked.

"You got to be kidding! With those shysters! I wouldn't send Dave Tressler to see them – if he were still alive. Something's going on here, and I don't like it. They're trying to pull some shenanigans. I promise you this – these slime balls mess with my daughter..."

"Calm down, Will," Betsy said. "Let's try to think about this thing logically before we go off the deep end."

"Either you get hold of Lexie right now, or I am going to. We're going to get to the bottom of this," Will said.

"She's in class, but I'll call her the moment she gets out," Betsy said.

"I'll be here. I'll send out and get a sub for lunch. I'm not going anywhere until I hear from you. These fucking assholes mess with my baby...I wish I could prove they were behind that bomb..."

"Settle down. I'll be back to you shortly."

Betsy hung up.

Betsy immediately called Jack to tell him about the e-mail she received from Lexie. His silence was deafening. Finally, Jack told her he would look into the matter and get back to her.

Betsy called Lexie on her cell phone and told her the appointment must be a mistake – "Do not respond and do not go."

CHAPTER 42

After calling Will back about the e-mail Lexie sent on the appointment with Club Tropic, Betsy came out of her office and walked down the hall. Barreling around the corner came Carson Crown who ran straight into her. They hit so hard his glasses almost fell off.

"Ooof! You stepped on my foot," Betsy said. "You better watch where you're going, Carson, or you're going to hurt somebody. It might even be you."

"I'm sorry, boss lady," Carson said. "I guess I'm preoccupied."

"Anything I should know about? Been out on a good appointment? Bring in a multi-million dollar new account?"

Betsy waited for Carson to answer.

"Just coming back from Rotary," he said. "The speaker was Frank Romero, who's on the Fantasy Fest committee. You know him I think. He works for the Tourist Development Council. Should be a great fest this year. Rotary's going to have a T-shirt booth."

"And I thought you were out on a business call. I should have known better," Betsy said.

"This is good for business. Old CC's out bustin' his hump getting that WB name in front of the community. By the way, I'm going to Fantasy Fest as a gator."

Carson made a snapping motion with his arms extended straight out horizontally.

"How original!" Betsy said. "That's because you always snap up those new accounts. I'll be looking for the tidal wave of new relationships that should start rolling in. I assume you will have an adequate supply of new account forms in the booth to handle the avalanche?" Betsy said sarcastically.

Carson barged ahead.

"Anyway, I had heard before Rotary that there are some disgruntled Club Tropic investors in Key West who are saying that renovations are running way behind schedule. I asked Sol Schwartzman about it at Rotary, and he snapped my head off. He grabbed me by the arm and squeezed so tight he left a bruise as he pulled me aside. He said renovations are handled by a separate company that Club Tropic only has a close working relationship with, not Club Tropic itself, and besides, he had not been served with any formal complaints, and that even if he had heard of a possible complaint, he wouldn't be free to comment," Carson rattled. "Lord, he wasn't just rude, he was scary. His eyes bugged out. He lowered his voice and actually threatened me – said if he ever heard I was spreading any rumors about Club Tropic, he'd make me sorry I was ever born."

"Well, Carson, your question was pretty stupid, even if I have to say so myself," Betsy said. "Do you have to repeat everything you hear just to make small talk? You need to learn when to keep your mouth shut. My mother used to always say it's better to let people wonder if you're a fool instead of opening your mouth and removing all doubt. What did you expect Schwartzman to say? You think he's going to admit that he may have a mini investor revolt going on?"

"I guess I didn't think…"

"No, you didn't think," Betsy said. "Carson, when are you ever going to learn?"

Betsy left him red-faced and embarrassed.

After she put back some papers she had gotten out earlier, Betsy returned to her office. She could hear Carson telling a joke to one of the administrative assistants as she returned.

Walter Wanderley was sitting at Margaret's desk drinking a cup of coffee when she walked in.

"Walter, got a sec?" Betsy asked.

"Got plenty of seconds until this coffee cup either runs dry or gets cold," Walter replied and followed her into her office.

"Heard anything about any problematic issues with respect to Club Tropic renovations?' she asked.

"Matter of fact I did," Walter replied. "I heard that twenty Royal Island Club Tropic investors have sued in federal court," he said. "They are alleging that they were promised a world class Keys resort. Instead they were left holding the bag on a virtual ghost town generating no income, with their apartments now worth half of what they paid for them."

"Do you think Club Tropic has a house of cards getting ready to come down?" Betsy asked.

"Who the hell knows? We both realize that these boys are pretty slippery. They showed up down here in the Keys a few years ago, and it seems there isn't anything they don't want to either own or sell. This suit gets even more specific than that. The investors are saying they were promised at least $30,000 worth of improvements on each apartment. They listed granite countertops, a plasma TV, crown molding and swanky furniture. Instead they say they got a coat of paint and some cheap-ass 'glit' furniture."

"What's 'glit'?" Betsy asked.

"You know, glue and shit," Walter said grinning.

"Oh, good old pressed board," Betsy laughed. "Like you get at Kmart or Big Lots?"

"Precisely!" Walter said. "But it doesn't stop there. The suit goes on to accuse Club Tropic of reneging on the lease-back payments and never getting the units zoned for a transient rental license."

"No wonder Schwartzman was upset," Betsy said.

Walter looked puzzled but continued.

"There are other issues in the suit. The buyers' claim that Club Tropic promised them that the lease-back payments would go on for two years or until the upgrades were finished. Club Tropic quit paying the owners after the coat of paint got slapped on the units, which was well before the two years was up. The investors hired an independent rental agency that looked at the units and declared them unrentable. The rental agency found things like old mattresses pushed up against the walls and worn-out filthy carpet. They determined that the bathrooms were so dilapidated that they were unusable."

"Anything else?" Betsy asked incredulously. "Sounds like pig sties."

"Oh yeah, I almost forgot," Walter said. "The leaseback agreement said the renter was supposed to pay for electric, water and sewer. Since there were no renters, Club Tropic had these bills sent to the buyers."

"Real sweethearts, aren't they?" Betsy commented.

About that time, Walter's cell phone rang. He looked at the keypad and punched the "on" button. "Walter Wanderley…"

He rose and silently waved at Betsy on his way out the door.

One week later.

Naples – In a suit filed October 10 in Collier County Circuit Court owners of Regal Collier Club Tropic allege Club Tropic Hospitality utilized their money as an investment, which real estate agents are banned from doing. The suit also lists four appraisal companies the plaintiffs believe inappropriately valued the property based on projected worth tied to promised renovations.

"I don't know how you could perform an appraisal for something that doesn't exist," said Bob Leggett, a Naples attorney who specializes in real estate law.

The suit alleges four appraisal companies – Blue Ribbon, Ponderosa, Wood Ridge, and Spring Hill – did just that.

"The values set forth in each of the appraisals were premised on representations by Club Tropic Hospitality defendants that the resort would be completely renovated," according to the report. "There was no basis for any competent appraiser to arrive at these conclusions."

Spokesman Carmine Scarpetti said the company had not been served with the complaint and therefore could not comment on it. A lawyer for some of the plaintiffs said Club Tropic Hospitality would be served by the end of the week. Club Tropic Hospitality will have 20 days to redress the claims.

CHAPTER 43

Will heard a rumble coming down the street and he knew it was Reuben Nolan's vintage sidecar Harley-Davidson. He laughed to himself and thought this wouldn't be Buccaneer Estates without Reuben.

The Harley transported Reuben and Esther. When Reuben saw him he waved and braked the big bike.

"How are things going with you two?" Will asked.

"Been better," Reuben said. "Just got back from the Club Tropic Dive Center. You know that sucker's closed. Gave a phone number to call for special appointments for group charters. Apparently, that's all they're doing. Sheeet! I don't know what's wrong with this Club Tropic bunch. Shafted a good friend of mine too.

"You remember Jonesy – buddy of mine – played guitar at my wedding. He was singing, man, at their place in Marathon, and they laid him off last week with absolutely no notice. He told me they've laid off some other musician friends of his as well at other resorts they own. I feel for him, man. He used to play on a regular basis down on Duval Street. He gave up those gigs 'cause this bunch promised to take care of him. Now he ain't got shit, and the joints on Duval say they can't use him no more. Those low-life turd tappers. I guess they deserve what I heard Marvin Cheney is doing to them."

"What? I haven't heard," Will lied. What's Cheney doing to them?"

"He originally developed Leisure Bay Club Tropic, Royal Island Club Tropic and Sandy Beach Club Tropic."

"I know," Will said. "He recently substituted his management group for theirs – said he didn't like the way they were running things."

"Well, word circulating is he's gone further now that those lawsuits have broken out again against Club Tropic," Reuben continued. "Not only has he taken over management, but he's declared them in default on the money they owe him and filed a foreclosure suit. I was told Marvin took some of his toughs into Sandy Beach Club Tropic and kicked their candy asses out completely – even changed the locks on the doors."

"I bet Schwartzman was livid over that move," Will said.

"I heard that's the understatement of century," Reuben said. "I heard he pulled a gun on Cheney momentarily. They said Cheney and his men didn't even blink. Cheney must have balls of steel."

"One New Jersey goon should be able to handle another New Jersey goon. You put a hoodlum in a Brooks

Brothers suit, and you know what you've got?" Will asked with a laugh.

"Yeah," Esther said. "A well-dressed lowlife."

Reuben and Esther were still laughing when they roared off down the street.

Over the next several weeks news stories and articles about Club Tropic continued to break. A letter to the editor appeared one day in the *Citizen*.

CLUB TROPIC POISON FOR HONEST INVESTOR

Your newspaper claims it publishes truth. I'm about to tell you REAL TRUTH. You have good developers and you have bad ones like Club Tropic/a.k.a Sol Schwartzman.

The fact remains that there was fraud – and not just one piece of fraud, almost everything that took place about their transactions was full of fraud. Their empty promises to create five-star hotels and condos were nothing but lies. As far as them spending millions on furnishings, we purchased two condos which were both supposed to be fully furnished – but we only got 1 with furniture. An empty promise and a lie!

Bottom line is there is fraud and mismanagement. Club Tropic got greedy, did not finish the projects they started (unless that was the plan the whole time; I am not sure), and left hundreds of people in financial ruin. It has affected our entire community. They defrauded banks and owners out of millions of dollars.

Penny McGraham, A disillusioned investor, Islamorada

The following day a press release ran in the *Citizen* about a new acquisition:

> A Club Tropic affiliate today announced the acquisition of the Americas Billfish Xtreme Release League, a Caribbean fishing tournament series formerly televised on ESPN. The ABXRL, now under Club Tropic management, started the series in Marathon two years ago but halted operations after staging two of six scheduled tournaments.

Will was thumbing through the paper when Betsy got out of the shower.

"Here's the Cheney story Jason and Reuben told us about."

CHENEY TAKES REINS FROM CLUB TROPIC

> Developer Marvin Cheney will take back control of three Keys resorts that have recently been managed by Club Tropic following Club Tropics announcements of employee layoffs, temporary restaurant closings and investor unrest.
>
> Cheney and Club Tropic had previously announced a partnership on Leisure Bay Club Tropic, Royal Island Club Tropic and Sandy Beach Club Tropic, all of which were financed and built by Cheney's hedge fund.
>
> Club Tropic will retain a minority ownership interest in the resort's assets, but previous plans for Cheney to sell the resorts are off the table.
>
> "The current arrangement is not attractive to me," Cheney said reiterating his long-term plan to stay in the hotel business.

Confusion between Club Tropic's management and Cheney led to an affordable housing snafu at Leisure Bay Club Tropic. Marathon officials have recently learned that the resort had been operating without fulfilling its onsite affordable housing requirement.

"Just what Jason and Reuben told us," Betsy summarized.

The following day a quotation was published once again from Sol Schwartzman.

"Our inability to provide the capital necessary to fund negative cash flows at some of our resort properties impacts the visitor experience, recurring tourism, and long-term viability of the property's brand. As we continue to fight numerous challenges, we are implementing qualified solutions for our property owners, while addressing the ongoing sustainability of our business."

"Do you know what he said?" asked Will.

"Are you kidding? He doesn't even know what he said," Betsy said.

The adverse news just kept coming.

$37 MILLION FORECLOSURE FILED

Club Tropic and its large backer Golden States Investments are listed in three foreclosure suits claiming outstanding mortgage bills totaling $37 million. The two are accused of not paying bills on properties purchased from Lake Shore Investors Ltd. which is headquartered in Chicago according to three filings recorded in Monroe

County Circuit Court on Plantation Key. Club Tropic Construction is also listed in the suit.

"The borrowers have defaulted under the note by failing to timely and fully pay to Lake Shore Investors the amounts owed. As a result Lake Shore has been damaged to the tune of $15 million in each of the first two suits and $7 million in the other," stated Lake Shore vice president Jonathan Edwards.

It is not immediately clear which properties Lake Shore is targeting for foreclosure.

Before the week ended, Schwartzman announced that the company was hitting some significant challenges as he regretfully reported the resignation of Club Tropic's vice president of operations. He simultaneously published a press release announcing Club Tropic's pending expansion through the purchase of Walker's Cay in the Bahamas.

"I'm getting dizzy trying to keep up," Betsy said to Will.

"If you think you're dizzy, Sol Schwartzman must feel like he's on a tilt-a-whirl," Will said.

CHAPTER 44

Will laughed to himself as he perused the morning paper and sipped his coffee. He was waiting for the market to open. His laughter was stimulated by a newspaper article about a guy who was arrested on misdemeanor drug charges who insisted police allow him to take his duffel bag with him to the police station. While being booked at police headquarters, additional drugs and paraphernalia were found in his bag. He told officers he smoked "weed for medical purposes."

Will smiled to himself as he thought, what a moron. 99% of the people the police question anywhere always deny knowing the origin of something found in their possession when they were interrogated.

Will's administrative assistant stuck her head in the door. "There's a Mark Michael Moore here to see you," she said.

"Oh yeah, that oddball," Will said.

"And he's got another gentleman with him."

"Did I do something to piss God off?" Will asked.

She gave him a disapproving stare and returned to the lobby to show Mr. Moore and guest in.

The two men entered and closed the door.

"Mr. Black, Mark Michael Moore. It's so good to see you again. The markets have been treating you well I hope. My recent successes have been stunning. I can't wait to share some of these triumphs with you. I hope you aren't taping this."

He laughed and winked at Will.

Will asked, "And who may I ask do you have with you today, Mr. Moore?"

"This is my cousin Vinnie from New Jersey."

Vinnie stuck out his hand and said, "Vinnie Costello."

Vinnie was a small wiry man with a mustache, a pasty complexion and dirty fingernails. He wore dark polyester clothes and a fedora with a wide band that reminded Will of the hat Frank Sinatra had worn on the cover of the "Come Fly With Me" album. Vinnie took off his hat to wipe his brow. His wispy hair had been greased with oil and combed back. His one concession to the tropics was a pair of cheap, dark wraparound sunglasses. He wore scuffed black shoes with thick soles. He was chewing on a disgusting-looking cigar.

"I thought since I haven't heard back from you that I'd stop back for a visit. I assume you've been working on getting the security matters into place that we discussed on our first appointment," Mark Moore said.

"Mr. Moore, as I tried to say on your last visit..." Will tried to begin.

Mark Moore continued as if Will had said nothing. "The reason I want you to meet my cousin Vinnie is so he can testify that my stock trading system really does work and deliver the results we discussed."

"Is Mr. Costello an investment professional?" Will asked.

"Yes and no, actually Vinnie is a bail bondsman from New Jersey. You might say he invests in people. He's down here in Florida to subdue a dangerous felon who fled New Jersey – a fellow named Joey Gambino."

"Yeh! You might say I'm a bond underwriter," Vinnie said. "I underwrite the bond; you pay interest. The bond covenants are very clear. If your credit rating falls below investment grade, there's a call feature. If you default on the bond issue, I knock your head and then take your dick and wrap it around your piece of shit neck like a rubber band like I'm going to do when I find that asshole, Joey," Vinnie said.

"You wouldn't have a picture of Joey Gambino, would you?" Will asked.

"Never go anywhere without one," Vinnie snarled. "You don't fuck over Vincent 'The Bull' Costello and get away with it. If I ever find that piece of shit, he's going to pray to the Virgin Mary he were dead."

Vinnie showed Will a battered photo.

"As much as I hate to deprive you of the joy of killing him," Will continued, "somebody has already beat you to it."

"What do you mean by that?" Vinnie said.

Will pulled a newspaper article out of the stack of newspapers on his credenza and showed it to Vinnie and Mark.

"That's Joey, all right. I can see that dick wad's face in my sleep," Vinnie said, almost chewing his cigar in two. "I'm not surprised somebody got to that weasel. There's some pretty big men who went to jail on account of Joey's blabbering loose lips."

Will decided to take another chance. He pulled out another article with a picture of Aldo Colletti's picture in it.

"Ever seen this guy?" he asked.

Vinnie and Mark both looked at it and then at each other.

"That's our cousin Aldo. He's on our mother's side," they both said at once. "Why do you have his picture?"

"His body was found near here not too long ago – in fact shortly before Joey died. There's some people who think the two deaths may be connected," Will said.

Nothing else was said about an RST brokerage job for Mark. Mark and Vinnie now had other fish to fry. They left Will's office with minimal good-byes. They took off on Mark's Vespa. Just before Will saw the SUPR INVSTOR tag disappear into traffic and go around the corner, he saw Vinnie's right index finger waving in the air as he gestured behind Mark. He was waving so violently it almost threw the scooter off balance.

CHAPTER 45

Will and Betsy invited the Masellis for Sunday brunch at Mangrove Mama's.

Will and Betsy drove into the pearock driveway on the side of the restaurant and walked around to the back into the outdoor patio area adjacent to the bar. Missy, their favorite waitress, waved at them. Will purposely picked out a round resin table that had an umbrella by the front corner. Chris Case, the one-man pan band, played a snappy Arrow soca number Will had heard many times, *Hot Hot Hot*.

Ole, ole, ole, ole
Feeling hot, hot, hot

Chris waved to Will and Betsy and continued to sing. Moments later, the Masellis walked in. Soon all had settled in and ordered a round of mimosas and sangria. The sangria was served in an old Ball canning jar. Will told Missy that they weren't in any hurry to order food yet.

"Wave when you're ready to order," Missy said. "I'll be here until five o'clock."

"I think we'll be able to make up our minds before then," Betsy said.

"So how'd your week go?" Jack asked.

Betsy told them about some of the things that had happened that week at the bank. Will related the story about his visit from Vinnie and Mark.

"Have you ever heard of a Vinnie Costello from New Jersey?" Will asked. "He said he's a cousin of your former investor, Aldo Colletti."

"Costello, no, I never heard of him, but I remember Aldo Colletti well," Jack said. "How can I ever forget him? He was in my office the day before he died out on No Name Key. Shit, he had just paid full list price for two preconstruction units."

Jack took a slug of his sangria before continuing, "But I certainly never would have related him to this Vinnie creature, and I certainly never connected him to our dead salesman, Joey Giambi. What a small world!"

"I'm always suspicious of coincidences," Betsy added.

Jack looked puzzled, "Surely you don't think..."

"As I said, coincidences are sure worth a second look," Betsy said.

Jack took another drink.

"I hate to speak ill of the dead, but I'll tell you in confidence, I never did like Joey Giambi," he continued. "Something about him just never felt right."

He stopped, drained his Ball jar, and then continued, "Even if he was handpicked by Sol Schwartzman."

"Did you ever know anything about his New Jersey background?" Will asked.

Jack shook his head, and Will started telling him about the story in the newspaper regarding Garden State Check Cashing.

"According to the story, Garden State was letting construction companies write them checks on phony baloney subcontractors and then cashing them. Garden State was making a handsome commission off each check. The construction companies were then laundering the money, taking bullshit tax deductions, and screwing the IRS to the wall. Giambi was running one of Garden State's ventures called Quick Buck Cash Flow Financing. He screwed all his buddies to get a lighter sentence and then skipped out without even fulfilling that obligation. When he skipped he left a bail bondsman holding the bag."

Joan had been saying nothing this whole time, but it was like a light came on in her head. She looked at Jack. He returned her look, and all of a sudden he too got it.

"And so Vinnie Costello..." he said.

"Sounds like something more than coincidences to me," Betsy said.

"I still think the Colombians are up to their necks in some of the odd occurrences that have been happening at Club Tropic," Jack said "It seems that's all anybody at work talks about anymore – you know, that Jorge Carlos."

Will and Betsy nodded. Jack went on.

"Sol has discussed him at length in our sales meetings. Told us to tell everyone…that it will make buyers froth at the mouth that they are fortunate to be involved with us. He owns Centennial Partners and will soon invest one hundred million of their capital in Club Tropic. Sol said this is just the first investment. There will be more coming. I just don't trust those Colombians, especially ones with an illegal history."

Will and Betsy nodded.

Jack continued, "It's public record that Carlos had some trouble with the SEC a few years back. Check on it if you don't believe me. Carlos paid over $250 million out of his own pocket…"

"$50 million out of his own pocket," Will interrupted. "$200 million out of the corporate account."

"To settle some dirty dealings…"

"Fraudulent market timing," Will completed Jack's thought.

"Everyone must know about this," said Jack, surprised at Will's knowledge. "Boy is that great for us – we're going to be identified with a known felon."

"I wouldn't say it's common knowledge," Will said.

"God, I hope not. Shit! That's all we need at the office. I need to go to the little boy's room. Would you order me another sangria?" Jack asked.

Jack excused himself and walked in the men's room behind the bar. It was hard not to notice the signs that decorated the room. One over the urinal said DEAD END. Another series over the men's toilet next to it announced a series of pronouncements: PRIVATE ROAD, NO DUMPING, $500 FINE, AND PLEASE WAIT TO BE SEATED.

A small, sweating man in dark clothes, a wide banded fedora, chewing on a cigar, was just zipping his pants. He looked completely out of place for Mangrove Mama's or any other place in the Keys. Jack couldn't help but almost stare.

He looked Jack straight in the eye and said, "What you staring at, faggot."

When Jack broke eye contact, the man left the restroom without washing his hands.

Jack came back out to their table.

Will said, "I told Missy we're ready to order."

Jack said, "I just saw a man in the restroom who perfectly matches that bail bondsman you told us about from New Jersey. You don't think he's trying to find out what happened to his cousin, do you? Maybe he's working for Schwartzman. Maybe Schwartzman sent him here to watch us. He looked dangerous. I don't know how much more of this I can take."

Betsy put her hand on Jack's and quietly said, "Jack, you're letting your imagination get the best of you. You're starting to see boogie men everywhere you go. You're going to talk yourself into a nervous breakdown if you don't get control of yourself."

Jack said nothing.

"I wish we were back in New Jersey," Joan said.

CHAPTER 46

Will's sales assistant poked her head in the door. "Ernie Kemp just called. Said he will be here in fifteen minutes."

"Wonder what he needs. I always enjoy seeing him," Will said. "He's a nice, very pleasant, low maintenance client. Wish I had a hundred more just like him. He and Nan are really a nice young couple."

A few minutes later Ernie came in his office.

"So how's the market?" Ernie said after he sat down.

"Not bad – markets appear to be headed higher, even though they're not probably going off the register. We think there'll be the usual volatility as we go into earnings report season. Looks like interest rates will be stable. That always helps. So what can I do for you today? You're looking good. You must have been out fishing."

"Thanks. I wish I felt as good as I look. I need to start taking $3,000 a month out of my investment account," Ernie said.

Will thought for a second before answering. "That's a pretty stiff distribution rate, Ernie. I thought you were trying to build this account to enhance your net worth down the road. That's $36,000 a year on a $250,000 account. You'll be taking almost 15 percent a year out of a balanced account."

Ernie looked uncomfortable. "I know, Will. I wish I didn't have to, but I need to do this for now."

Will continued, "You know, the account probably won't make 15 percent a year every year. We have you positioned 75 percent stocks, 25 percent bonds, which is a pretty conservative mix for someone your age. If the stocks make 10 percent and the bonds make 6 percent, that gives you a total return averaging about 9 percent...And that is pretax. At some point you will be cannibalizing your principal. Will you continue to add money to the account?"

Ernie looked more uncomfortable. "No, I'll have to suspend contributions for the time being."

"Is this merely a short term cash crunch? Have your investment objectives changed? Have you found an investment with more opportunity?" Will asked.

Ernie didn't answer.

"I hope there are no problems at home," Will said.

"I was hoping I wouldn't have to tell anyone this, but I've got a bit of a situation not related to you to resolve, and I don't know exactly how long it's going to take me to work through it."

Will remained silent.

Ernie started out hesitantly, "I know this is going to sound stupid. Normally I'm a very conservative, prudent person, but I've gotten in over my head in a real estate investment. Now I've got to try to see it through."

"We all make mistakes, but I'm sure it'll work out. I've always known you and Nan to be an ambitious and hard working couple," Will said.

Ernie sighed before continuing.

"We committed to a $18,000 reservation agreement for a membership in the Gulf Shores Club Tropic. I can't believe it looking back. Even though we didn't know which unit we were buying, what the sales price was, how big the unit was, or what the view was going to be like, the Club Tropic salesman convinced us we had been fortunate enough to secure our spot in a great, once-in-a-lifetime investment.

"Three months later the same salesman called and said he had an opportunity for us in the Orange Beach Club Tropic. He said if I would write him a check for another $10,000 he would reserve unit number 322 in the Orange Beach complex. We had heard that panhandle resort property was growing like a weed. He said this unit was further along and we were lucky there were any slots left. I was reluctant, but he said we'd be sorry if we passed. He said he was calling us because he wanted to see us get ahead. He said financing wouldn't be an issue with our impeccable credit. I finally said yes. We tried to get financing for Orange Beach, but since we had committed to the Gulf Shores unit, we ran into some roadblocks borrowing the money. The salesman told us that he just happened to have someone who wanted to live in Orange Beach. He also said it would be easier to finance our investments if we owned two units in the same complex and offered to flip our $10,000 into a second unit in the Gulf

Shores project. He said the financing problems could be solved down the road. He also showed us appraisals saying that our first purchase in Gulf Shores was worth $100,000 more than what we paid for it. He suggested that I should be the owner of one unit and Nan be the owner of the other."

Will just listened.

Ernie continued, "We got our sales contracts about three months later. There should have been a red flag in our minds because Club Tropic seemed totally disorganized. The contracts were riddled with blanks that hadn't been filled in. Also the sales prices had been inflated over what he originally told us and the closing costs had been left blank. Just recently, when I complained, we were given addendums to the contracts we were never shown at that time justifying the inflated sales price and showing the items the developer was responsible for. He told me he had given me those documents originally and I must have misplaced them. I can't prove it, but I would swear on a Bible he was lying.

"I then started in earnest to try to get financing on our two units. The salesman gave me contact information on a José Rodriquez at some place named Trans Gulf Mortgage Brokerage. I tried to call him a few times, but he never returned my calls, so I started working on financing on my own. I called the sales rep back for updated appraisals. He gave me appraisals from Blue Ribbon Appraisals showing that each unit had gained an additional $60,000. We were annualizing well over twenty percent a year. I couldn't believe I was having this much trouble finding a lender for such a great deal.

"Anyway, after six months of no success in finding a lender, the salesman sent me to Roger Packard over at Interstate Bank. He was able to use the appraisals from Blue Ribbon. We finally got a loan. We used a title company in Gulf Shores called CT Title on a mail-away basis. We didn't have anyone to close the loan. He instructed me to take the loan documents over to my bank and have them notarized. I then had to put an additional 5 percent down and had to come up with $18,000 in closing costs. These expenses drained our savings account, and we sold the stock in Nan's stock purchase program to come up with the difference. This property appeared to be so hot it didn't seem to matter. We were going to be fine as soon as the lease-back checks started coming in."

Will said "Ernie, I don't want to meddle in your affairs, but aren't you aware of some of the allegations and innuendos that have been brought forward against Club Tropic? Some a while back, but more have come recently. Some have been related to high-pressure sales practices. As for the lease-back program, just recently an investor in Naples has filed a suit alleging failure to pay leaseback payments. This investor is also accusing Club Tropic of gypping investors on common areas in their complex."

"What do you mean?" Ernie asked.

"I mean they are being accused of telling investors they owned a pro rata part of the common areas when they were actually owned by Club Tropic who was then charging the investors excessive fees to maintain and manage these areas."

Will continued, "There's also accusations of hard selling Club Tropic's corporate financial stability by claiming they were merging with a public company any time now but then doing an about face by announcing this merger has now been put on hold but everyone should be assured it will come to fruition next year. That's just a couple of matters that were just released over the last week or so."

Ernie squirmed in his chair but continued.

"I wish I had seen some of the publicity on them before I was in so deep. I never worried about these investments because the appraisals were always so much higher than what we had paid. It seemed like we couldn't lose even in a worst case scenario. Besides Nan and I had money in the bank we thought would cover the payments for two years. Our strategy all along was to hold the property for a minimum of one year and one day or no longer than twenty four months. When we got to the one year target, I called our friend, the salesman, and told him we were interested in selling our units. He talked me out of it, telling me to wait and take advantage of the full period of the lease-backs. He also said that there was going to be a strip mall going up near our condo which was going to create a lot of buzz so, the longer I held off, the more capital return we would realize.

"I waited for a couple of months, but Nan convinced me to put in my request for the $28,000 'refundable' reservation deposit we were told we were entitled to even though it was supposed to be getting a good rate of return in Club Tropic's escrow account. I waited for a month but never heard back from our rep. I sent a follow-up e-mail. He sent one back telling me we would get our refund as soon as they were able to put a replacement buyer in our position. Now I was starting to feel very uncomfortable and told the salesman so. He sent me a cancellation form to fill out. I breathed a sigh of relief and sent it back. I didn't hear anything else from Club Tropic. Two weeks later when I called, he told me he was still trying to find a replacement buyer and couldn't release the money until he did. He assured me, however, that if he couldn't find a replacement buyer soon he would personally take our place. It was that good a deal. Still nothing happened. Finally, when I hired an attorney and threatened to sue, we finally got our $28,000 back. I used it to pay off the loan at the bank we had taken out to raise part of the money originally. I later read that we were some of the lucky ones. Some people never got their refundable deposit back."

"Everything with them was like pulling teeth, wasn't it?" Will said.

"Was it ever? We made a trip up to Gulf Shores, but I saw no evidence of a strip mall going in and our complex had barely broken ground, so we decided once and for all to sell. The price was just too good to pass up. When I told the salesman of our decision, he told us there was a real estate investment trust (REIT) that wanted to buy our whole complex and they would give us a profit of $100 a square foot. I waited for six months but nothing happened. He said just be patient. Hell, for that kind of profit I was willing to wait another six months. Finally I called them back, and once again they tried to convince me to wait just a little bit longer. Nan and I got antsy decided 'screw it', we're just getting out, take our profits, and run no matter what they advised.

I called Club Tropic's recommended real estate company. The woman quoted me $425 a square foot – a lot less than our original salesman had said it was worth. She said it was a volatile market. Plus there was going to be an 8.5 percent brokerage fee plus closing costs and some miscellaneous costs.

"I decided to have a confrontation with the salesman. His office turned out to be a doublewide trailer in Key Largo. I even prepared a Microsoft Excel spreadsheet to show them that if we couldn't sell we were going to be out of pocket $34,469 over the next year, and we plain didn't have it. I even took the e-mail from the realtor showing what was supposed to be the going price per square foot of our units."

Will sat there in disbelief. No wonder the poor bastard needed money.

Ernie caught his breath and concluded his sad tale. "The sales rep danced around every question Nan and I threw at him. He even tried to sell us an additional unit in a new complex they are starting in Crested Butte, Colorado. He kept throwing irrelevant bull shit back at us asking us things like did we write off the entire furniture package. He also suggested that a solution to our problem would be to deed our units into a corporation and do a one time write off.

"Four months later we got a newsletter from the salesman saying that the REIT deal had been consummated, but that the buyouts of the units would not start for another eighteen months. At the same time we got our last check for the lease-back, but it was only half of what I had been told we would get. It's been a year and half now and I haven't heard anything more about the REIT. That's why I need money out of my investment account. I guess I'm just going to have to see this matter through."

After Ernie left, Will looked at his sales assistant and said, "Is it too early for a drink? Ernie just depressed the hell out of me. I wonder if he's seen this morning's *Citizen*. After listening to his pitiful story, I couldn't bear to show him one more piece of bad news."

He pulled his copy out and showed it to her. The headline read

**BIGHT DEAL WITH CLUB TROPIC
FALLS THROUGH**

CHAPTER 47

Will pulled off his tie when he came in from work. He heard Betsy's car on the pearock driveway and looked out the kitchen window to make sure it was her. The dogs were eagerly waiting by the front door for her to get home.

"Looks like it's going to be a perfect sunset tonight," she remarked as she came in.

"That it does," agreed Will. "Why don't we take the boat on a spin out to Picnic Island and enjoy it from there."

"I'll put a few munchies and a six pack in a cooler," said Betsy. "Just give me a second to change clothes."

Within twenty minutes, Will and Betsy were sitting out at Picnic Island. There were virtually no other boats there. The solitude was a welcome change to the stresses of the day as the water gently lapped the boat and the sky turned pink.

"This is the life, isn't it?" Will remarked. "What did we do to deserve this?"

"I still miss Vero Beach," Betsy said, "but I'm glad things fell into place down here. People just don't appreciate the Keys lifestyle until they've lived it."

"And we get to live it every day; not just on an infrequent vacation, but every day," Will agreed.

The statement didn't require a response. Betsy just took a sip of her beer and looked out over the horizon, letting the events of the day gently fade away over the water.

Finally Will commented, "All I heard about all day was that investigative report in yesterday's *Citizen* about Club Tropic's source of funds for the Key West Bight deal."

"They make a pretty compelling case for the fact that one of Sol's many investors is a private real estate company from New Orleans which is strongly suspected of having underworld connections that may track back to a Colombian drug cartel."

"I bet the bight board is glad they disentangled themselves from that whole affair when they did," Will said.

"My buddy, Chief Wanderley, was in my office today," Betsy said. "He said the bight board has now been approached by our neighbor, Marvin Cheney."

"He does get around, doesn't he," Will murmured. "But enough business talk – we came out here to watch a breathtaking sunset."

While Will and Betsy were enjoying beer and the sunset, Al Soltero was paying Jack Maselli a visit. It seemed a good time to do so since he only saw one car in Jack's driveway and Joan was likely not home. He rang Jack's bell.

"Come in, come in," Jack said when he answered the door. "Isn't it a marvelous sunset? A perfect end to a day in paradise. I was just having a cocktail on the porch. This sure beats the hell out of New Jersey sunsets. Would you like to join me?"

"A rum and water on the rocks doesn't sound bad – easy on the water," Al agreed.

As they sipped their drinks, Al said, "I assume everyone at your office is talking about losing the Bight deal."

"Yeah," Jack said. "There's a lot of paranoia with all the things that have happened to Club Tropic over the last six months. Hell, I'm sure six months ago the bight restaurant lease deal would have been in the bag."

"I read about some of the investor allegations," Al said.

"Yeah! Those sure didn't help matters any," Jack said.

"Or Marvin Cheney's seizing management of some of the properties he had sold Club Tropic," Al continued.

Jack looked uncomfortable but nodded in agreement.

"And they still haven't come up with a cause of death for Señors Levitt or Driskoll, have they. Such a shame – such a shame. Such a horrible way to die. Can you imagine being buried alive?"

Suddenly, Jack's cocktail was not helping his already delicate stomach and fragile mood.

"I guess if I were working for Club Tropic, I would certainly be thinking about taking steps to make sure I protected myself if it became necessary. I hope you don't think I'm overstepping my bounds by making that statement," Al said softly as he looked into Jack's eyes.

"What exactly are you referring to? Do you know something I should be aware of?" asked Jack.

"I'm only speaking in generalities. I truly don't want to interfere..." Al began.

"Al, please, let's not play word games. I value your opinion highly. You have been very successful in your various endeavors," Jack said.

"Well, if I were a Club Tropic sales manager, I would want to try to make sure I didn't get blindsided by future disclosures. I would want to try to anticipate problems before they occurred not merely react to them after the fact as most of my less successful colleagues would do."

Al paused to let the effect of his words sink in with Jack.

"I would sure protect myself and those around me who could help me build a power base."

He paused again.

"And I'd want to make sure that if there were matters awry, they couldn't be blamed on me and result in my dismissal or, worse yet, my being incriminated as a legal scapegoat by those higher in the corporation."

"What are you suggesting?" Jack asked.

"I would take advantage of my ability to look at company files and possibly make copies of anything I found that I might need to strengthen my position going forward or might enhance my people's situations. As I said, it is not my wish to meddle. I just know what I would do if I were possibly vulnerable."

"Would you give me your confidential opinion of any questionable documents that I find?" Jack asked.

"If it is your wish, of course, I will be of any humble assistance that I can," Al replied.

"Thank you, and I'm not speaking strictly hypothetically. I do currently have a copy of one document I Xeroxed earlier today. It's been bothering me all day. I came into possession of this letter inadvertently. No one knows I have it. You're the first person to see it – I haven't even shown it to Joan. Would you mind reading it?" Jack said.

"It would be a privilege, my friend, if that is your desire."

Jack retrieved the letter from his briefcase and brought it to Al.

It was a letter from an attorney for Marvin Cheney addressed to Sol Schwartzman advising that legal actions had been initiated against Club Tropic to dissolve the management contracts and lease-purchase arrangements for the partnerships of the Leisure Bay Club Tropic, Royal Island Club Tropic, and Sandy Beach Club Tropic. In addition to Club Tropic not providing the affordable housing in connection with the Leisure Bay Club Tropic, the management of the three resorts by Club Tropic had resulted in investor unrest, subsequent lawsuits from many investors, loss of sales, employee layoffs, closing of many resort amenities and as a consequence a substantial downvaluing of all these resort assets.

Al smiled and looked back at Jack, "As I said knowledge is strength. With knowledge like this you are in a much better position, my friend, to be a survivor."

He drained his glass.

CHAPTER 48

Vinnie spread his arms as wide as they would go, a beer in one hand and a lit cigar in the other. A passerby on the sidewalk had to dodge him so she wouldn't get hit with the outstretched stogie. She gave him a dirty look but then thought better about saying anything when she saw the pistol in Vinnie's waistband.

"So what you think, paisano," Vinnie said, showing off his new flamingo print shirt he had bought at Key West Fashions. He had to have selected the loudest shirt in the store. "Do I look Key West or do I look Key West? Bring on the honeys."

Mark didn't want to burst Vinnie's bubble by telling him that he'd look more local if his legs weren't so white in his baggy plaid shorts and if he would trade his white socks and brown Hushpuppies for a pair of flip-flops.

"Yeah, life is good, isn't it?" Mark said.

"Crap, usually I'm getting ants in my pants to go back to Jersey after I've been away this long. Maybe I'm cut out for this tropical shit. I just didn't know it until now," Vinnie continued. "Bring on the broads."

Two hours and several Duval Street bars later Vinnie and Mark were starting to get ripped but still hadn't found any female companionship.

They found themselves in the Bull and Whistle listening to Yankee Jack.

Everyone gets paid in the Key West serenade
Get your money ready
'Cause the weather's hot and sweaty...

"He's right. It is damned hot down here," mumbled a drunken Vinnie. "Look at the tits on that broad…and look at those shorts ride the crotch on the one with her. I think I'm in love. With a pair of honkers like those, the bitch must be Garden State Italian. Look it says Carnival on her shirt."

"Mama mia! That kind of carnival was made with me in mind. I could get lost and drown in tits like that. I think they want us to come over too. I think they just looked our way," Mark agreed.

Yankee Jack overheard them and nodded at security.

Mark and Vinnie stumbled over and tried to start a conversation with the ladies.

The girls paid for their drinks leaving a twenty on the bar and quickly left, hoping to avoid trouble.

Vinnie headed out the door right behind them. Mark stumbled to keep up.

The security man watched them exit, glad to have them out of the Bull and Whistle. They awkwardly tried to approach the girls again on the sidewalk. The security man saw a cop and pointed them out to him. The cop made a beeline down Duval Street toward Vinnie and Mark. When he caught up with them, he asked the girls if they were being bothered. Vinnie tried clumsily, with arms waving, to dispel the cop's suspicions.

It probably would have worked too, except at this point Vinnie bent over and his pistol fell out of his waistband. Now it was not going to be so simple.

The next thing Vinnie and Mark knew, they were at the Key West police station and feeling very sober. Over the course of the next several hours, it was determined that Vinnie did not have a concealed weapon permit. The arresting officer told Vinnie that he was in trouble with a serious violation. Vinnie demanded to see the police chief.

The officer went to find the Chief. Before he met with Vinnie, Wanderley asked the arresting officer for a summary and was filled in on the details of their arrest.

"I'll talk to him," Wanderley said. "Put him in interrogation room number two."

Vinnie told Chief Wanderley that he had valuable information on a recent death in Monroe County he was willing to trade for leniency on the concealed weapons charge. Wanderley only promised to listen, but told Vinnie he was willing to possibly negotiate a deal as a professional courtesy to a bail bondsman.

Vinnie talked about his cousin Aldo Colletti who had been trying to break a sales contract with Club Tropic. He then told the Chief that the Club Tropic sales rep, Joey Giambi, was a bail jumper from New Jersey by the name of Joey Gambino, who had cost him a lot of money.

"I been looking for that dirt bag for a long time," Vinnie said.

Vinnie told Wanderley about his conversation with his cousin the night before he died.

"He called me and said he'd run into Gambino hiding out down here working for Club Tropic. Aldo said he didn't think Joey knew who he was, but he sure as hell knew who Joey was. He filled me in. That's why I came down to Florida, but when I got here my cousin was dead. Joey Giambi or Gambino killed my cousin just as sure as I'm in this room. He was trying to stay hid, but he didn't know Aldo had already called me. Aldo was looking after me... after all we're blood."

"I guess you know Joey's dead too," Walter said.

"I found out when I got here," Vinnie said. "I don't know who did Joey, but I can tell you this, Joey Giambi or Gambino ran with some bad motherfuckers. You can make book on the fact that one of those mothers did him in. Check out the name Juan Strazzuli."

Walter told Vinnie he was going to let the current matter of the gun possession slide, but since he had no further business in Key West, he wanted him on the next plane headed back to New Jersey.

"Capice," he said.

"Capice," Vinnie agreed.

"And that's exactly what happened," the Chief told Betsy the next morning over coffee at the bank. "I don't think we have to worry about seeing Vinnie around here anytime soon. Chalk one up for the good guys."

CHAPTER 49

Luis Gonzales was just walking out of his small Spartan office at Rum Reef Club Tropic in Islamorada when his phone rang. He almost didn't answer it but thought better of his actions at the last moment. Instinct told him it could be urgent.

"Luis," a smooth voice said, "How is my dear Maria's favorite son?"

Luis Gonzales instantly knew the identity of the caller.

"Uncle Adolfo," Luis said. "What a pleasant surprise to hear from you."

He knew this was not a social call. Uncle Adolfo was a busy man and did not make frivolous social calls, even to favorite cousins. Adolfo was not his uncle but his cousin, yet family members called him "uncle" out of respect for the power he could wield.

"I recently returned from Colombia. Your mother wants you to know she is well and very happy in the new home my colleagues helped arrange for her," Al Soltero continued.

"That was very generous of your friends," Luis said. "As with all your favors, we are eternally grateful. The house will be a comfortable place for my madre to spend her declining years. I only wish there was some way I could repay your kindnesses."

"Actually there is a minor favor you can do for me," Adolfo continued. "It is only a small thing, but it would help me a lot in some upcoming negotiations."

"You know all you have to do is ask. You have been very good to me and my family," said Luis.

"Am I right to assume this conversation is private?" Adolfo continued.

"I am alone. I would die before I would repeat anything you told me in confidence."

"And I you," Al said. "That is the bond that makes us family. We must never forget we are of the same blood.

"It would be helpful to my negotiations if various problems or accidents would happen that would temporarily disrupt normal operations with your employer. I will leave the particulars to you. There are funds and people who can be made available if they are needed. All of your kindnesses as well as those of your compadres will be remembered if there happened to be a change in management at your company in the future. I will let you know when normal operations should resume. By the way before I have to pick up my next call, I would be remiss if I did not tell you how glad I am we were able to arrange transportation for brother Jorge's baby to go to the doctor in Medellin. I hope the child is well.

Anyway I must go now. Good day, my friend. I will be in touch."

Two days after Adolfo and Luis spoke, the air conditioning system at Rum Reef Club Tropic suddenly died. It was unfortunate because a large undertaker's convention was scheduled to begin there the following day. Parts were not available locally and were on backorder from the wholesaler. Sol Schwartzman instructed them to move all the convention booths to The Sporting League of Club Tropic in Islamorada. In a twist of fate after everything had been relocated, the refrigerators and freezers at The Sporting League also quit working. It was not discovered until all of the food in the hotel spoiled. Especially cumbersome to move was a display of caskets that Club Tropic had to hire a special truck to move. Several were dropped by the transportation company, Five Star Latin Movers. After it was found out that the parts would also take several days to be delivered for the refrigeration equipment, all the convention booths had to be dismantled a second time and taken by Five Star to Deep Water Club Tropic in Key Largo. The organizers of the convention who expected by now to be drinking rum punches were irate and insisted that the convention be discounted by fifty percent across the board to compensate them for these inconveniences. They also insisted that Club Tropic pay for all the moving expenses in full as well as arrange limos to transport their group to the new hotel. Exacerbating their impatience was that the undertakers had to share the hotel with the southeastern NAACP workshop that had already been booked at Deep Water for the same week. A livid Sol took out his frustrations on his already overworked staff.

On the second day of the undertaker's convention a three-foot iguana suddenly sidled in a door to the meeting room at Deep Water Club Tropic that had been left ajar and slithered across the floor toward the speakers' podium.

The undertaker's recording secretary from Vermont, who had never been to the Keys or seen an iguana, suddenly panicked and screamed, at the top of his lungs, "A komodo dragon, a komodo dragon!" as the invocation was being said.

Conventioneers started jumping on tables. One turned over the American flag and smashed a water pitcher. Others, including the speaker, ran out of the door.

At the same time in the NAACP workshop a filthy bearded man invaded the main assembly, waving a sword at the special celebrity speaker, Al Sharpton, screaming about Jesus. He ended up in a duel of sorts with Sharpton's bodyguard, slicing a chair that the bodyguard was holding to defend himself. The man was finally subdued with a Taser that had been brought to the meeting by a nearsighted eighty-five year old attendee who also zapped the person next to him by accident. By then, however, most of the workshop participants, including Sharpton, had fled the room. Some of the unruly mob ran into the room where the undertakers were meeting, fueling even more chaos. As Sharpton and the speaker from the undertaker's convention fled their respective rooms, both collided with Carmine Scarpetti, flattening him in the middle of the hall. Carmine's thugs beat up both Sharpton and the undertaker before realizing that both were VIP hotel guests not one of the perpetrators of the confusion. It was later found that the swordsman was a homeless man on a bad LSD trip who lived in Key West. He had sometimes been seen dragging a cross down Duval Street. It was never determined how he had gotten from Key West to Key Largo, but his cross was found leaning against the mile marker in front of the hotel. No one was sure how it got there either.

When he heard about the day's events, Sol Schwartzman backhanded his computer monitor off his desk.

On Sunday, a raw fish head was found floating in a large pot of conch chowder that had been prepared for Sunday brunch at Leeward Cay Club Tropic. It was found by a hyperventilating woman going through the buffet line as she ladled her soup. She then threw up on the salmon before accidentally pulling the tablecloth off the table. Schwartzman barged into the kitchen and fired all the cooks. He then ordered the remaining kitchen staff to prepare and serve brunch. He had armed men stand in the kitchen to prevent a reoccurrence of the sabotage. They inspected every platter as it left the kitchen. By this time it didn't make any difference - most of the guests had left.

On Monday morning, Sol Schwartzman called all of his senior staff to a meeting at Deep Water Club Tropic and berated them over the events that had occurred the days before. He threatened to replace everyone if they were not able to find the perpetrators. Sol screamed at staff members that their top priority was to track these people down until his blood pressure and laryngitis forced him to be silent. All other matters were to be put on the back burner. One staff member suggested that some of the events could possibly have been an accident. He was terminated instantly and escorted off the premises.

"If you don't get another goddamned fucking thing done this week, I want some names by this weekend. NAMES! DO WE UNDERSTAND EACH OTHER," Sol shrieked after he drank some water.

When the staff returned to their jobs, they began interrogating and grilling everyone employed in their facility. Morale tanked before noon. All that was heard was griping about work conditions.

The following day this headline appeared in the *Citizen*.

**FISHHEAD GRINS AND WINKS AT
GUESTS FROM CONCH CHOWDER AT
LEEWARD CAY CLUB TROPIC**

The article then told Sunday's events in a tongue-in-cheek manner.

Schwartzman called the staff to another hastily put together meeting at Deep Water Club Tropic and demanded to know who released the story to the press. He screamed for somebody's head. He continued to scream at the staff nonstop for over thirty minutes.

On Wednesday morning Sol Schwartzman picked up his phone.

"Schwartzman," he said in a flat slightly hoarse tone.

"Mr. Schwartzman, this is Jim Lenaghan up at Leeward Cay."

"What do you want? I don't want to hear shit from you or anyone else unless you have the names of the people responsible for disrupting my facilities."

"I wish I did, Mr. Schwartzman," Lenaghan said. "You know I'd tell you, but I was just calling to tell you most of our maids called in sick today. Would it be possible for you to send me some maids from another hotel?"

"I'll see what I can do and get back to you. You said this is Lenaghan at Leeward Cay?"

"Yes sir. Thank you."

Within sixty seconds the phone rang again.

"Schwartzman."

"Mr. Schwartzman, I know you're a busy man..."

"You're goddamned right I am! Who is this, and what to you want?"

"This is Emerson from Rum Reef. All of our maids called in sick today, and I need temps."

"I'll get back to you. My other phone's ringing."

Before Sol could hang up, he answered the next call

"Mr. Schwartzman, this is Jillby from..."

"Are you calling to tell me your maids called in sick?"

"Yessir, how'd you know?"

"What the fuck is going on out there? Jillby, you're from The Sporting League right?"

"Yessir."

"I'll get back to you."

Finally Sol said, "Misty, get Carmine on the phone. I want to talk to him, NOW!"

"Why do we have to hire those wetback maids?" he yelled at no one in particular.

Sol's phone rang.

"Carmine here."

Sol told Carmine, "Drop whatever you're doing and find out what's going on with our sorry, piece-of-shit wetback maids. I've had three phone calls in five minutes about them not showing up for work. If there's a revolt going on, bust some heads if you have to. Find out who's orchestrating this little coup, and we'll serve him his balls for lunch."

Within ten minutes Sol received similar calls from Bimini Cay Tropic and Paradise Club Tropic. Maids had called in with the flu. Sol broke his coffee cup and screamed at Misty to clean it up.

Carmine called back about mid-afternoon.

"Sol, I can't pinpoint the source of the trouble. It seems confined to our Hispanic help. I tried getting tough with a couple of the Hispanic supervisors. The strange thing is they don't seem scared of me or my men. They don't seem to give a damn. Who could be protecting them? I should have them quaking in their shoes. Somebody's gotten to them, promised them something, and is willing to look after them," Carmine said.

"I don't like this. I don't like this one little bit," Sol said. "There's somebody big backing these people and giving them a backbone, and we're going to find out who it is."

"Somebody is out to fuck things up for both of us," Carmine agreed. "We got to get him or them before he gets us - even if it means taking him out of the picture altogether."

"But who are they?" Sol said.

The following week, however, unplanned and unorthodox events continued to occur. It seemed like there was always a fire to put out.

CHAPTER 50

There wasn't a cloud in the sky. Sol was in a good mood for the first time in a week. He had decided to stop by Leeward Cay Club Tropic and catch some breakfast. He told the waiter to give him an outdoor table. It was just too beautiful to be indoors. It was a very quiet beginning to what the press would later call Freaky Friday. Sol's wife was going to Miami with some other wives to see a play and go shopping. He had lined up a nice little piece of ass for the weekend. He planned on taking her out to the Dry Tortugas on his thirty-two foot schooner. He got a hard-on at the table as he visualized peeling off her bikini bottom and taking her from behind. Sol had even ordered some of those pills that were advertised on late night TV that promised to "make a certain part of a man's anatomy larger and make him last longer." Yes, it was going to be a marvelous weekend.

Sol ordered an omelet and some home fries. He told himself he needed a good breakfast to get himself up for the big weekend ahead. After all his emphasis wouldn't be on eating while he was out on the boat. He fantasized about the weekend as he drank his coffee. I wonder how many times I can do it in one weekend at my age, he thought. He got a roaring hard-on all over again just thinking about his companion lying out on the deck topless with her hair cascading over her shoulders.

The waiter brought Sol's omelet. It smelled marvelous. He took one bite, ate some home fries, and was about to take a second bite of each when his cell phone rang. It was Andrea from his office. Andrea had replaced Misty after she quit following one of Sol's recent tirades.

"Mr. Schwartzman, I just got a call from the manager at Deep Water Club Tropic in Key Largo. He says there are a group of picketers outside his complex. They have signs accusing Club Tropic of buying produce from farmers who are using pickers who are underpaid illegal aliens. He said there were a couple of dozen picketers marching and waving signs at passing traffic. Across the street flagging the traffic going in the opposite direction is a group of commercial fishermen who are upset that we are buying imported frozen fish and not supporting the local fishing industry. They were also accusing Club Tropic of mislabeling fish on its menus. He said the two groups have begun yelling at each other."

Sol's omelet suddenly had no taste or smell; the home fries felt like a greasy lump in his stomach.

"Call the goddamned sheriff's department right now. I'll get there as soon as I can," he screamed.

He quickly speed dialed his cell phone

"Carmine," he screeched as he drove up U.S. 1, "get your ass to Deep Water, now. We have a situation."

"I would go," replied Carmine, "but I've got to put out a fire at Rum Reef. Some asshole has dumped a load of chicken manure all around their tennis courts. The automatic sprinklers came on last night and now the whole place smells like shit. Rum Reef has brought in Billie Jean King to conduct a tennis workshop this morning. We advertised the event all over the Southeast. The hotel is full of quests who signed up. I'm sorry; did you ask me what happened? Best I can gather, Rum Reef ordered a load of mulch and got this instead. Those dickheads didn't know the difference until it started stinking. The hotel manager said Billie Jean is throwing a tantrum and demanding her fee whether the clinic goes on or not."

"OK, OK, Carmine, you deal with Rum Reef; I'll handle Deep Water," said Sol.

Sol continued to race up the highway. His phone started ringing again. "Mr. Schwartzman, your secretary told me to call you. This is Jillby at The Sporting League..."

"What the fuck do you want? I'm busy," Sol screamed back into the phone.

"Mr. Schwartzman, I have a group here demanding to see a top officer in the corporation. They call themselves the Mangrove Action Project. They say we have some mangrove violations," Jillby continued.

"Blow smoke up his ass. Do something to earn your pay. I'll get there as soon as I can. I have another problem more pressing right now," Schwartzman growled.

"When can I tell them that will be?"

"When I goddamned get there, that's when," said Sol and hung up. He called Andrea and barked orders to her again.

Then she said, "Mr. Schwartzman, I just got a call from the sheriff's department. They say they got an anonymous call telling them that some partially opened paint cans have been illegally dumped in the water off Leeward Cay Club Tropic. They're coming over to check it out. They say if they find out the cans were dumped by us or someone we subcontracted to do work for us, we could be subject to fines. Also the Dolphin Center wants to talk to you. They say there's a problem. I don't know what about."

The phone rang yet again. "Mr. Schwartzman, where are you? This is Deep Water Club Tropic again. We need help."

"That's a stupid question. I'm trying to get to you, fag! Where in the hell, do you think I am? You think I'm goddamned Dorothy and can just snap my fingers and reappear in your office."

"Well, you better get on up here. One of the commercial fishermen has a dog, and he's bitten a guest. The guest got into a fist fight with the pet owner. Now the humane society's on their way over here."

"Oh, Jesus Christ! Anything else? Is the Pope looking for me too? The FBI?"

"Well there is one last thing, Mrs. Pandora from the Health Department called."

Sol almost threw the cell phone out the car window.

CHAPTER 51

How many times have you heard the comparison of the length of time it takes to build a great success versus how little time it takes to destroy what you have built? As with most generalizations this is not always the way things play out – especially when the Goliath was not built on a solid foundation but instead had been fashioned on a deep layer of muck. It may not disappear overnight but instead would just slowly sink into the cesspool from which it rose, gradually dragging those trapped in the quagmire into the filth, gasping and grasping until they are exhausted and choking on the very thing that had given them sustenance.

It had taken only two years to build Club Tropic from an unknown upstart into a major financial force in the Keys. Now this seemingly unstoppable steamroller was being transformed into a gigantic serpent with an insatiable appetite which had begun devouring and digesting both its owners and investors and tainting everyone it came in contact with. It seemed utterly out of control with federal and state violations, out of compliance loans, ownership disputes, labor problems, investor lawsuits, endless depositions, factionalism, possible homicide investigations and criminal proceedings. Was there any other shit left to hit the fan?

New $24.8 Million Foreclosure Filed

"I'm glad Carson's feel about Club Tropic was so much better than underwriting's. I sure hope he's reading this report," Betsy said sarcastically as she drank her coffee.

"I wouldn't bet on it. He's probably out on the golf course with Sol trying to get him to come into the bank and let them help restructure Club Tropic. I'm telling you, old CC's an old fashioned banker's banker. Don't you wish you had a dozen more just like him?" Will said.

"Riiight!" Betsy said. "Then you'd be reading about us in the paper. Let me read this latest story in the *Citizen*."

> Club Tropic and its CEO Sol Schwartzman are listed in two new foreclosure suits claiming outstanding mortgage obligations totaling $24.8 million.
>
> The two are accused of not paying bills on properties they purchased from Centennial Properties, a private real estate firm. Combined the two owe Centennial $24.8 million, according to the two filings recorded in Monroe County Circuit Court on Plantation Key. Club Tropic Marine Construction is also listed in the suit.
>
> It is not immediately clear which properties Centennial is targeting for foreclosure.
>
> This is just the latest signal of Club Tropic's escalating financial troubles as buyers are beginning to pile on the lawsuits against a shrinking Club Tropic.

A Calculated Conspiracy

"Yada, Yada, Yada. You know the rest of the story," Betsy said.

"Don't I remember C.C. saying something like, 'You're all conspiring to ruin my career'?" said Will.

"You must have been a horse-fly on the wall," Betsy said with a laugh.

"A horse-fly drinking a 'coldbeer'. Don't I also remember Sol making a statement suggesting that your short-sightedness and small thinking cost the bank the largest customer it would ever have in the Keys?" Will continued.

"Well, I guess short-sighted is better than no-sighted...or being on the unemployment line. I've seen some financial disasters in my career, but this one has to rank right up at the top!" Betsy said. "I may not have connections in the world of international high finance like Schwartzman and company, but I have managed to survive over twenty years in the business world, and it wasn't by being deaf, dumb, blind, and greedy."

"Or by being crooked as a dog's hind leg," Will said.

Betsy came out of her Monday morning meeting. Margaret greeted her with several call-back messages.

"Chief Wanderley is in your office," she said, softly enough so as not to be overheard. "He came in about ten minutes ago. I gave him a cup of coffee and a Danish out of the kitchen."

"Walter, you're out and about early for a Monday morning," Betsy said smiling.

"I guess you saw that article about the latest foreclosure suit against Club Tropic," he said.

285

"Yeah, the Centennial Properties – a twenty-five million dollar suit, and that's on top of the thirty-seven million dollar suit filed by Golden States Investments. These things are starting to pile up. Keep on going, and we're going to be talking about real money."

Walter waved his index finger and said, "I've said all along this bunch is not on the level. I said that when they made a run on the leases on Key West Bight. They never snowed me like some city officials I won't name. I know just as well as I'm sitting here that this rash of killings is stemming from Club Tropic's recently disclosed internal problems. Have you seen some of the toughs that work in security for that outfit? They look like deviant grease-ball graduates of Paris Island. We've had some reports about them strong arming some of Club Tropic's help. I can't believe that an above-board company in the Florida Keys needs that kind of muscle unless there's a reason. This ain't New York or Los Angeles, for God's sake," Walter said seriously.

"Or New Jersey," Betsy added with a smile.

"I'd bet a week's pay that every one of those killings will eventually be tracked back to Club Tropic," Walter said. "Aldo Coletti, a Club Tropic property owner from New Jersey; Joey Giambi, a Club Tropic salesman, from New Jersey; Myron Levitt, a Club Tropic accountant, from New Jersey; Terry Hayes, a Club Tropic hotel manager from New York and I bet, New Jersey, truth be known and Percy Driskoll, assistant hotel manager for Club Tropic, from guess where."

Walter went on, "Any fool could see what these victims have in common, but you know, beyond Club Tropic and New Jersey, we so far can't prove a damned thing. Nada! I keep waiting for the perps to make a mistake, but so far they're living a charmed life. I'd love to get the low-down on these sleazes and put them away forever. We do not need these swindling hoodlums in Monroe County. We have enough local talent to fill the job openings just nicely."

"And weirdos and burnouts too," Betsy said.

"We got a few of them as well, but as a rule they're fun…or at least an entertaining diversion," the chief said. "They make the Keys the Keys. Schwartzman, Scarpetti and company do not. They just give the place a bad name – like New Jersey."

CHAPTER 52

Wade Wiseman was drunk, broke, but very happy. He had been to a "gentleman's club" up at mile marker 81. He'd gotten lap dances. He'd gotten whiskey. He'd listened to Big Dick and the Extenders. Shit! Life was good. Easy come, easy go. It wasn't his money anyway, and there was always more where that came from.

Wade turned up the stereo in his black Tundra pickup. He was feeling mellow on his way back to Key West. Damn! That sweet young thing had been shaking those marvelous boobs right in his face. He definitely had to go back to that place soon.

Groovin' on a Sunday afternoon
Really couldn't get away too soon

Wade sang along and loud to The Young Rascals. He swigged on the roader he had taken with him. He changed lanes again, effortlessly going around the slow-moving traffic. The whole world seemed to be slow traffic today, but it didn't matter. Everyone couldn't have a happy buzz like he had.

"It don't make no never mind," Wade said out loud and then laughed at his own joke.

Wade didn't hear or see the patrol car come up behind him. He didn't see the flashing lights.

Life would be ecstasy, you and me endlessly
Groovin' on a Sunday afternoon
Really couldn't get away too soon

He lazily noticed the siren and the flashing lights behind his truck. Oh, shit! Where'd that guy come from?

"Sir, are you aware you were going 70 in a 45 zone? And you almost cut off that car in back of you. May I see your license?" he heard the officer say over the buzz in his ears.

Suddenly it wasn't such a groovy day.

Walter Wanderley had just come back from lunch when he was told he had a call from the sheriff's department. The deputy was inquiring if anyone with the initials PCD had reported a toolbox missing to the Key West police department. Wanderley told the deputy there recently had been a homicide on Stock Island of an individual with those initials.

"Well, you may want to talk to the person we're holding then. We picked up a Wade Wiseman on a DUI, and this toolbox was in the back of his truck. We still have him in custody."

Wanderley interrogated Wiseman at length. Wiseman, now sober and scared, was willing to talk after the chief told him he could be a possible suspect in a homicide and at this point, he was their only suspect. Wiseman quickly started to spill his guts. He said he was a cable installer and admitted that he watched for unlocked houses in the neighborhoods he worked. When he found an easy target and there were no witnesses around, he would let himself into the house or the garage. He never stayed long. If he saw some item of value, he would load it into the back of his company van. He said he never took much, just portable items. That's how he obtained Percy Driskoll's toolbox. He simply walked into Percy's garage, picked it up, and carried it out like it belonged to him. He certainly never killed anyone. He'd just engaged in a little petty larceny. He didn't even know Driskoll, for God's sake. He had no idea who lived in the house. He'd never seen the man and he certainly didn't know Driskoll was dead. He would never have taken a chance like that.

Wiseman seemed to be telling the truth. He was much too nervous to lie. After the interrogation, Wanderley asked the sheriff if he could take the toolbox with him. He tested it when he got out to his car. It was locked. He knew who to call to get a key. He'd go over to the bank and get a spot of coffee as soon as he got back to the station.

"Didn't you tell me that Percy Driskoll gave you and Will a key to keep for him when you met him?" the chief began as he sipped his coffee at Betsy's office.

"Sure did! Mr. Driskoll said it was a key to his toolbox, but when Will and I went by his house we couldn't find a toolbox anywhere," Betsy said.

"That's because Percy's toolbox had been stolen, but now it's turned up," Wanderley said.

He told Betsy about Wade Wiseman's little moonlighting job, and how the toolbox had been found in his pickup when he was pulled over for a DUI.

"It's a good thing Percy put his initials on the toolbox," Wanderley said. "Otherwise no one would have suspected it didn't belong to Wiseman. It was good police work for the deputy to realize that a toolbox with the initials PCD on it might not belong to someone with the initials WWW. Wiseman only has himself to blame. He had WWW on the door of his truck and then a toolbox with PCD in the back. Otherwise the deputy probably never would have thought about it," Wanderley said. "I'm glad he was thorough enough and sharp enough to call us. Yes, sometimes we get lucky. Do you have the key with you?"

"Actually we locked it in a safety deposit box. We hid it after our house was ransacked and suspected the key to be the reason," Betsy said. "Do you have the toolbox with you?"

"I will go get it and bring it over here."

"I'll have the key." Betsy said.

Within thirty minutes Walter was back at the bank with the toolbox. They closed the door to Betsy's office for privacy and told Margaret to hold Betsy's calls.

"Not much of a toolbox," Betsy said. "If you took the PCD off of it, it would just look like a cheap metal box from Home Depot."

She picked it up. "Not very heavy either. Must not have the first tool in it."

"Yeah," Wanderley observed. "Must be why Wiseman never appeared to even try to open it. He admitted he had thrown it into the bed of his truck intending to look at it later and forgotten it was there."

Betsy turned the key in the lock, and the toolbox opened without hesitation.

"No wonder it's so light," Walter said. "All it contains is some papers rolled up with rubber bands."

He unrolled the first papers. It was a printout of a Googled Wall Street Journal article with a picture. The man in the picture was identified as Paul Miles.

"He looks just like Terry Hayes, the missing hotel manager from Royal Island Club Tropic," Walter said. "I'd love to know where that boy is so I could ask him some questions."

Wanderley started reading the article aloud. It said Miles was adjudged to be dead by authorities in New York. He had run a hedge fund in New York and had been charged with conspiracy and fraud. While out on bail he had committed suicide. His luxury SUV had been found abandoned on a bridge going over the Hudson River. The words *Suicide Is Painless* had been found scrawled on a VHS tape in his car. The tape was of the M*A*S*H episode with the same title. Investigators determined he must have drowned, but they were never able to find the body.

The article said Miles scammed people into investing more than $500 million into his fund, then announced nonexistent profits and gave investors fake audits to validate the inflated results. It maintained he made millions for himself charging exorbitant commissions on losing trades for the fund.

Wanderley said to Betsy, "Driskoll must be telling us Paul Miles rose from the dead and became Terry Hayes in his next life. Miles certainly didn't want that to come out in an interview."

Betsy agreed, "He scammed the investors; then he tricked law enforcement and the courts, and he got away with it for a long time. We've always been told expatriates and the Keys are a ready match for each other."

"And for all we know, he may still be getting away with his crimes since he's disappeared again," Walter said. "I'll check with New York police and confirm what you and I both are pretty damned sure of already. It seems Percy heard some things he wasn't supposed to hear."

There was a second roll of paper in the toolbox. Wanderley unrolled it. It contained photocopied pages of a financial ledger.

The financial statement reflected a summary of sources and uses of funds for the Royal Island Club Tropic for the most recent twelve-month period ending June 30th. Substantial amounts of funds had been designated as "uses" to Sol Schwartzman. In fact, the "uses of funds" far exceeded the sources from investors, earnings etc. A notation in handwriting (presumably by Percy Driskoll) suggested the same practice of large periodic withdrawals of funds had occurred at the other two Cheney-owned resorts of Leisure Bay Club Tropic and Sandy Beach Club Tropic. This was substantiated by a copy of an e-mail from Schwartzman to Percy advising not *excess funds* but a set amount monthly should be transferred to his personal bank account. This monthly recap reflected a deficit each month which totaled over $2.5 million for the twelve-month period.

"What do you want to bet the little ole mealy-mouth peon Percy was blackmailing Mr. 'high and mighty' Schwartzman. No wonder he couldn't sleep at night. I think Percy was playing with fire and got burned. I guess Percy was never meant to be a big leaguer," Betsy said after examining the pages. "No wonder he gave us the key to this box to keep safe for him. This was Percy's retirement plan."

"Yeah, but he took an early permanent retirement," Walter said.

The box also contained a hand-written note about the death of Myron Levitt. The note placed the blame on Sol Schwartzman's henchmen. According to the note, Levitt had not covered up discrepancies in the financial statements of Club Tropic which Myron Levitt was using to blackmail Schwartzman.

The information said Schwartzman ordered Carmine to have Levitt killed and dumped in the ocean. Instead it appeared Carmine, in his efforts to send a message to Jack Maselli, dumped Levitt's body in the canal in front of Jack's dock. An attached hand-written note stated that Myron's lack of action on the financial discrepancies had thrown a red flag in the face of the Colombian investor. Schwartzman purportedly was not only livid over the

Colombian questioning these financial issues, he was further angered because Levitt had revealed to the Colombian the extent of the company's use of illegal aliens in an attempt to "encourage" Schwartzman to pay his blackmail funds.

CHAPTER 53

Will and Betsy walked into Looe Key Tiki Bar with Guy and Penny Walsh. They saw Nira and Ruthie and were motioned over to the table. After everyone hugged, a round of drinks was ordered.

"Tonight looks like a real treat," Will said, waving at the musicians on the bandstand. "Ron and Terry jam together frequently, but tonight C.W.'s with them too. This place will rock."

The bar was full of the usual eclectic assortment of locals. A man in a long grizzled beard wearing a Chinese rice farmer's hat sat at the bar. Next to him was a woman eating chili while playing computer solitaire; she was covered with tattoos like the one across her shoulder blades announcing VIVIAN in heavy Gothic. Several sweaty-looking plumbers wearing baseball caps saying Dry Tortugas Plumbing sat drinking beer at the bar. A retiree in a tank top was bragging to another local about his dolphin catch earlier in the day. A local skin diver stood by himself, barefooted, stoically drinking a beer, watching the jam session. A Harley rumbled out back.

Ron Bauman finished a rousing harmonica solo on *Orange Blossom Special*. They then moved into Terry's original composition about the bat tower, and then on to a popular C.W. Colt number.

Mi amigo mosquito, adios
Makes you want to scratch and itch and scratch and itch

The patrons laughingly sang the familiar lyrics, following the song's instructions to scratch or slap.

And slap...

When the song was over C.W. toasted the crowd with his Jack Daniels saying "Let's have a drink on the count of three - Three!" and Terry announced that it was the end of the set.

As he walked to the bar to order another beer, Terry stopped by the table to visit with Will and Betsy.

"Terry Cassidy," Will asked, "Do you remember our friends from Vero Beach, Guy and Penny Walsh?"

"Sure," Terry said, shaking hands with Guy and hugging Penny. "Good to see y'all again. Glad to have you back in the Keys. So what's new?"

"We've been gone for over a week. We stopped by Vero Beach on the way back and convinced Guy and Penny they needed a few days of Keys R and R," Will responded. "Went up to Mississippi to see my folks. Anything been happening around here?"

"Nothing unusual...unless you work at Club Tropic," Terry said.

"Oh, yeah! What's going on there now?"

"Lake Shore Investors won their foreclosure suit against Club Tropic. Club Tropic owed them $37 million. Three of their properties are going to be auctioned off. The company sure looks like a candidate for melt-down."

Will whistled. "And people thought they'd take over the Keys."

Guy interrupted and looked at Will, "That reminds me. I never told you about my almost experience with Club Tropic about four months ago, I had a client ask me what I knew about Club Tropic. He said word was circulating that they had an exclusive opportunity for smart money. Out of courtesy I told him I'd research it. I went on my computer and looked up Club Tropic resorts. I found a web site for them, but when I went to pull it up the web site was blocked. Out of curiosity I found a phone number and placed a call. I got an answering machine.

"A few days later out of the blue I get this phone call from a woman named Danielle Casas. She said she was a licensed real estate agent for Modern Investment Realty in Park City, Utah. She had one hell of a high pressure sales pitch. She informed me that the company had multiple investments for discriminating investors and faxed me pricing on some of their more attractive units as well as information on what she called their *preferred lenders*."

Guy had Terry and the group's attention now.

"She said one option was to participate in what she called *the fund*. She said they had created a special company to manage *the fund* – called Cedric and Lucian Asset Management LLC. If I chose to go this route, it was realistic for me to expect four to seven percent returns every month."

Will, Terry, Betsy and Penny were transfixed. Guy went on to describe the two year lease-back deal Will and Betsy had heard of before.

Guy continued, "She said this fund was not publicly advertised and there were special documents I had to sign before I would be allowed in, and I had to participate in a confidential conference call with Cedric and Lucian's principals. Despite my being non-committal, she even set up a tentative time for the call. I told her to send the documents to me."

Guy stopped momentarily to take a swig on his gin and tonic. Then he continued.

"I received the documents, just as she promised, by UPS the next day. One was a non-disclosure/non-circumvention agreement. It seemed to have two purposes. First, to prevent me from sharing information on this investment with anyone – I strongly suspect their main concern was my leaking word to law enforcement, and second to make me deal through their investment organization, i.e. they wanted to make damned sure I couldn't cut them out of the deal.

"The second letter in the package was called a non-solicitation letter. This was to protect them if I later claimed they had solicited my participation in this scheme. It was also worded in such a way that it would be difficult to accuse them of securities fraud."

Holy shit!" Terry said. "You didn't invest money with them, did you?"

Guy gave Terry a patronizing look, "Surely, you jest, my friend! I never even called them back. I just shit-canned the documents...I should have kept the damned things...Anyway, about a week later my phone rang. It was a conference operator telling me that my conference call with Mr. Cedric and Mr. Lucian would begin at eleven o'clock. I said 'what the hell.' During my call, they told me they had never had a month where the investor didn't make money. I was also told that even though the sales rep had said four to seven percent a month, they actually locked it in at five percent each month provided I invested at least $150,000. It would be capped at 4 percent for investors smaller than that. They told me C &L's profit for any given month was to keep anything above five percent. Cedric said he was going to be very honest and tell me that some month's returns had been as high as thirty percent, and if that happened again, I would still only get five percent while he would keep the other twenty-five."

"Mighty decent of him to be so candid," Terry said with a laugh.

"I'm telling you, these Club Tropicers are really princes, aren't they. I don't see how anyone in his right mind could refuse a deal like that," Will said sarcastically.

"I don't either," Guy said, "but somehow I found the willpower to do so. Yah! Mon! That's my story and I'm sticking to it. I wish the best to exclusive members of *the fund*. I'm glad to be back in the lower Keys."

"They'll probably require more than luck," said Will.

"Good to see you again, Guy. I guess I'd better go earn my money so I'll have some when Cedric and Lucian call me," Terry said, lightly squeezing Guy's shoulder.

Will looked at Guy after Terry started playing his next set.

"Foreclosure? I'm not surprised," Will said, "I wonder what will be the next shoe to drop."

CHAPTER 54

When the avalanche began, there was no stopping it. Perhaps it is difficult to visualize the occurrence of an avalanche – particularly in the Florida Keys. However, it did start in the Keys, moved up the state of Florida, spread east to the Bahamas and then west, as far as Colorado.

The collapse of the Club Tropic companies and their real estate schemes was out of control. There were no counter stories of potential investors to offset the media headlines. Defrauded investors filed individual and class action suits. Lenders obtained judgments against guarantors of various Club Tropic projects when the numerous Club Tropic entities failed to pay their loans.

The feds, through U.S. Attorney's offices in Florida specifically, got tough on loan and mortgage fraud, stating that, "Law enforcement has been given a clear mandate to go after loan/mortgage fraud and prosecute violators to the fullest extent of the law." Many compared this aggressive approach with the war on drugs declared by the federal government some twenty years earlier.

The results of this financial debacle were an economic catastrophe. Club Tropic developments, resorts, condominiums, clubs, construction, rental and sales firms, mining ventures, distributors, restaurants and marinas filed bankruptcy to stall foreclosure actions and auctions. Investors were left with debt on worthless real estate and related investments. Thousands of Club Tropic employees were laid off. Suppliers and vendors went unpaid for the goods and services provided to the many Club Tropic entities.

So went this financial descent . It appeared to impact almost every aspect of the economy in the Keys, the state of Florida and beyond to other areas "fortunate" enough to have had a Club Tropic experience. Individual investors lost all or part of their savings, retirement accounts and credibility for borrowed funds. The real estate schemes also generated widespread fraud charges, tax evasion, and legal maneuvering that brought law enforcement (from local, state and federal levels) and flooded the justice system. About the only beneficiaries of this fiasco were the attorneys.

CHAPTER 55

"Listen to this," Betsy said to Will as she went through her home e-mails.

To the Blacks,

I am sending this communication anonymously to help justice be done in the Joey Giambi matter. Do not try to identify me. I would deny any knowledge of the whole affair if questioned by authorities. I WILL NOT BECOME DIRECTLY INVOLVED.

Joey Giambi was killed by Carmine Scarpetti at the orders of an organized crime boss named Juan Strazzuli. I will leave it up to you to find Strazzuli, but I will warn you before you look, there is nothing you can do to him. When and if you identify him it will become clear why he wanted Giambi dead. If you doubt what I say, check Carmine's bank account for two large incoming wire transfers which were immediately re-wired off shore. You will see one occurred the day prior to Giambi's death, the other the day following, With a little thought I believe you can put the rest of the pieces together.

Good luck. You will not hear from me again,
A friend

"What do you think about that?" Betsy asked. "Do you think it's on the level?"

"Why would someone go to this much effort and risk to stir up trouble?" Will responded.

"Let's forward it to Walter at his personal e-mail and get his reaction," Will said. "I don't want it going into the police station as an official document until he's read it."

"Good idea." Betsy hit the forward button to the police chief.

Within five minutes their phone rang. It was Walter, wanting to know if they knew who sent the e-mail.

"I wish I did," Betsy said. "It just showed up."

"You know I need to consider this official business and provide this information to the sheriff's office and the FBI," Walter said.

"We figured as much, but we thought we'd let you make that decision," Betsy said.

"You also realize that if this thing is true, we are dealing with some very dangerous people who will stop at nothing to keep their secret a secret," Walter continued.

"We also thought about that," Betsy said.

"We will get a techie over to your house and try to trace the origins of this message before we go any farther," Walter said.

Walter was waiting for Betsy when she got out of her morning meeting.

"I've got an FBI techie lined up," he said. "When can we get him in your house?"

"Unfortunately, I'm booked all day, but I'll get Will to let you in."

Walter and the FBI techie arrived at Will and Betsy's home. He found the IP address and the provider from the e-mail. The person who sent the message had taken some effort to disguise his identity. After just a little work, however, the techie identified a location on Greene Street in Key West as the location from where the e-mail had been sent.

The FBI technical person told them he would contact the AT & T provider to see what addresses on Greene Street used their services and match that with the IP address.

Within minutes he had an answer. An Internet café on Greene, just a block from Simonton was the location from which this e-mail had been sent. However, they would have to visit that Internet café and provide them a date and time from the e-mail to identify the sender through video surveillance.

Walter and the FBI techie left Will and Betsy's home to return to Key West.

"I'll call you later," Walter said.

Walter came by that afternoon on his way home from work.

"A cold Greenie tastes awfully good on a hot day," he said.

"Took the words right out of my mouth," Betsy said.

Will opened the fridge to retrieve three Heinekens.

Walter took a long first sip.

"So?" Will said impatiently.

"The video surveillance from the Greene Street Internet café revealed the e-mail's sender to be your neighbor Jack Maselli. I actually identified him on the video for the FBI," said Walter.

"Good grief," Betsy said.

"This certainly puts a new wrinkle on matters," said Will.

Walter quickly added, " I don't want you to say anything to Maselli about this matter. Even though the investigation is ongoing, we do not yet have evidence that his assertions are valid. But I do know this, Juan Strazzuli is a wise guy. And not just a low-ranking wise guy either. He's currently a guest of the federal government at Fairton Correctional Institution in Heislerville, New Jersey. He's got eleven more years to go on his sentence. I'm told he's one bad mother who none of us would want to mess with."

"How would Jack Maselli get the down and dirty on someone like that?" Betsy asked.

"What put him there?" Will asked.

"Seems like he got convicted in a racketeering, money laundering, and fraud case with a company called Garden State Check Cashing," Walter said.

"Wasn't that the name of the company that Joey Giambi was affiliated with?" Will asked.

"I remember reading about that company . You mean this Strazzuli was with them too?" Betsy asked.

307

"Not with...He was running the whole damned show. Giambi was just a peon who had a similar operation, an outfit named Quick Buck Cash Flow Financing," Walter said. "And Giambi is the reason Strazzuli is in the can right now. Joey pitched Juan under the bus to save his own sorry skin...in retrospect, probably not the brightest thing he ever did."

"Do I understand that Joey's death was possibly retribution from a Mafia don getting even with Joey for the Garden State affair?" Betsy asked.

"It looks very possible and probable," Walter said. "I'm told these people don't forget their enemies, and a rat is the worst kind of enemy. Apparently Joey was hiding out down here in the Keys after he jumped bail, and somehow Juan Strazzuli may have found him. People like Juan can be almost as dangerous from prison as they are on the street."

"But how would a nobody like Jack Maselli know about this? He doesn't seem to be the mafia type," Will asked. "And why would Jack want to risk involvement?"

"I don't know, but I'd keep my eyes open with good old Jack in the future. There may be more to that do-gooder sales manager than appears on the surface. Let's just keep this entire affair to ourselves for now. It will not only be more productive, but a helluva lot safer for you two financial wizards. Agreed?" Walter concluded.

"Agreed," said Will.

"Agreed. But it's not like Juan Strazzuli is free to run the streets," said Betsy.

"Tell Joey Giambi that," Walter said.

Walter Wanderley came by the bank a few days later. "Haven't seen you last few days. Things been busy?" Betsy asked.

"Definitely been interesting. Now I know what it must feel like to be a big city cop," Walter said.

"Anything that pertains to my e-mail?" Betsy said.

"All of it, and now something's happened we won't be able to keep out of the paper. The sheriff's department picked up Carmine Scarpetti for questioning in the death of Joey Giambi. Fortunately, he was carrying a 9mm pistol with a silencer so there was an excuse to book him. As you might expect from a guinea wise guy, he totally clammed up. You know, the *omerta* bit."

"*Omerta*? As in the underworld's oath of silence?" Betsy asked.

"Exactly. The FBI grilled him for hours. He never even came close to cracking. Then early this morning when the jailer checked his cell Carmine was dead. The medical examiner is telling me he ate or drank something that was poisoned. The medical examiner is still doing extensive lab work to figure out what."

Betsy gasped.

"Do you think Strazzuli was afraid he'd break down and talk?" she asked.

"That is being investigated, but so far, as they say in the sewer, nobody didn't see nuttin', nobody didn't hear nuttin', nobody knows nuttin'," said Walter.

"And I thought Juan was of minimal concern since Juan isn't currently free to roam the streets," Betsy said.

"Like I said the other day, please be careful. These are not your typical white collar criminals."

CHAPTER 56

"Boss lady, boss lady," an excited Carson Crown announced. "Fred Barnes told me at Rotary that the Club Tropic merger might be in for a little trouble and setback."

"Fred Barnes? Isn't he the Rotarian you told me a few weeks ago was 91 years old – the one you gave a fifty-year pin to?"

"Yeah, he's been one of the stalwarts of our club. He was the biggest fund-raiser for the Fourth of July fireworks for ten years in a row."

"I think I remember the newspaper saying that was in the 1980s. Didn't it also say his caregiver brings him to Rotary every week because he doesn't drive any more?"

"Well, old Fred has slowed down a little, but he still knows what's going on around town. After all he is a Conch, and his granddaddy was once mayor of Key West."

"As usual, your source is unimpeachable," Betsy said. "Not that I would want to correct Fred Barnes, but it will be announced tomorrow that the deal is deader than a doornail."

"Where'd you hear that?" C.C. asked.

"I have my sources," Betsy said. "Don't you have a meeting you're late for?"

The headline in the *Citizen* the following morning confirmed what Betsy had said.

CLUB TROPIC AND CLUB TROPIC HOSPITALITY CALL OFF MERGER

At the various Club Tropic companies, it seemed like it was every man for himself. Some executives quit. Others formed new companies that tried to assume old and pending Club Tropic deals. More investment partners stepped forward to try to take back control of Club Tropic assets. And, of course, everyone involved either sued or was sued. More investors brought suits alleging they were sold a bill of goods. Not only were Club Tropic properties the subject of foreclosure filings but some executives' personal homes, many of which were company-owned, were foreclosed as well. Jack and Joan Maselli's house was one of them. The once-maligned brand that many locals had feared would take over the Keys was now disappearing. Phone calls went to disconnected numbers.

Club Tropic Hospitality not only ended its merger talks with Club Tropic but dissolved as a corporation. The stock was suspended on NASDAQ. There were no bids for the stock as market makers and the transfer agent abandoned it, making stockholders' investments effectively illiquid and worthless.

A Calculated Conspiracy

The Florida State Attorney's Office pressed forward on its investigation into complaints that Club Tropic's vacation rental company had kept homeowners' money and would-be renters' deposits. Club Tropic Rentals, with offices in Islamorada and Key West had closed, announcing rental fees would not be returned. This company had been responsible for about 70 exclusive homes throughout the Keys. Its managing officer was Gina Grabetti, the girlfriend of Carmine's nephew, Rocky. It was unclear how much the rental company owed or how many people stood to lose money. Authorities were unable to locate Grabetti or her boyfriend to question them.

The only comment from the State Attorney's Office was, "Candidly, it is going to be a very long investigation because there are numerous complaints, and there are complaints coming from both sides of the rental equation."

Former Club Tropic properties had to be put back on the market even after an unsuccessful mortgage-holder bidding. Prices ranged from 60 to 75 percent below their appraised market value. Jorge Carlos of Centennial Partners retained Al Soltero to bid on the properties. Soltero's efforts were successful, coming in on the low end of the range since he was the sole bidder.

Club Tropic was dead. It had not been a pretty death, and there were still plenty of unanswered questions. Many people were pondering these issues. One was Sergio Mendosa from Immigration and Naturalization. He was staring at an anonymous communiqué that had arrived at his office telling him to talk to Luis Gonzales and Terry Hayes if he wished to know more about illegal alien activities at Club Tropic. One of the things puzzling him was when he attempted to follow up on the lead, he found that Hayes had quit his job at Club Tropic months ago. In fact, he had not been seen in the Keys since. If he and Luis Gonzales had been in bed together, he needed to find out how. The person who could give him that information was probably Luis. Now, how was he going to get Luis to talk? If anyone could probably sweat the info out of Luis, he knew it would probably be a fellow Latin.

Luis Gonzales was at first resistant to cooperate with Mendosa until Mendosa reminded him that his green card could be revoked or not renewed if he were deemed to be an undesirable alien. This changed matters dramatically.

Mendosa finally sweated what he thought was as close to the truth as he would ever get from Luis. Per Luis several months before he disappeared, Terry Hayes approached him about where he might obtain a new set of documents in case it ever became necessary to flee and change his identity once again. Luis gave him a name of a fellow countryman who might have connections to accomplish a mission of this sort. He swore to Mendosa he had no further involvement after that. He said he never even asked Hayes if he had followed up on the matter.

Luis then told Mendosa that when Terry's true identity was uncovered, Terry approached him again to see if he could arrange transportation to get out of the country. Terry said he was willing to pay and had the money to do so. Once again Luis reported he gave Terry a lead and told him he could use his name as an introduction. Luis then swore that he could only assume that Terry had arranged transportation.

He also swore that he had no idea where Terry ended up or what his new name was. All he knew was that just like the New York incident, Terry Hayes had once again vanished.

Sergio Mendosa went back to quiz Luis Gonzales further the following day, only to find that Luis had disappeared as well.

CHAPTER 57

A moving van pulled up to Jack and Joan Maselli's house.

"You guys leaving?" Will asked as he and Betsy were walking the dogs.

"There's nothing to keep us here now. I guess you know this house was owned by Club Tropic, and it was foreclosed on," Joan said. "We're returning to New Jersey."

"Is that truck big enough for all your furniture?" Betsy asked.

"Oh, no, the furniture stays here. It belongs to Club Tropic. All we have to do is get our personal belongings out of the house," Jack said. "I resigned yesterday...like it was necessary. Hell, there's nothing left to manage anyway. The sales force all quit last week. Sol wasn't even gracious to any of them on the way out the door. He came into our office and told them all just to 'get the fuck out.' He announced that if anyone had any belongings left in their offices at the end of the day, he was going to pitch them all out on the street."

"He always was such a class act," Joan said.

"He also had his bullies go through my guys' boxes to make sure they weren't taking any Club Tropic records with them," Jack said.

"What are you going to do in New Jersey?" Will asked.

"I don't know. All I know is there's nothing left for us down here. If anyone saw on my résumé I had been a sales manager for Club Tropic, I probably couldn't get a job on a bet in these parts. Something will come up. It always does. We'll have a final drink with you and Betsy before we leave. After all we have had some good times together. You've heard of an Irish wake; just call this an Italian one."

Jack and Joan walked back to the dock.

Another car pulled up. They all heard a car door slam and turned to see Sol Schwartzman who came towards them, half walking, half running and stumbling. Will could tell Sol was sloshed.

"I want to make sure you're only taking what belongs to you, you piece-of-shit conspirator," he said gruffly to Jack. "Let me see those boxes."

"What do you mean conspirator?" Jack asked.

"You didn't think I'd find out who you are," Sol continued. "Well, I didn't know until recently, but I do now."

He turned to Joan, "I've thought for a long time you seemed familiar. You're that loser, Judy Westfield's mother."

"Don't you talk about Joan's daughter that way," Jack said.

"You think I had something to do with that deformed bitch's suicide, don't you," screamed Schwartzman.

"Yes, I'm Judy's mother," said Joan. "In a sense I'm glad you finally know my identity. That girl was devoted to you. She worked for you seven days a week, and how did you pay her back? You scammed her on her medical insurance policy. You cheap bastard! You withheld money from her payroll every week, but instead of paying the premiums on her medical insurance, you pocketed her money. You're such a low-life, Sol Schwartzman! I know you didn't know she was going to need a liver transplant. You didn't anticipate when she found out there was no insurance to pay for it, she would go into a depression and end it all, but you killed her just as sure as if you had held a gun to her head."

"It's not my fault you raised a wacko daughter," Sol sneered. "Don't try to lay off that guilt shit on me. I don't buy it. I didn't know there'd been a mix-up on paying her premiums. I had more important matters to tend to than worrying about every pissant employee's insurance coverage. If your daughter had any sense, she would have kept closer tabs on her own damned insurance. Devoted to me? She wasn't even that good of a secretary. You say she worked seven days a week. Maybe it was because she was too slow and inefficient to get things done during normal hours."

"You lying sack of shit! Don't talk about Judy," Jack yelled. "Mix-up, my ass. You pocketed that money, and it cost Joan her only child. I'm glad to see your fraudulent goddamned company go up in smoke. It made it worth devoting a couple of years of my life to get even. You don't know how satisfying it is to see the mighty Sol Schwartzman get screwed to the wall and humbled. I fucked you over for

A Calculated Conspiracy

two years providing information on you and your associates to the FBI and the Securities and Exchange Commission, and you never knew it. You even paid for me to live in a Club Tropic house while I was doing it. You got a well deserved fucking for the fuckings you gave – a tooth for a tooth."

Jack laughed and pointed his finger.

"And you thought you'd get even, you minor league wimp, by costing me my company...MY COMPANY! I'm going to kill you like I killed that other piece of shit, Myron Levitt. Unimaginative rats like you don't deserve to live on the same planet with visionaries like me."

Sol was by now completely out of control. He drunkenly picked up a gaffing hook and swung at Jack with all his might. The gaffing hook glanced off the boat. He swung again. Will threw a life jacket he grabbed off the ground and wrapped it around the hook. When he jerked, the hook came out of Sol's hands. Sol looked for another weapon. He spotted Jack's machete lying on the ground and went for it. Joan tripped him as he reached for the weapon. Sol fell on the machete which sliced through his chest. Mr. Club Tropic tumbled into the canal. Will jumped in and grabbed Sol's body. Sol Schwartzman was as dead as the company he had founded.

CHAPTER 58

A wet Will Black vaguely remembered hearing Betsy say, "I called 911" as he sat on the dock next to Sol's bloody lifeless body; still in shock, he wasn't sure exactly who was talking. Within minutes a variety of vehicles started pulling up in front of the Maselli's house. He heard feet running across the pearock and looked up to see a uniform. He heard Betsy and Joan both trying to explain to the deputy at the same time what had just happened.

On the heels of the deputy, other vehicles arrived. Paramedics, drivers, the medical examiner, more deputies. He glanced up and saw Walter Wanderley striding up the drive. Suddenly he was barraged with questions from the sheriff's department. It was like a three-ring circus.

Walter was talking to a deputy. "Let me get this man some dry clothes. He just lives next door. I'll take responsibility."

Betsy was rapidly talking to another deputy, "It was self defense...I saw it all."

Before crime tape could be placed on the property, Walter broke away from Will momentarily to shoo a reporter away from the crime scene. He told Betsy to wait and finish her statement in the back seat of the deputy's car. He then guided Will back toward the house to change into fresh clothing. Will could see neighbors huddled on the street and on the canal talking to one another. He looked up again and saw Adolfo Soltero standing alone on his porch, smoking a cigarette, quietly absorbing the scene below him.

Will told Walter that he was fine and wanted to stay. He pulled Walter off to one side so just the two of them could talk.

"Walter," he said, "Schwartzman admitted he killed Myron Levitt. The son of a bitch did it himself. He said so."

"I guess I shouldn't be surprised," Walter said. "And you know, if he had kept his mouth shut, he'd probably have gotten away with it. No one in law enforcement found anything on him."

Will then told Walter the details of Joan's daughter, Judy Westfield's death.

"I guess in a sense he was tried, convicted and sentenced by the person who wanted him dead the most, Joan Maselli, since he was indirectly responsible for her daughter's death," said Walter.

After several hours the excitement was over. The official personnel were gone. Sol's body had been taken away. The neighbors had gone back to their homes. The Masellis had gone to a motel for the night. The only people left were Walter and the Blacks. As they sat on the porch, Walter sighed.

"Well, I guess we're about as close to a wrap as we're going to get on the crimes from the Club Tropic affair. In a perfect world we would want everything tied up in a neat package with a pretty bow on top, but this isn't a perfect world. I guess three out of five isn't bad."

"That's 60 percent. Not too long ago, we'd have loved to have been at that number," Betsy said.

"Yeah, you're right. Aldo Colletti – disgruntled Club Tropic real estate investor of the year. We've known for some time he was killed by Joey Gambi, but we didn't know why. Because of Vinnie Costello, we now know Joey had skipped bail on Vinnie, who got lost from him in Florida because the name he used was Joey Gambino in New Jersey. Vinnie's cousin Aldo recognized him and was threatening to turn him in - so Aldo had to go," Walter said.

He continued, "We've also solved the Joey Giambi (aka Joey Gambino) murder; Joey helped mastermind a crooked check cashing service in New Jersey with Strazzuli. To Strazzuli, Joey was an *omerta* rat, the lowest of the low. Strazzuli finally admitted to the FBI he hired Carmine Scarpetti on a contract hit because he wanted revenge on Joey for ratting him out and getting him sent to the pen. This was a recent confession for a legal concession for Strazzuli."

"You two solved the Myron Levitt murder this afternoon when Schwartzman admitted doing it. Myron was another prince of a fellow. In New Jersey he was a former corporate VP who sank to convicted felon status after he helped hatch a tax scheme involving illegal aliens. That leopard sure didn't change his spots at Club Tropic. According to Percy Driskoll's documents, Myron was blackmailing Schwartzman after he found out Schwartzman was keeping two sets of books.

"Terry Hayes or Paul Miles or whatever the hell you want to call him – swindler extraordinaire. Let's face it, he was working for the Latinos as well as Club Tropic. He was helping Luis and Myron with the illegal worker operation at Club Tropic. I figure the wetbacks either killed him or he hauled ass again with a new alias. We may never know... but who knows, he may reappear somewhere down the road. We know he's good at disappearing, but you never can tell. He might not be perfect. And I figure if he is alive, he won't be going straight. He'll end up in some kind of racket somewhere. It's just his nature. The wetbacks may have even helped him disappear. You know that Luis has vanished too – probably with some help from his Colombian friends.

"And that leaves Percy Driskoll – mealy-mouthed, little two-faced, lying weasel that he was with his dynamite hidden in his lethal little toolbox. There were a lot of people who wanted him dead. He had cut himself in on Myron's action; he took over blackmailing Sol. He found out who Terry Hayes really was. For all we know, he might have been blackmailing him too. So as I said we solved three out of five of these dirty cases."

"You forgot one," Betsy said.

"Carmine."

"Oh, yeah! That vicious thug! The wise guy who thought he could play every angle against the middle and get away with it. Every indication is that Strazzuli had him poisoned through a Hispanic food service worker at the Stock Island jail. Unfortunately, when the deputies tried to pick this guy up for questioning, he had disappeared. Last night his body was found floating in the harbor at Stock Island. You'll never guess who this latest victim was kin to – Juan Strazzuli."

"I thought Strazzuli was Italian," Will said.

"Only on his father's side – his mother was Colombian. I guess that's why his first name was Juan."

Will looked at Betsy and smiled, "Remember when we were thinking of moving to the Keys, and you told me there is never any serious crime here."

Betsy smiled back. "Now wait a minute, big boy, you're the one who said that."

They looked at Walter and said, "RIGHT!"

Walter laughed. "Well, I guess we should congratulate ourselves. Maybe now the Keys will be a little cleaner and safer place to live."

EPILOGUE

The Brazilian sky was blue and cloudless. There was just enough of a breeze to feel comfortable. The surf murmured as it gently slapped the beach. The sand was immaculate. The only people stirring were waiters and attendants for the hotel's spoiled, elite clientele.

Victoria Schwartzman stretched out on a teak chaise lounge, her face mostly hidden by a big floppy hat and oversized designer sunglasses. On the chaise lounge next to her lay Paul Miles aka Terry Hayes dozing in the hot sun. She tapped her toe as she listened to a local group, Bossa Rio, singing a sexy bossa nova interpretation of *Old Devil Moon*, which wafted down the beach through outdoor speakers. They were flanked by three more matching chaise lounges. On each one lazed a young man – men obviously much younger than Victoria was. People who were passing by tried not to stare at the three gorgeous young men. Each had a sun tan that had been bronzed to perfection. Their hairless bodies did not have one pound of excess fat. Each wore a Speedo as tight as a skin. One was bright red; one was white; the other was a royal blue. Only when a passerby glanced at them did he notice one other characteristic. The three magnificent Latino studs were identical triplets.

Victoria looked at the one to her left slyly from behind her sunglasses. "What absolute perfection," she sighed.

Paul stirred and agreed with her.

She glanced from the young man's face to his Speedo and almost licked her lips. "There's no padding in that bathing suit," she thought. "I know too well."

"As do I, my dear," Paul said and sighed contentedly.

She got slightly damp thinking of the night before. Paul got slightly hard.

She glanced at the young man on her right and sighed to herself at the mass there. A stray dark pubic hair had escaped on one side and set her imagination aflame.

Victoria reached out and gently squeezed Paul's groin. He groaned.

My three A's. Adulio, Adan, the earthman and Apolinar. Victoria had a hard time telling them apart – especially when they were nude. That's why she had bought them Speedos in different colors. She almost wanted to peel the material off right here on the beach.

Victoria's reverie was interrupted by a waiter who said, "Miss Ferraro, I have a call for you." He handed her a cell phone. It was a steak house confirming her reservation for that night. Before the waiter left, Victoria ordered a piña colada for each of them.

"Victoria Ferraro Schwartzman...I don't need the Schwartzman anymore," Victoria said and dozed momentarily. The waiter brought a drink for each of them. All of her companions gathered in the sand around her chaise lounge.

"To the Keys, my dear Sol, and the good life," Victoria said. "But you don't know what I'm saying, do you my Latino darlings? Not one of you speaks English, but with what each of you is packing in those bathing suits, you can be understood in any language. Isn't that right, Adulio?" She smiled at Adulio; He smiled in return.

"Well, old Sol said I never was much of a conversationalist. I always knew how to make him understand though. Ain't that right, Adan."

She popped her gum. Adan smiled.

"And Sol, wherever you may be, I left without thanking you for the Club Tropic fortune you stole. It's more money than I could ever spend. Right, Apolinar?"

He smiled back at her.

"I still can't believe you found three identical Brazilian hunks" Paul said. "If you lined them up naked with bags on their heads, I'd be real hard-pressed to tell the difference. Just three gorgeous pricks for you and for me. Boys, you are the fulfillment of our fantasy – all action and no smart mouth."

Victoria smiled at Paul and said, "Men never knew I was listening after I fucked their brains out. To them I was just a bimbo with hot pants. Myron couldn't hold a candle to these boys in the sack, but he loved to talk afterwards."

Paul agreed. "It's truly a shame Percy Driskoll found out about that disc Myron had pirated from Sol. And I've felt so bad about Myron. I guess you just shouldn't have told Sol where the disc was hidden. How did we know he'd overreact like that and kill Myron? And it's really too bad your 'Uncle' Juan Strazzuli found out that Carmine screwed up the Giambi hit like he did.

Victoria added, "I swear I didn't mean to accidentally copy Jack Maselli on the e-mail about it. I never was good with computers, even when I was a secretary."

She smiled at Apolinar; he gave her a blank look and grinned back.

"Well, my friends. You know what they say, shit happens. A toast to Club Tropic and the spoils. It was good while it lasted, but this is better. I guess I'm just a dumb bimbo after all…a dumb bimbo who can afford three of you. I wonder which one of you I'll have when I go back up to the room. Maybe I'll have all three of you at the same time."

"Save one for me," Paul said teasingly.

"Haven't I always shared?" Victoria asked.

Victoria again smiled expansively at all four of her lovers. She adored life in Brazil. It beat the hell out of New Jersey.